Destiny's Captive

Center Point
Large Print

Also by Beverly Jenkins and available from
Center Point Large Print:

The Blessings Novels:
  Bring on the Blessings
  A Second Helping
  A Wish and a Prayer

The Destiny Series:
  Destiny's Surrender

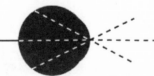

**This Large Print Book carries the
Seal of Approval of N.A.V.H.**

Destiny's Captive

Beverly Jenkins

CENTER POINT LARGE PRINT
THORNDIKE, MAINE

This Center Point Large Print edition
is published in the year 2014 by arrangement with
Avon Books, an imprint of HarperCollins Publishers.

The text of this Large Print edition is unabridged.
In other aspects, this book may vary
from the original edition.
Printed in the United States of America
on permanent paper.
Set in 16-point Times New Roman type.

ISBN: 978-1-62899-361-5

Library of Congress Cataloging-in-Publication Data

Jenkins, Beverly, 1951–
Destiny's captive / Beverly Jenkins. — Center Point Large Print edition.
    pages ; cm
    Summary: "After giving him one of the worst nights of his life, Pilar
steals Noah's ship! Now he is on the hunt, and he'll stop at nothing to
find this extraordinary woman . . . and make her his"—Provided by
publisher.
    ISBN 978-1-62899-361-5 (library binding : alk. paper)
    1. Large type books. I. Title.
PS3560.E4795D467 2014
813′.54—dc23
                                                                    2014034522

This book is dedicated to Alexe Boone.
It's my way of saying thank you
for the beautiful bracelet.

Prologue

1874
Pacific Ocean off the coast of San Francisco

"Hold him while I teach him some obedience."

The knife sliced through the cheek of eighteen-year-old Noah Yates, and the searing pain made him cry out as he struggled against the three men keeping him in place.

"Yer face is too pretty anyway." Captain Alfred Simmons chuckled malevolently, holding the bloody blade in his hand.

"My mother will pay for my release!" Noah pleaded, hating that he was begging, but it was all he had.

The watching crewmen laughed and a voice rang out, "Got us a mama's boy, do we?"

"She as pretty as you?" another yelled.

Bruised from all the fighting he'd done since being shanghaied last evening, Noah Yates was weary, and yes, afraid of what might happen next. His older brothers, Logan and Drew, were undoubtedly turning San Francisco upside down in an effort to ascertain his whereabouts, but they'd never find him—not on a ship far out at sea. His fate and that of the others unwillingly forced aboard the ship rested in the hands of the foul-breathed Captain Simmons.

"I'm going to ask you one more time: Do you want to sign on with my crew?"

"No!"

"Take him belowdecks and put him in irons! He'll change his tune. Bring that next one over here."

So Noah was dragged belowdecks and chained to the floor by his wrists and ankles. Earlier, the captain expressed an aversion to confiscating religious items, so he'd let Noah keep the gold cross hanging from a chain around his neck, but his boots had been taken along with his other possessions, leaving him clad in his shirt and trousers. Two other men eventually joined him in the dark, damp hold. One, who appeared to be about Noah's age, introduced himself as Kingston Howard, a dockworker from Los Angeles. The third offered neither name nor conversation. He simply sat and wept.

Blood from the knife wound seeped into the corner of Noah's mouth and as he used his shirted shoulder to staunch the flow, the pain burned bright. Closing his eye until the fiery wave ebbed, he tried not to think about how frantic his family must be over not knowing his fate and how terrified he was about what might lie ahead.

And what lay ahead were weeks upon weeks of darkness, rats scurrying over his body at night and being given just enough food and water to stay alive. Captain Simmons never ventured below.

Noah and Kingston tried to maintain their sanity by telling each other stories of their lives. Kingston spoke of his wife and son. Noah, who'd been abducted while celebrating his eighteenth birthday, talked about his family and his love for music and books. The third man was seasick for days on end and the hold was filled with the stench of his retching . . . He was finally taken above deck but never returned.

Over time, due to the damp conditions and lack of nourishment, infection settled into Noah's wounded cheek, bringing with it fever, and as the poison spread though his body, delusion. Kingston told him later that the ship's doctor came down to treat him, but Noah had no recollections of the visit, only the body-wracking chills and monstrous dreams filled with the face of Captain Simmons.

Noah had no idea how many days had passed when he and Kingston were roughly awakened by members of the crew. Their chains were undone and they were prodded to their feet. Noah's legs immediately gave way, as did Kingston's. The crewmen laughed and forced them to crawl up to the deck. It was the first full sun Noah had been under in what seemed years and the brightness stung his eyes. The air, unlike the cool breezes of his Northern California home was thick and humid, letting him know he was somewhere far from home. He saw Kingston clearly for the first time since their capture and was shocked at his filthy clothes, full growth of beard, and how emaciated the once big man appeared. Noah looked down at his own filthy self and guessed Kingston's condition mirrored his own.

Captain Simmons sneered, "How'd you like the hold?"

Noah's eyes blazed hatred.

"Have to admit, you got more stones than I gave you credit for. Figured you'd be begging to be free of the chains weeks ago. You ready to sign the crew articles now?"

Noah thought how easy it would be to just surrender and give himself over to the man who'd stolen his life, but he refused. "No."

Simmons shrugged and turned to Kingston. "How 'bout you?"

"Go to hell!" came his weary-toned reply.

Simmons chuckled. "And that's where you're going. Throw 'em in the longboat, boys!"

Noah did his best to resist, but in his weakened state he was easily forced into the longboat where one of the crewmen held a pistol on him and Kingston as they were lowered to the surface of the sea.

Simmons called down from above. "Be back to get you—someday. In the meantime, enjoy yerselves!"

The crew's derisive laughter rang out as they were rowed away from the ship towards an island in the distance.

Simmons was right. It was hell. An island prison camp. Noah had no idea how the captain knew about the place but it didn't matter. He and Kingston were turned over to uniformed soldiers and led away.

During the day, it was the job of the one hundred male prisoners to transport felled trees to the small dock, where tied up ships waited in the shark-infested waters. At night, they were herded like cattle into the confines of an old stone prison left behind by the Spanish and locked in without food, water, or protection from each other. With no guards to ensure peace, it was every man for himself against murderers, rapists, and the deranged. The first night, Noah got no sleep because of the screams—some of which were his own. As his stay lengthened and the horrors continued, he prayed the nightmare would end, but was convinced God wasn't listening.

To feed themselves after hours, prisoners roasted rats over makeshift fires. Others ate cockroaches, lizards, and anything else unfortunate enough to cross their paths. Noah and Kingston joined them. It was either that or starve.

In the months that followed, Noah grew stronger from the forced labor and from fighting to stay alive. Both he and Kingston were challenged by those who'd carved the prison's population into fiefdoms and were looking for more subjects to rule, provide them with food, and be their lovers when called upon, but the two men proved their mettle by being as craven and fierce as their opponents and were eventually left alone. The uniformed guards, themselves disgraced Spanish soldiers, turned a blind eye to the nocturnal mayhem. They spent their days patrolling the work sites—bayonet-fitted rifles at the ready— and their nights buying favors from the local women. Their only concern was that the work be done, and that each morning enough men were still alive to ensure that it would be.

After six months on the island, Noah no longer identified himself with the pampered youngest son of his illustrious California family. The night before, he'd thrust a man's face into a fire for ambushing Kingston and breaking his collarbone. He'd become as feral as the tigers that hunted in the mountains, and as deadly as the sharks circling the coasts. His humanity had been shed in order to stay alive and he had no way of knowing if he'd ever reclaim that other self again.

A week later, he and Kingston, whose arm still hung in a makeshift sling, were pulled from their work detail without explanation and driven by wagon to the docks. Waiting there stood the smug Captain Simmons. "You boys ready to sign on with me now?"

Neither man hesitated. They affixed their signatures to the articles and followed him back to his ship.

Chapter 1

Summer 1887
Havana, Cuba

Pilar Banderas scanned the slew of vessels anchored in Havana's crowded harbor. She needed to steal a ship. Disguised as an old woman and wearing a worn head wrap, a shapeless blouse, and dusty skirt, she leaned on a cane and continued her slow walk down the docks. Two brigs belonging to the hated Spanish navy were quickly ruled out as candidates due to their size and the surety of punishment should she be caught aboard. There were other vessels about, both smaller in design and tonnage, but these required more crew members than she had access to, so she quickly eliminated them as well. The most likely candidate was a two-masted schooner named the *Alanza*. Having sailed similar ships in the past, she knew it would easily make the journey to Santo Domingo for her rendezvous with the gunrunner and wouldn't need a large crew. She'd had her eye on it since beginning her surveillance yesterday and the more she observed it, the more she cottoned to it. From intelligence gathered from friends inside the city, she knew the *Alanza*'s owner to be a wealthy American named Noah Yates, and that he docked in Havana annually to sell Oriental silks, spices, and other exotic goods to those with the coin to waste on such extravagances. Last night, he was seen escorting one of the city's fabled beauties to the theater and after returning her home, he'd spent a few hours at a popular gambling hall where he won a sizeable amount of gold. Were he to lose his ship, he was undoubtedly wealthy enough to commission another, so she felt no remorse.

Pilar was an *araña*, a "spider," one of many who gathered information on behalf of the Cuban rebels determined to rid their beloved island of Spanish rule. The last attempt at independence, known as the Ten Years' War, ended in 1878 with a negotiated surrender by the rebels, but she and her compatriots were convinced the next campaign would be a success mainly because of the prowess of rebel leader General Jose Antonio Maceo, affectionately called the Bronze Titan by his followers for the color of his skin and his fearlessness on the battlefield.

Her decision on the *Alanza* made, she picked her way through the crowds and moved back to the three-legged stool that marked her spot on the busy dock, where Cubans of every hue, age, and size hawked everything from food and drink to religious medals in an effort to supplement their paltry incomes, all under the watchful eyes of the increasing numbers of Spanish soldiers on patrol.

For the past few months, hundreds of new troops had been brought in to help keep the crown's boot on the neck of the people. In a shameless effort to quell the rising dissent, thousands of people tied to the rebels had been rounded up and forced into squalid camps filled with despair, disease, and too little food. But instead of breaking the spirit of the movement, the calls for freedom were intensifying with the dawning of each new day.

In spite of the island's underlying tension, the air near the docks was alive with the smells of food cooking on small braziers, the sounds of peddlers and musicians and the tangy scent of the sea.

"Where's your badge, old woman?"

Pilar slowly raised her attention to the man who'd spoken in such a sneering tone, and eyed him for a moment. He had a thin, light-colored face, was dressed in a tight, Spanish-cut suit, and his hair was slick with pomade. "What badge?" she asked as she lined up the fish she was selling as part of her ruse.

"The badge that gives you the right to be on the docks."

The graft in Havana was so pervasive even beggars were required to pay a bribe to beg. "I don't need one." Out of the corner of her eye she watched her friend Tomas ambling innocently in her direction. He was posing as her fisherman son in order to be part of her eyes and ears. He was also good in a fight should the need arise.

"Everyone needs a badge to be on the docks or you'll have to leave."

"Says who?"

"Says me."

"And who's your master?" she asked careful to keep her voice in the register of the aged.

His scowl announced he was not enjoying being challenged. "I have no master."

"I think you do. His name is Gordonez. Yes?" She knew who ran the docks.

He stiffened.

"My name is Banderas. Tell him I am here on business and I don't need his people fouling my web."

Apparently infuriated by her refusal to be intimidated, he drew back his fist, but her steely glare gave him pause.

"Do you see that man there in the green shirt?"

He took a look at Tomas, who'd taken up a position a short distance away while the crowd flowed around him.

"He has a knife that can fly from his hand to your heart before you can blink an eye. If you prefer to die today, go ahead and strike me."

His eyes widened.

She used her true voice: "Go give your master my message before I have you killed just for blocking my view."

Plainly furious, he gave her a final glare before striding away.

Tomas walked over and added a few more freshly caught fish to her stacks. They'd been friends since infancy and shared the common pain of having their fathers hanged by Spain during the Ten Years' War. "Who was he?"

"One of Gordonez's men. I sent him away with a message that I hope he'll take to heart. I'll not have this ruined because he wants a tribute."

"Let's hope he does, because our prey approaches."

Two men, both tall and brown skinned, wove their way down the crowded walkway, eschewing the offerings of the legion of hawkers. "Which one?" she asked.

"On the left. The other is his business associate, Kingston Howard."

Pilar saved evaluation of Howard for later and discreetly focused her attention on Yates. His thick black hair was pulled back in a queue. Its texture and length heralded a man of mixed blood. As he drew nearer, she realized he was even taller than he'd initially appeared. His shoulders in the well-cut gray suit were wide and powerful. There was a silent power in his carriage, giving the impression that he was not a man to be underestimated or toyed with. As she took him in, from those shoulders to his expensive boots, an uncharacteristic frisson of nervousness coursed through her and she wondered if choosing another target might be more prudent. As he turned his face from his companion, she noted the cool depth in his dark eyes and the wicked scar that ran along his cheek. "*Dios!*" she whispered sharply. The scar was startling, but seemed to heighten the granite lines of an arrestingly handsome face.

"He won't be easily bested, Pilar. Taking him on might be a mistake."

She agreed, but the rebels needed those guns. At the conclusion of the Ten Years' War, personal possession of firearms had been outlawed, so the populace was forced to deal with smugglers. "There's no time to search out anyone else. If we don't meet Octavio tomorrow night, he'll sell the guns to another buyer." The old smuggler was a family friend but business always outweighed the personal, and he wouldn't wait forever, no matter how much gold he'd been promised.

By then Yates and Howard were abreast of Pilar's position, so she called out in her crone's voice, "Won't you try this fine fish, gentlemen? It's fresh."

They shook their heads and continued walking.

"Fish is good for bed games," she added. "Makes you strong and hard. Helps a handsome man last 'til sunrise."

That earned her a slight grin but they shook their heads again and moved on.

"Bed games?" Tomas asked over a chuckle. "What do you know of that?"

Rather than admit the truth, she offered up

instead, "I know we have to have his ship." She stared at the retreating back of Noah Yates, hoping this wouldn't be a mistake.

She was about to say more, but was interrupted by the return of Gordonez's man.

"He wants to see you."

"And if I refuse?"

He gave her a cold smile. "Then he will alert the authorities of your presence in the city, and we both know you can't afford that."

She looked to Tomas, who was observing the man malevolently.

"Alone," the man added smugly.

"No," Tomas replied coldly.

Pilar put her hand on his arm. "I'll be fine." She doubted Gordonez wanted his illegal operations impacted by General Maceo's wrath should something happen to her. He might be a snake but he wasn't a stupid one. "I'll meet you after we're done."

Tomas nodded tightly, but promised. "If she is harmed in any way, my knife and I will come hunting—you."

The confident smile withered.

Victorio Gordonez lived in a fine house on the outskirts of the city. He cultivated the façade of a wealthy businessman, but what lay beneath stank of corruption, extortion, and murder for hire. When Pilar arrived, his man escorted her to a study that was overly decorated with statues of saints and nude women. "He will be with you shortly."

"Shortly" dragged on for over an hour. She knew the delay was an attempt by Gordonez to upset her, so instead, she used the time to devise her plan for Yates. She decided on one that was both simple and direct because that always worked best. Attempting something complicated and involved meant too many things might go wrong.

"Ah, Pilar. I wondered which Banderas sent the message."

She turned to the portly man who'd once been her mother's *novio*. She didn't return his smile.

"That disguise is so dramatic, but your family was always known for their . . . theatrics."

She ignored the dig. She also kept to herself how utterly ridiculous he looked in the white powder he wore in a failing attempt to mask the dark skin passed down to him by his enslaved African grandmother. "Why did you wish to see me?"

He walked over to the desk and took a seat in the red upholstered chair, which resembled a throne. "Have you no time for pleasantries? How is your beautiful mother? And your sister and aunts?"

She folded her arms and waited.

"Ah, always the rebellious one. That will be your downfall one day, let's hope it isn't soon."

She ignored that as well.

"The reason I invited you to my humble home

was to welcome you to the city and to inquire as to why you're here."

"And if I say it is not your affair?"

"I'm sure my man gave you my message just as he gave me yours. Why are you in Havana, Pilar?"

"On business for the general." She saw him take that in and try and determine just how far to push.

"Ah the illustrious general. Is he still in hiding and licking his wounds, in, Bolivia, is it?" He opened a small elaborately decorated tin box sitting on the desk and took out a chocolate that he popped into his mouth. "Would you like one?"

"No, thank you."

He sat back and studied her momentarily. "General Maceo would be better served by concentrating on farming, as he was raised to do. He and his Mambi hordes know nothing about running a country as advanced as Cuba. During the Ten Years' War the crown proved that they knew very little about fighting as well." And he laughed.

The Mambis were the members of General Maceo's army. More than eighty percent were of African-Cuban descent. They took their name from Eutimio Mambi who'd successfully fought the Spanish in Santo Domingo.

"Are we done?"

"Again, why are you here?"

"Again, not your concern, but to ease your fears, it has nothing to do with you or your enterprises."

"I want you out of Havana."

"As soon as I've accomplished my goal, I'll take your desires into consideration."

"You know, had your mother chosen me instead of your wastrel father, you'd be my daughter, and you'd both be living in Havana, enjoying a rich, full life instead of starving in the rat mazes of Santiago with the rest of the vermin there."

"How did it feel when she didn't show up at the church on your wedding day?"

"Get out!"

"Gladly."

Tomas was outside, waiting atop a wagon, just as she knew he would be.

"What did he want?" he asked as she climbed up to the seat.

"Other than trying to determine the general's whereabouts and slurring my parents, nothing."

"Bastard."

Gordonez was that and more. His lies had sent her father to the gallows. She swallowed her hate. "Forget him. Let's go steal a ship."

Chapter 2

On board the *Alanza* in the small quarters below-decks that served as Noah's office and bedroom, he and Kingston prepared to part company. Kingston would be journeying by ferry to Florida to take the train up the East Coast to rendezvous with his wife and son now residing in Boston. Noah would be raising anchor in the morning to head home to California to attend his mother's wedding. A decade had passed since Simmons led the two men away from the island prison camp. Due to that shared experience they were as close as brothers. The articles they'd signed bound them to the heinous captain for two long years, but once free they'd formed Yates and Howard Imports and amassed a small fortune selling merchandise from all corners of the world.

"How long do you plan to stay in California?" Kingston asked.

Noah shrugged. "I'm not certain. I find I can only stomach being on land a short while, but I am anxious to see my family. I'll wire you if I get antsy."

The smile on King's face made Noah ask, "What's so humorous?"

"That old woman and her fish. Just thinking back on her touting its, uh, qualities."

Noah rolled his eyes. "At her age I doubt she can even remember what it was like to be in a man's bed."

"Speaking of which, what did you think of Senorita Bernita Mendoza?"

"She's lovely as a sunrise but has the brains of a barnacle."

Kingston laughed.

"I think my mother may have given her parents the impression that I was seeking a bride." The family was distantly related to his mother and had recently settled in Cuba after fleeing the war and upheaval in Santo Domingo.

"But you aren't."

"Of course not. The sea is my mistress and doesn't bore me with talks of gossip and gowns, which is all the girl talked about last night."

"You need a wife to bring light into that dark soul of yours."

"I like my dark soul but if you find me a woman willing to live on the sea, I may consider changing my stance."

"I'll see if one can be found. What are your plans this evening?"

"I foolishly agreed to escort Bernita to the opera. After that I'll come back here and prepare to sail for home."

"Fine. Then, I'll take my leave now."

The two men shared a brotherly embrace.

"Godspeed, Noah."

"And to you as well. My regards to your wife and son."

Kingston departed, leaving Noah alone.

Noah walked up the short stairway that led above deck and stood looking out over the congested harbor. He couldn't wait to weigh anchor and feel the roll of the waves beneath the *Alanza* and the wind in his face. He and a skeleton crew would sail west to Brownsville, Texas, and dock the boat at a shipyard he'd used in the past. The men would make their way to their homes and he'd take the train to San Francisco with the hopes of arriving in plenty of time for his mother's wedding so he could walk her down the aisle. After his father Abraham's death, she'd raised Noah and his brothers alone. It was time she found love for herself, and he considered Max Rudd, an old family friend, to be a perfect match for the strong-willed matriarch. It had been almost a year since he'd seen his family. On his last visit to Destino, the ranch where they'd all grown up, he'd been pleasantly surprised to find his oldest brother, Logan, married to a feisty golden-eyed seamstress from Philadelphia named Mariah. Since that time, they'd presented his mother with her first grandchild, a baby girl named Maria, who, he'd learned by correspondence, had inherited her mother's golden eyes. Even more surprising was the recent letter from his mother informing him that his second eldest brother, lawyer Andrew, was now married as well. Drew, who everyone believed would spend the rest of his years sowing his wild oats from the Bay to Mexico, married? The thought of that made him smile. He couldn't wait to meet the woman who finally saddled him. Noah was glad his brothers had also found love and in a small way envied them their happiness, but he had no intentions of marrying because he enjoyed his solitary seafaring life and he doubted any woman would willingly embrace what King called his black soul. The optimistic, carefree young man he'd been lay buried beneath the experiences set into motion by Captain Alfred Simmons. He wore the darkness left behind like a heavy winter coat and it hampered his ability to reclaim the joy he'd once found in life. Although he'd never admit it to anyone, he had vivid nightmares about those terrible months on the island. Still. They'd tapered off somewhat in the past few years, but not enough to declare himself free of the nocturnal terror that made him bolt awake, shaking and drenched in cold fear-fed sweat. Yet another reason he eschewed taking a wife.

"We're going ashore, Captain. See you at dawn."

It was one of the mates, the red-haired Irishman Henry Dennison. With him were the other crewmen who'd be making the sail back to the States.

"Enjoy the ladies," Noah told them, knowing where they were headed this last night in Cuba.

Henry returned wryly, "Oh we will."

After their departure, Noah went below to read and rest up for his evening at the opera with Bernita "the Barnacle" Mendoza.

Bernita leaned over in her seat and whispered, "By the scowl on your face one would think you're not having a good time."

"One would be correct."

Not even the theater's darkness could mask the shock on her lovely face.

"I'm just being truthful," he informed her.

She huffed around and fanned herself angrily.

It was difficult to be pleasant when her need to change gowns—twice—had made them arrive at the opera house so late they'd been denied entrance to the performance until the first intermission. Onstage the caterwauling woman attempting to pass herself off as Bizet's Carmen was making the long evening in her company even more exasperating. Behind him Bernita's duenna was snoring loudly enough to be heard over the orchestra.

"Then at the next intermission I demand you take me home."

"My pleasure."

The fan moved faster. "You are no gentleman."

"I agree."

True to his word they left during the intermission and after the hired coach was brought around, Noah saw the ladies home. He stepped inside to say good night to Bernita's parents, who glanced between the silent American and their furious daughter with confusion.

Noah lied: "I wasn't feeling well and Bernita was gracious enough to allow me to return her home early."

She scoffed derisively.

Her parents' eyes widened.

Deciding further explanation was unwarranted, he bowed and made his exit. Outside, he descended the stone stairs and undid the tie at his throat. Feeling much more relaxed, he crossed to the waiting coach. As his hand grasped the handle, suddenly something pointed and sharp was pressed hard against his spine. He froze.

A pleasant-sounding female voice instructed, "Please stand still, Mr. Yates. This rapier in your back has tasted men's blood for fifty years. I'd hate to add your name to the list."

Noah didn't move. "If you want my wallet it's in my coat."

"We're not petty thieves. Climb into the coach, please."

Havana, with all its gaiety and vices, was a dangerous place, and beneath his coat was a holstered pistol, but the chances of getting off a shot before the woman ran the rapier through his liver were slim. Two men stepped out of the darkness and flanked him. Both had their faces hidden beneath bandanas and were carrying machetes—Cuba's weapon of choice. He chose to follow orders.

The door was opened.

"Slowly, now," she cautioned.

He complied. As he stooped to enter, the sight of the two men occupying one of the benches made him pause. Now, there were at least five of them and only one of him. Six, when he counted the driver, who he assumed was part of their gang. The rapier was still pressed dangerously against his spine. The man on Noah's left reached into his coat and pulled the pistol free of the leather holster. "Please take the seat next to my friend by the window," the woman ordered.

Again he did as he was told. After she and her masked companions were seated, the coach pulled away.

Sandwiched between the two men on his bench and facing the two men and the caped woman seated opposite him, Noah asked, "If you're not after my gold, what do you want? My life?"

"No."

"Then what?"

No response.

That he might be shanghaied again began to play on his nerves and he swore he'd find a way to kill them before being forced into servitude again. "Who are you?"

Again, no response.

Filled with frustration, he wished he could see her more clearly. He wanted to be able to give the authorities a credible description should he somehow manage to escape, but her hood and the coach's shadowy interior hid her face and the voluminous folds of her black cape negated his ability to accurately gauge her size or weight. He had no problem seeing the rapier, however. She held it at rest across her lap and the silver glittered malevolently as the open windows caught the light of the passing lamps as the coach sped by.

After a short passage of time, the tang of seawater drifted to his nose. He turned his head to try and gauge his location but the partial view from the window offered only the blackness of night. The coach slowed and then stopped. He heard the sound of waves nearby.

"We're all going to step out now, Mr. Yates. No sudden moves or shows of bravado you Americans are so famous for. There are six of us and only one of you. We'd hate to have to shoot you with your own gun."

Noah didn't want to be shot with his own gun either, yet every fiber of his being demanded he take some action to change the odds. He had no idea whether she'd lied about taking his life, but in truth they'd already had the opportunity to do so, so what was this about? His curiosity was high but in order to get answers he had to play along, at least for the moment.

The coach's door opened. The woman and the men seated with her stepped out first, followed by the man to his right. The man to his left stuck the nose of the gun in his side and prodded him to follow. He moved to the door and as he stooped to exit, two thunderous blows exploded across the back of his head and he pitched forward. It was the last thing he remembered.

Chapter 3

"The next time, can we pick a much smaller man? *Dios*, he's heavy," Tomas groused. He and Eduardo held the unconscious American between them with his lifeless arms slung over their shoulders. The toes of his expensive boots dragged on the surface of the worn dock. There weren't many people about. The vendors with true homes were gone for the day, while those who used their stands as their abodes were huddled in the shadows. A few orphans played in the moonlight and on the dark water, a few lights could be seen shining within some of the ships filling the harbor.

"Halt!"

Three soldiers out on patrol. Pilar had planned for this possibility, so she and the others stopped and waited for them to approach.

"What's going on here?" one of the soldiers asked.

Pilar pulled back her hood to reveal her aged face and replied in her crone's voice, "Drunk American. We're taking him back to his ship."

The soldiers surveyed them. "He have any identification?"

"He has ship's papers and a passport in his coat."

The soldier rifled through his clothes and extracted the items, along with his billfold. It was nearly impossible to read by the light of the moon but he attempted to do so. "And you found him where?"

Glad she'd had the forethought to remove Yates's holster, Pilar explained, "My bordello. Stupid American couldn't handle the girls or the rum."

The soldier shook his head as though sharing her disdain. American attempts to annex Cuba went back to the time of President Thomas Jefferson. Spain hated the United States as much as the Cubans hated Spain.

"You know which boat is his?"

Grimacing beneath the American's weight, Tomas managed to say, "Yes. I'm her son and a fisherman. Made his acquaintance this afternoon. Rowed him out some of my catch."

As if weighing their story, the soldier in charge eyed them for a long moment, then looked to his two companions. They replied with shrugs. After helping himself to the money in Yates's billfold, he handed it back, along with the passport and papers, and dismissed them with a wave. "Go."

Pilar righted her hood and she and her companions continued on.

Under the light cast by the full moon, Pilar and her friends raised the anchor and slowly sailed out into open water. Yates was secured in his room belowdecks and would probably awaken soon, but for the moment, she stood at the bow and momentarily let go of her immediate worries to enjoy the journey. She'd been born at sea twenty-five years ago and she loved being out on the ocean. Her first voyages had been with her paternal grandfather, who traced his lineage back to the corsairs of North Africa's Barbary Coast. Part pirate, part smuggler, he'd loved thumbing his nose at the European navies almost as much as he'd loved her and her sister Doneta. When Pilar was ten years old, he'd lost his life aboard a ship during a hurricane, after which, her father, Javier, took up the family mantle. He too had lived outside the law, providing well for his wife and daughters by smuggling everything from guns and fake paintings to antiquities and rum. When the Ten Years' War began, in 1868, he'd declined to participate because it hadn't mattered to him who ruled the island of Cuba as long as nothing interfered with his clandestine endeavors. But when his three brothers joined the rebel army and were subsequently hanged for their participation, he fervently embraced the cause in order to avenge them, only to forfeit his own life during the war's closing years.

Now, she, her mother, sister, aunts, and cousins were a female coven of smugglers, counterfeiters, and forgers united by skill, blood, and a deep abiding hatred for Spain.

"Pilar. He's coming around." It was Eduardo.

Giving the moon-laced water one last look, she headed below to check on their host.

Noah came to, groggy and disoriented, in a dimly lit space. He was vaguely aware of lying on his back but there was nothing vague about the way his head ached. It throbbed like he'd been kicked by a horse wearing anvils. He tried to sit up. Realizing he was restrained immediately plunged him into panic and he struggled against the bonds while the nightmare of being chained in Captain Simmons's ship rose and took hold. A second or two later he saw that he was in his cabin and relaxed somewhat, until he remembered his abduction and fury followed; fury aimed at himself for being still susceptible to his inner fears and fury at his captors for evoking the response. He was spread-eagled atop his four-poster bed, tied by his wrists and ankles. His angry attempts to loosen the bonds were in vain. The intricate knots in the ropes had been fashioned tightly and well.

The cloaked woman, flanked by two masked men, entered the cabin and Noah stilled. Within the raised hood, a black veil covered her features. "My apologies for our methods, Mr. Yates," she offered. "But it was necessary. If your head aches, I can offer you something that will ease it."

"All I want is to be freed from these ropes," he snarled.

"You will get your wish—when it's time."

"What do you want from me?"

"We already have it."

"And that is?"

"Your boat," she replied simply.

He stiffened. "What do you want with my boat?"

"I can't tell you everything, Mr. Yates. A woman must have some mystery."

He struggled again against the ropes.

"You may as well lie still. When my grandfather taught me those knots, he said they'd hold a dragon if need be and he's been proven correct."

"What was he, a pirate?" he spat scathingly, hoping to offend her with words, since he had no other weapons.

"As a matter of fact, he was. Stealing boats is in my blood, I suppose."

"I demand that you release me!"

She shook her head seemingly with pity. "We all have dreams, Mr. Yates."

He shot back. "Pirates hang, you know."

"Only those caught, and we have no intentions of doing so."

"Why my boat?"

She shrugged. "It fits our needs, and I've shared all the information I plan to. Are you hungry?"

"No."

"Do you wish to relieve yourself? I wouldn't want you to be any more uncomfortable than is necessary."

"No," he gritted out. What he wanted she

wouldn't allow—which was to get his hands on her.

"Then I shall leave my companions to watch over you." Offering him a nearly imperceptible nod of farewell, she took her leave.

And as she did, Noah bellowed with fury-fed frustration.

In the silence afterwards, he glanced over at the two masked men she'd left behind. "I'm a very wealthy man. I can pay whatever you ask if you'll cut me free."

Silence.

"Do you value your lives so lowly that you'd let a woman lead you to the gallows, or does what she offer between her legs—"

Instantly, the gleaming blade of a machete was pressed against his throat. "Say one more word," the man invited sinisterly from behind the bandanna, "and I will slit you from stem to stern. You know nothing of her or us. She's not a whore."

Their eyes warred for a silent moment and Noah sneered, "It's easy to threaten a man tied down."

His companion pulled him away and they returned to their positions by the door. Noah schooled his anger but he hated being in such an impotent position.

An hour later, the woman hadn't returned and Noah's shoulders were on fire from being in such an unnatural position for so long a period of time.

He was certain that even if he could get free it would be a while before his arms functioned normally again.

When she finally arrived she had the silver rapier in hand, and he wondered if that was something else bequeathed to her by her pirate grandfather.

"It's time for us to part company, Mr. Yates. You've been an excellent host."

He added her sarcasm to the list of things he didn't care for about his evening.

She walked over to the foot of the bed and took up a position between his spread-wide legs. When she slowly raised the rapier he instinctively shrunk back and he swore she smiled from behind the veil.

"My friend is going to cut you free. Make one false move and I will geld you."

His jaw tightened.

"Do you understand?" she asked in a voice as soft as the shadows in the cabin.

He nodded tersely.

"Good." And she silently signaled the man with the machete to approach. The blade sliced through the rope as easily as if it were a mango. Noah's right arm dropped free and he moaned with relief in spite of himself. The man walked around to the opposite side of the bed and a second later the left arm was cut loose.

As his ankles were released one by one, she

cautioned during the process: "Remember. Don't move." And because he believed her earlier threat, he complied.

No longer bound by the ropes, it might have been the perfect moment for him to mount an attack to change the odds but his arms weren't strong enough to pick up a spoon, let alone take on the pirate git with the rapier and her machete-armed companions. All he could do was lie there and pray the burn in his shoulders, ankles, and knees would subside soon.

"I'll give you a few moments to regain some of your strength," she said to him, "and then we'll go above deck."

Noah had no idea what awaited him but with each delayed moment, small amounts of life returned to his limbs.

She was apparently astute enough to anticipate that. "Let's go."

Faced with the overwhelming odds and having his own pistol trained on him by one of the men, he moved slowly to the door.

Above deck, the night was bright with the moon and stars. If he had to meet his death, he preferred it be under the stars.

"Into the rowboat, please."

He stilled.

Under the light of the lantern held aloft by one of the men, he studied her. Only then did he realize how short-statured she truly was. "The rowboat?"

"Yes, Mr. Yates. I told you we weren't after your life. Just the *Alanza*. That's Spanish. Is it named for your wife?"

"No. My mother."

"Ah."

Noah tried hard to see her face but the darkness, in combination with the veil, made it impossible.

"Shall we?" she asked, gesturing with the rapier. And in that split second of movement the light from the lantern fell on the only thing that might help him identify her in the future. An old scar in the form of an *X* gleamed palely on the back of her brown hand. "There's water and food from your stores. Your coat and papers are there also. I'd row west were I you."

Noah studied the small woman who'd been the root of this maddening adventure and vowed aloud with soft menace: "I will find you if it takes the rest of my life, so stay alive until I come for you, my little pirate, because I will be coming."

She visibly stiffened in reaction, giving him the evening's only measure of satisfaction.

Without another word, Noah climbed into the boat and was lowered down to the black surface of the sea. He checked the stars overhead in an effort to fix his position and forced his protesting arms to row west while his beloved ship sailed east and out of sight.

Pilar left the piloting to the crew and went back down to his quarters to see if he'd left anything of value behind; after all, she was from a family of rogues. Before bringing Yates aboard, she and Tomas did a hasty search for weapons and such to insure that if he somehow freed himself from her grandfather's dragon knots he wouldn't be able to mount a counterassault. The cursory inspection uncovered a few rifles and some knives, which she planned to turn over to the rebels, and now as she studied the space it seemed to resonate with his presence. *I will find you if it takes the rest of my life, so stay alive until I come for you, my little pirate, because I will be coming.* The hairs on the back of her neck stood up at the memory of his parting words and although she doubted he'd ever make good on the threat, the certainty in his tone made her heart pound with unease. Determined not to think about it, she walked over to the nightstand and picked up a framed photograph that was there. Staring back was a strikingly beautiful woman with dark hair. She was seated, wearing an ornate gown and flanked by three boys. She wondered if this was his mother. Looking closely at the boys, she was almost certain that the solemn-faced youngest of the three was Noah Yates. The eyes were the same, as was the then unscarred jaw. His brothers perhaps? Having no answer, she set the frame down again and crossed to a worn desk. It held two drawers. The top one was filled with charts, maps, and a ship's log. The bottom drawer revealed a large number of papers, which she withdrew. They were musical charts and she found that surprising. Having no musical training, she didn't know what tune the notes represented but penned across the top of one of the sheets were the words *Requiem for the Sea* and below that his name. Surely he wasn't a musical composer? As she slowly leafed through the seven pages, Tomas entered.

"Find anything we can sell?" he asked.

"Not yet, but I did find these."

She handed him one. He scanned it and asked, "Music?"

"Yes, and his name's on one of the sheets. I think he may have composed them."

"No one will want to buy this. What else did you find?"

In spite of Tomas's dismissive response, she thought the music impressive. It made her wonder who Noah Yates was beneath his wealthy and yes, angry exterior. She knew a few songs taught to her by her grandparents but they were either religious or borne of the sea, and they certainly weren't the composers.

"Now, these will bring us some funds," Tomas exclaimed over the open lid of a chest. In his palm were two pairs of expensive gold cuff links. They'd fetch a fine price indeed but for some reason her conscience balked.

"We'll not be selling his things."

"What? Why not?"

"We've already taken his ship. Doesn't seem right to steal what's inside, too."

"Since when did you become so holy?"

She cut him a look.

"So, we just leave what's here to rot, or are you planning to give him back the ship someday?"

She had no ready reply.

"Did he scare you with that talk about finding you? Is that what this is about?"

She shook her head. She didn't know what she was about. All she knew was that for some reason she was conflicted over what was usually a fairly straightforward decision. In the end, she gave in to what was best. "You're right, they'll fetch a fine price."

Tomas continued to observe her closely. "Are you all right?"

"I am. Pay me no mind. Let's see what else is here."

The chest held a couple changes of clothing, some bedding, a shaving set, and another surprise: paints and a brush. Further exploration turned up an easel behind the bed. On a wall hung a seascape that she'd noticed earlier but hadn't paid much attention to. Now she viewed it with interest.

"Do you think he painted it?" Tomas asked.

She shrugged.

"First music, now paints. Never knew Americans to be so cultured."

She agreed. The small painting was a night scene

of a storm on open water. Dark, brooding clouds were above an angry wave-tossed sea in shades of black and indigo. Flecks of gray capped the roiling waves. Her sister Doneta was the family's art forger and Pilar wondered what she'd make of his talent. To Pilar's untrained eye it appeared to be fairly well done.

"Worth anything, you think?"

"We'll let Doneta decide."

Tomas placed everything they planned to sell inside a pillow slip taken from the trunk. He added the painting to the haul.

Pilar gave the space one last scan. "I think we're done."

Tomas agreed. "I'll place this with the guns we found."

As he departed, the American's ghostlike presence continued to fill both the space and her mind. Knowing she had more pressing matters to worry over, she shook him off and went above deck to join her companions.

When the sun rose, the exhausted Noah was picked up by a ship belonging to the Spanish navy and taken aboard.

After hearing his story, the captain, a reed-thin man in a too-large uniform asked, "A pirate, you say?" He didn't appear too impressed by the tale. "More than likely smugglers or at the very least, rebels. They negotiated a surrender the last time, but lately they've been causing trouble again."

"I don't care who they are or what they call themselves, I want my ship back," he said while pacing angrily.

"That's understandable, but they could be anywhere by now, and with no other description than the leader wore a cape and veil . . ." His words faded and he shrugged. "I will file a report when we reach Havana. Maybe your ship will show up at one of the other ports."

"I need to find my ship!" he declared, pounding on the desk for emphasis.

"Mr. Yates, I know you Americans think the sun rises and sets on your desires, but we may be on the verge of war again, and we can't drop everything to go searching for a ship stolen from you by a woman."

The man's derisive tone stung. Noah was already embarrassed enough at being a pawn in the woman's game. The sarcastic reminder only added to his frustration, but he reined in his temper. "My apologies for being so rude and overbearing. Were it not for your kindness I'd be still oaring my way back to Havana." He ran his hand over his tired face. He owed the man his thanks. Another captain might have simply sailed by. Noah prided himself on keeping his emotions in check, but this situation had him at his wit's end.

"We will do all that is possible to learn the fate of your ship, Mr. Yates. I promise you."

"Thank you."

A short while later the ship dropped anchor in Havana's harbor and Noah was rowed ashore. After thanking the sailors, his first order of business was to find his crew. He could only imagine what might be going through their heads upon finding the ship gone. To his relief they were holed up at one of the boardinghouses that catered to Americans.

"What's happened?" Dennison asked. "We thought maybe you'd sailed off without us."

Noah told the tale once more and the men stared, stunned. Before they could ask the many questions he knew they were harboring, he waved them off. "We can discuss the particulars later. Right now, I need to see about securing more funds—did I mention that I was robbed as well?" Just thinking about the pirate git threatened to raise his temper again. "While I'm gone, ask around about another ship going west. I'll pay your passage." He strode out, leaving the still gaping crewmen behind.

Dawn was just breaking when Pilar and her crew reached the eastern tip of Cuba for the final leg of their journey home. The guns they'd picked up from their smuggler contact in Santo Domingo were safely aboard and now they were slowly sailing up an inland river bordered by rocks and vegetation in an area near the coast. "Watch those rocks, Tomas," she called out as he piloted the narrow passage.

"I'm minding them, Pilar. Just stop your nagging."

His tone held a smile and an answering one curved her lips in reply. They both knew the waters like the backs of their hands. Between what she'd learned about these waters from her grandfather and Tomas from his fisherman father they could've navigated the way blindfolded. There were spots so shallow the rocky bed all but scraped the schooner's hull and other stretches wide and deep enough to support a brigantine. That they'd been able to successfully accomplish their mission without a hitch was elating. No one was hurt, the guns were secured below, and other than having to deal with the very angry Noah Yates, stealing the ship had been as easy as the breeze lightly filling the sails. She wondered if he'd had to row the entire distance back to Havana or been picked up by a fishing boat. The waters near the capital were fairly bustling with activity after sunrise, so more than likely someone had come to his rescue. He was still furious, no doubt, and she supposed he had ample reason. After all, they had separated him from his property, and that it had been accomplished by a gang led by a woman was probably even more galling—no man enjoyed being bested by a member of the opposite sex.

Even though she had bested him, his parting words continued to resonate ominously. Something she had no words for had passed between them at that moment and she was still feeling oddly unsettled. She'd taken great pains to keep her features and those of the men with her hidden so he'd not be able to identify them later and she felt confident about having accomplished that as well. It was highly unlikely they'd meet again, yet since casting him adrift, she found herself thinking about him, with his scarred handsome face, even though she had no business doing so.

Her reverie was broken by the sight of the water-fall ahead. This end of the island was mountainous, untamed, and filled with a lush green of paradise, where stands of red bananas, cocoa, coffee beans, and coconuts grew unimpeded. Waterfalls dotted the area, too, offering places to swim, fish, play, and in this case a place to hide. Her grandfather and his most trusted pirate comrades used the cave behind this particular fall to shelter their ships and booty from the prying eyes of the British and Spanish navies. Pilar was reasonably certain the Europeans had no idea what lay behind the cascading water because their ships were too large and bulky to navigate the way, but behind it lay a cave vast enough to safely hold a ship the size of the *Alanza* and not be seen from the outside. She and the men hauled down the sails as they neared the rocks. Everything above deck would be soaked by the deluge as they passed through the powerful flow so they all held on as Tomas slowly steered them through and into the shadowy darkness of the cave.

Once inside they set the anchor and transferred the oilcloth-wrapped guns and powder to the rocky ledge. Eduardo and his son Jose had relatives who lived nearby, so they immediately set out to retrieve a wagon that would be used to transfer the guns to Santiago.

She and Tomas sat on the edge of the rocks to wait. He asked, "Do you think Yates has been found?"

She shrugged. "I wondered about that, too, but I'm sure he has been."

"Still worried about him finding us?"

She lied, "No, so let's not talk about him."

He nodded.

When their friends returned, she and Tomas swam out with their cargo and once it was loaded into the wagon's false bottom, they headed south for the two-day journey home. In ten days, they'd return for the *Alanza* to get her refitted, then sail to Santo Domingo for another rendezvous with the gun smuggler.

Chapter 4

Alanza Yates didn't think there was any woman in the world happier than she. Two of her sons were now married and had gifted her with daughters-in-laws and grandchildren she absolutely adored. She'd gotten a big kick out of watching Philadelphia seamstress Mariah Cooper tame her stepson, Logan. Middle son, Andrew, and his wife, Billie, had had an interesting courtship as well. Both married couples lived on Rancho Destino property, the sprawling ranch she'd inherited from her late parents, and having them near gave her joy as well. In a few weeks, her third son, Noah, would be docking his ship, the *Alanza*, in San Francisco, and the thought of having all three boys with her again filled her heart.

"You're awfully quiet, Lanz."

Alanza snuggled closer to the man holding the reins of the buggy. "Just thinking about how happy and blessed I am to have my family—and you." The two of them would be marrying in a bit over a week and that made her the happiest of all.

"You're not going to get cold feet and run off on me, are you?"

"No," she said with a laugh. "Even if I did, you'd just hunt me down."

"Very true."

She'd known Max Rudd most of her adult life. He'd been best friend to her late husband Abraham, but the circumstances surrounding her relationships with the two men were as different as night and day. Due to her being a foolish and spoiled child, Abe had been forced to marry her. He'd been a widower in those days, and his son, Logan, was six years old. In the years following the wedding, she and Abe grew to respect each other and she'd given birth to first Andrew and then Noah, but the marriage held no passion. After Abe's untimely death, she'd taken over the running of the ranch and Max, being true to the memory of his friend, stepped in to help. She'd no idea he'd been in love with her until recently. Even though she held feelings for him as well, she'd been afraid of being in another loveless relationship and had done everything she could to discourage his suit. However, Max was as stubborn as she was headstrong and refused to let her walk away from the happiness he wanted them both to share, so she, like her sons, surrendered to love. And now, just as soon as Noah arrived, they would become man and wife.

"You still want to have the wedding as part of your birthday celebration?"

"Of course." Her natal-day parties were legendary in both size and scope. In addition to her many Spanish relatives, most of the people in the surrounding valley would be attending. It wasn't uncommon for her annual celebration to last three days or more, so adding the wedding to the festivities seemed to be a natural solution. She drew back slightly to gauge his handsome face with its graying moustache and temples. "Would you rather I not have my birthday party?"

"Would you cancel it if I said yes?"

She studied him. "The wedding is in less than ten days and all the invitations have gone out. If you're getting cold feet, I need to know now, Max."

"No cold feet. Just being selfish. Don't want to share you. We're not spring chickens, Lanz, so I want to spend each and every moment that I can with you."

She cuddled close again. "That's so sweet. After the wedding we're going to be together so much you'll be downright sick of my company."

"Doubt that, but willing to test it out. Oh, and you might not want to have any wedding guests stay in your wing of the house though." Her home had two large wings: one for her personal use and one her sons shared growing up.

"Why not?"

"Don't want to have to shoot anyone for breaking down the door once you get to screaming on our wedding night."

She rolled her eyes. For the past few months, he'd been teasing her unmercifully about the intimate details of the wedding night. "Why do you keep saying that?" she asked on a laugh.

"Because it's the truth."

"Well, I talked to Billie about this whole screaming nonsense, and I doubt I'll get that carried away."

He began chuckling. "If you say so. I'd make you bet me, but you're going to be my wife. Not right for a man to take money from his wife."

Always ready to meet a challenge, she replied confidently, "I'll take that bet. What are you putting up, my handsome *vaquero*?"

"If you lose, you wear my choice of clothing."

"Your choice of clothing?" she asked dubiously.

He nodded. "I asked Mariah to run me up some things."

"For me?"

He nodded.

Alanza was so confused she wasn't sure what to ask next.

"And you'll not fuss at Mariah for not telling you, or ask her about my request. Think of it as a surprise wedding gift."

"But—"

"Promise me, Lanz. I don't ask much from you, but do this for me, and I promise the reward will be the sweetest thing this side of the Rockies."

Even more confusion set in.

He stopped the buggy, leaned over and kissed her with such practiced ease she momentarily forgot what they'd been discussing. He brushed his lips against hers. "Promise me *querida*."

Alanza was so lost she would've promised to turn herself into a prized steer as long as the kisses didn't stop. And when they finally did, and he reluctantly drew away, her eyes were closed and her senses were spiraling. She somehow managed to whisper, "I promise."

Still in the throes of his spell she missed his quiet smile as he got the buggy moving again and drove on.

The following morning, Alanza rode over to the small house belonging to Logan and his wife, Mariah. She had an appointment with her seamstress daughter-in-law to make the final adjustments on her wedding gown. Since leaving Max last evening, she'd been trying to think of a way to get around the promise she'd made to him in order to find out about the mysterious garment he'd commissioned. Fairly confident she'd hatched a reasonable solution, she walked around to the door that led to Mariah's small shop, which was built on the back of the house. Outside playing were her grandchildren, the sixteen-month-old "twin" cousins, Mariah's Little Maria and Billie's son, Tonio. Both were in the wooden pen the mothers fondly referred to as the Baby Jail. At her approach both toddlers ran to the edge of the pen, their little faces filled with joy and their arms raised for her to pick them up. At one point in her life, Alanza had prayed every night for grandchildren. Presently it seemed silly, but back then she'd been utterly convinced none of her sons would ever marry, because Logan was married to his duties tied to running the ranch, and Drew— well, he had a remuda of women that spanned the state. Now, her smile matched theirs.

"How are my two angels this morning?" She picked them each up and placed big fat loud kisses on their chubby cheeks. Tonio immediately squirmed—his way of intimating his desire to be set down. "Oh, no. Your mamas have you in jail for a reason. You're not getting your *abuela* in trouble this early in the morning." And she set them both back in the pen. Tonio stomped and whined, but she was as immune as the other adults in his life to his little fits of pique. "Tonio, one day you're going to wish you were still little enough to spend your entire day doing nothing." She blew them kisses and went inside.

Both daughters-in-law were there having a cup of coffee, and like their children greeted Alanza with ready smiles. "Morning, ladies, I'm here for my fitting."

"Give me just a few more moments of fortification," Mariah said over a yawn. "Maria woke up in the middle of the night screaming. I think she had a bad dream, and of course, once she calmed down she didn't want to go back to sleep. The sun was coming up before she finally drifted off."

"You look tired, too, Billie."

"I am. Having trouble getting a full night's sleep. I think it may be the baby. Drew's been getting up with Tonio so I can sleep in a bit and that's helped immensely."

Billie's baby was due next winter. Alanza could hardly wait to greet her newest grandchild.

"Where are my sons?" she asked as she walked over to eye her beautiful gold gown on the headless dress form.

"Logan is working in town."

"Drew's at the bank."

A few weeks ago, a deadly arson fire destroyed most of the buildings in town. In the midst of the ensuing chaos Billie and Tonio were abducted by a dangerous man from Billie's past. Drew finally found them but only after Billie freed herself from the man's clutches and Tonio was given to a couple in a false adoption. Everything turned out well in the end, and now, every man in the area was helping to rebuild the businesses that had succumbed to the fire. Max and Logan were heading up the construction crew and Drew, whose license to practice law had been laid low by bigotry, was now the town banker, a role he seemed to enjoy.

Once Billie and Mariah finished their coffee, Alanza's nearly completed gown was taken from its form and she donned it carefully to avoid all the pins. Mariah's dressmaking business was thriving. She had a plethora of orders from shops as far away as San Francisco and Seattle but she'd dropped everything in order to bring to life the creation she'd designed for her mother-in-law.

"This is the most beautiful gown, Mariah," Alanza gushed while viewing herself in the large stand-up mirror.

"Stand still, Mama, please," Mariah instructed kindly around the pins in her mouth. "We don't want this hem to look like your granddaughter had a hand in it."

Properly chastened, Alanza complied and added, "Speaking of hands in things, Max said he asked you to make something for me."

Mariah paused and looked up. "He did."

"I promised him I'd not fuss at you for keeping it a secret, or ask what it might be, so how about you simply show it to me. That way I won't break my promise."

Billie chuckled.

Mariah took the pins from her mouth. "Nice try."

"Please?"

Mariah replied with a smile and carried on with the hemming.

Alanza sighed dejectedly and pouted dramatically.

Billie's eyes sparkled with humor. "Now I know where Tonio gets that. His *abuela*."

Alanza stuck her tongue out at Billie, who laughed.

Alanza tried again. "If I'm to wear it I think I should be allowed to see it beforehand."

From her spot on the floor, Mariah replied, "Understandable, but you aren't going to. Have you heard from Noah?"

"I received a wire a few days ago. He's in Havana and should be on his way. Please let me see it."

Billie cracked, "She's persistent if nothing else."

"That she is," Mariah spoke. "So while I pin this hem, would you answer her, please?"

"Sure," Billie replied. "No, Mama."

"I'm beginning to hate you both."

Billie got to her feet and placed a kiss on Alanza's smooth cheek. "We hate you as well. I'm going to free the inmates and take them for a walk. Have fun."

For the rest of the time at the shop, Alanza continued her quest to extract answers from Mariah, who shook her head at her mother-in-law's persistence but held on to Max's secret and continued pinning away.

Hoping to hear something about his stolen ship, Noah cooled his heels in Havana for three more days, but each day, when he went to see the admiral in charge of the navy and ports, there was no news. Realizing the date for his mother's wedding was fast approaching, he finally gave up. He and his men caught a ferry to Florida. After parting ways with them, he boarded a train for the coast. Due to the rising trend of segregated seating, it was not his preferred mode of travel, but booking passage on a westbound ship that would get him to the States in a timely manner hadn't panned out, so a train had to do. Before boarding he sent Kingston a wire to let him know the *Alanza* had been stolen, and promised to wire him again once he reached home. He brooded over the disturbing turn of events for the entire cross-country journey. What would happen to his company now that they had no way of reaching the people and vendors who relied on them to transport their goods? Would he and King be able to find another ship, and if so at what cost? Would their contacts wait for Yates and Howard to get up and running again or would they move their business elsewhere? Presently, he had no answers and that was frustrating for a man who didn't care for turmoil or chaos. Since leaving Captain Simmons, he'd plotted each and every turn in his life so he would be the person in control. The *Alanza* was his livelihood and without her everything he and King had built for the past ten years was now in jeopardy, all because of a short, masked woman with a rapier.

He arrived at Rancho Destino three days before his mother was due to walk down the aisle.

"Noah!" she exclaimed excitedly as he entered the house and set his valise by the door. She ran to him and he caught her up and held her tightly.

"Hello, Mama," he said, smiling for what felt like the first time in weeks.

"So glad you're here. How are you?"

Not wanting to cause her worry, he lied, "I'm well. How about you? Haven't changed your mind about marrying Max, have you?"

"Of course not." She slipped a motherly arm around his waist. "Come outside and sit with me. Your aunts, uncles, and cousins will be arriving tomorrow so this might be my only chance to enjoy you without being interrupted."

"Where are my brothers?"

"In town but they'll be joining us for dinner."

He looked forward to seeing them. "Did Drew really get married?"

"Yes and he has a sixteen-month-old son."

Apparently the confusion on his face was plain, because she laughed lightly. "You go sit. I'll explain in a minute. Are you hungry?"

"Famished."

"Then let me talk with Bonnie and I'll come out and join you."

She disappeared into the kitchen and he continued out onto the grand stone patio and took a seat at the large table. Sitting there in the silence he felt the tension of the past week slide away. He was home. Surveying the familiar orchards and the mounted ranch hands going about their duties brought back pleasant memories: the riding, the fishing, the games with his brothers, the fights they'd had over everything and nothing, the love of their mother who'd worked herself until her fingers bled to give them a home. The young boy he'd been back then always came alive for a time when he returned home but as always slipped back beneath the darkness that ruled him. He looked up to find his mother watching him silently, concern in her eyes. He'd never revealed any of the ugly details about his shanghai experiences to anyone in his family, but they all, especially Alanza, knew something dire had occurred, because he was not the same person he'd been before. "Yes, Mama?" he asked quietly.

She came forward carrying a tray with glasses of lemonade and a sandwich. "Nothing. I'm just glad to have my youngest near."

"Your youngest is glad to be near," he echoed rising to take the tray from her hands.

While he ate she sat silently and stared off into the distance, mining unspoken thoughts.

"So," he asked, hoping to lighten her mood. "Tell me about Drew." He knew she wanted to discuss the changes she saw and sensed in him, but as always she was content to let it be, and he loved her all the more for that, because to tell her would plunge her into the darkness as well.

After Noah left her to go up to his room, Alanza remained out on the patio alone and pondered her youngest son. Why he'd changed so much from who he'd once been was a question she'd been wrestling with for ten years now. She guessed it had to do with his being shanghaied, because the day he finally returned home there'd been a bleakness in his once bright eyes. Although he'd talked about the prison camp and some of the terrible things that transpired there, she sensed he'd held back on a lot of the more troubling details, and as far as she knew, he hadn't shared the full truth with Drew or Logan either. Gone was the boy with the ready laugh and open heart; in fact he rarely smiled. Of all her sons, he'd been the most sensitive and the most loving but now seemed to move through his visits home like a ghost. Mothers knew when their children were in pain and he wore his like a shroud. She so wanted to help him deal with whatever was at the heart of it, but he was a grown man and she didn't want to lose him completely by pressuring him to reveal whatever was wrong. Would she ever know the truth? She didn't know but would continue to pray that he'd find healing and peace in whatever form God saw fit to send him, because this new version of her son was breaking her heart.

Later, upstairs in his bedroom, Noah glanced around at the familiar surroundings and again the carefree young boy he'd once been took pleasure in what he viewed: his beloved books, the desk where he'd done his lessons, his well-used easel still standing by the door that led out to his verandah, and in his adjoining sitting room, the Brahms Streicher piano his mother ordered for him all the way from Vienna. He walked over to it and visually lingered over its gleaming wood and ivory keys. It was an 1868 model and with its carved lacelike music stand and artfully shaped legs, it remained as beautiful as the day it arrived. He hadn't played since his last visit home because it was impractical to have such an instrument on a ship. He tapped out a few random notes, observing that it was still in tune and knew instinctively that his mother had engaged someone to come out and see to the tuning in advance of his arrival. Although both his brothers loved books, neither of them were musically inclined or enjoyed putting brush to canvas. Those passions had been reserved for him alone, it seemed, and he derived great pleasure from both endeavors. The young Noah had dreams of being a music teacher or a concert pianist, like his musical idol Beethoven, but—he turned his mind away from those long lost aspirations. Instead, he sat on the bench, flexed his fingers and began to play, first Beethoven and then Brahms before sliding seamlessly into Bach. Soon he moved into hymns, sea shanties, and tunes from operas and bawdy houses. He lost himself so completely in the intricacies of the notes and melodies that when he glanced over at the clock it showed two hours had passed. Allowing himself a small smile, he played a few minutes longer, then got up to prepare himself for dinner.

When his brothers arrived, they greeted him warmly. He'd met Mariah before but not Drew's wife, Billie, so introductions were made. He also met his niece and nephew and the sight of their chubby little faces touched his heart, and again a part of himself envied the couples' happiness. After that, they took their seats at the table. As always, their mother reigned at the head while a contented Max sat at the other end.

They were eating when Logan glanced over and asked, "So, Noah, how's the seafaring business?"

Deciding to go with the truth, he shrugged. "Fine, but it'll be better once I get my ship back."

Everyone at the table paused and stared his way.

Appearing puzzled, his mother asked, "Is it in dry dock?"

He shook his head and prepared himself for the razzing sure to follow. "No, a pirate woman stole it from me about two weeks ago."

Drew snorted a laugh. "You let a *girl* take the ship named after your *mama?*"

"Andrew!" his mother scolded.

"Was her name Califia by any chance?" Logan asked amusedly.

A smiling Noah took the ribbing in stride. He'd expected the teasing. "No. I've no idea what her name is, but I'll be heading back to Cuba just as soon as the wedding's over to hunt her down. Sorry, Mama, for not being able to stay longer."

She was still staring his way with confusion on her face.

"I'll get it back," he vowed, and he would if he had to track that little pirate git to the bottom of the seven seas.

Max weighed in. "So how did it happen?"

Noah sighed aloud and told the story, adding, "The Spanish navy believes the gang might be rebels. Apparently they might be on the brink of war there again."

"But why your ship?" Mariah asked.

"I don't know, the woman wouldn't say, but apparently it fit the bill for whatever they were planning."

"Is it safe to return there?" Billie asked.

"Doesn't matter. I need my ship."

Drew nodded understandingly. "All humor aside, let me know if I can be of any help. Bigotry may be making it difficult to practice law here, but Cuba can't refuse to let me practice, because I did my studies in Spain."

"Thanks, Drew."

After dinner he and his brothers stepped outside to enjoy the cigars he'd brought back for them and some tequila to celebrate his homecoming.

Logan drew on his cigar. "Girl pirates or not, Cubans make the best damn cigars on earth."

"Agreed," Noah said exhaling a stream of the

fine smoke. "Two years ago, I invested in a tobacco operation in Florida. The owner is a friend. A Cuban exile named Miguel Ventura. Business is booming and we're looking to expand. Would you two like in?"

Drew said, "To give myself access to these, hell yes."

"Once I get this ship business settled and talk with him, I'll let you know the details."

Logan raised his shot glass in a toast. "To brothers, tequila, and fine cigars."

Drew threw in, "And may we make a fortune."

They tossed back their drinks and set their glasses down. Logan poured more into each and they began to talk of old times: the pranks they'd pulled, the fun they'd had, the contests they'd constantly challenged each other to. "So, you think you can beat me at arm wrestling now, baby brother?" He'd been the king growing up.

Before Noah could respond, Drew scoffed, "He let a *girl* steal his damn ship, remember?"

"Shut up, Drew. I may not be able to best Logan but I can mop the floor with your fancy lawyer arse."

The laughing Logan spit tequila across the table. "Oh, really?" Drew asked.

"Really." Noah countered with a mischief in his eyes, and to prove the boast punched Drew in his chest hard enough to rock him in his chair.

Recovering, the grinning Drew stood, tossed

back his second shot of tequila and slammed the glass down. "Let's go."

Smiling, Noah stood to meet the challenge. Mimicking his brother, he tossed back his shot, slammed the glass down and the fight was on.

As they rolled around, knocking over chairs, breaking flowerpots, and trying their best to beat the tar out of each other, Noah was indeed mopping the floor with Drew. When a goading Logan pointed that out, Drew punched Logan in the nose and it turned into a three brothers' free-for-all.

Inside the house, Alanza could hear the ruckus outside, as could everyone else. Holding Tonio, Billie hurried to the dining-room window, which looked out over the patio, and snapped, "If they break those rose canes that I spent all summer reviving I will shoot them."

Alanza watched her sons rolling and punching and destroying the beauty of her patio and began spouting an angry stream of Spanish. Stalking to the gun cabinet in her study, she returned with her shotgun. As she primed it and started for the door, Max chuckled.

Watching the destruction, Mariah said to her daughter, "Papa's about to get a whipping." Little Maria's eyes went round and she stared up at her mother. "*Abuela*'s going to get him."

Tonio, on the other hand, seemed to be having the time of his life. Viewing the commotion, he laughed and clapped excitedly. In response to his obvious joy, Billie looked to the heavens and pleaded, "Lord, let me have a quiet little girl this time."

The next sound heard was the thunderous repercussion of the shotgun.

Outside all three sons froze.

"Get up, you idiots!" Alanza snapped in Spanish.

Trying to hide their grins, they stood before her as they'd done all their lives. Each had at least one black eye and a split lip. The seams of their suit coats had burst, and the rest of them was covered with dust and soil from the destroyed clay flower-pots. Blood trickled from their nostrils.

"Are you trying to ruin my wedding?" she yelled. "You're going to walk me down the aisle looking like you've been wrestling with bears!"

They dropped their heads in another effort to hide their now widening grins.

"If you so much as smile, I swear the padre will be handling three funerals, too!"

"Sorry, Mama," Noah and Drew said in unison.

Logan added, "Sorry, Lanza."

"No you're not! Go get cleaned up. May you live to have children as loco as you are!"

She stormed away, still muttering in Spanish. Once she was out of sight, they fell to the ground with howls of laughter.

Lying there in the silence afterwards, Noah said, "God, that felt good. Been wanting to punch something all week." This was the most fun in recent memory.

"Glad we could help," Drew said around the handkerchief he held against his nose.

Noah swung his head to his older brother. "Thanks Logan."

"Always here to help."

They helped each other up and stumbled inside to go clean themselves up.

Chapter 5

Pilar loved the city of Santiago. Its crowded, twisted streets were narrow and steep, and from different points one could view the tree-covered mountains and the beautiful blue waters of the bay that emptied into the Caribbean. Most of the buildings were of stone and constructed by Spain. The grander places with their expansive gated courtyards and ironwork verandahs housed the city's wealthy, but she and her sister Doneta were walking the cramped, crowded streets of the poor, which were lined with women selling fruits and vegetables; men offering to black shoes; old Vodoun women from Haiti peddling potions guaranteed to bring death to your enemies, make a person fall in love, and everything in between. Small children ran through the crowds, garnering stern warnings from local elders, and laundry hung in windows open to the breeze. The air was thick with the mouthwatering smells of braziers cooking yams, fish, sheep, and goat, and the people they passed spoke French and Spanish, and because many from the Far East had been brought to the island as slaves, Chinese could be heard as well.

She and Doneta were ostensibly on their way to sell the eggs they'd gathered from their hens that

71

morning, and although it was just past dawn the streets were as filled as if it were noon.

"Have you ever wanted to live elsewhere, Pilar?"

Somewhere in the distance came the sound of drumming and the syncopated rhythms put a lift in her spirit and step. "Not really. Why?"

"Thinking about the stories Mama used to tell about all the beautiful places she visited growing up. It would be nice to see at least one of those places before I die."

Born in Seville, their mother, Desa, was the daughter of a high-ranking Spanish diplomat. She'd been disowned for marrying their father. "I suppose."

"I'm twenty-three years old, Pilar, and the only place I've ever seen is—here. Is it wrong to want to be elsewhere with maybe a good husband and live in a nice house with nice things?"

"No, 'Neta. There's nothing wrong with that."

Pilar didn't hold her sister's dreams against her, because who wouldn't want to get away from the poverty that was their reality? But because she knew it was only a dream, she didn't long for it. Instead, she longed for changes in their world so that her younger cousins might attend school and learn to excel at something besides thievery. Hoping they could get an education was one of the many reasons she supported General Maceo and the rebels in their quest to gain independence from

Spain. As it stood now, only the children of the wealthy were allowed to study formally. People like her family and her neighbors, no matter their color, weren't offered the opportunity because of their station in life. And times were changing. With the growing presence of the soldiers in cities like Havana and Santiago, it was more difficult to make a living outside the law. The wealthy had begun hiring armed men to keep their homes safe, thus making it nearly impossible to slip in under darkness and slip out again with valuables that might help put food on the table for a few days. Doneta was an outstanding artist and in times past, her forgeries of the Old Masters sold to gullible art collectors brought in enough gold to keep their farm afloat for months, but the paintings took time and couldn't be rushed, so in the meantime other avenues had to be pursued to fill the coffers. With the passing away of their father's old fences and smugglers, those avenues were just about dry. Not to mention the Banderas name was now well known to the police. The secrecy that had shrouded their activities for decades was shattered last month when their cousin Juan, the adolescent son of one of her late uncles, was apprehended while trying to steal a prized statue from one of the city's museums, of all places. Having exhibited more bravado than brains his entire life, he'd done no planning beforehand, as far as Pilar knew, and as a result had been sentenced to ten years in a prison outside of Havana, leaving behind his three sisters and heartbroken mother, Ria. Now, everywhere they went, they were watched. Like now. There was a policeman about a half block behind them. He seemed to be just ambling through the streets, but at the last corner, Pilar stopped and looked back. When he met her eyes, he hastily glanced away and crossed the street. He trailed them still. "We're being followed."

"I know," her sister replied. "Maybe we should go over and ask him if he wants to buy our eggs."

Frustrated, they kept walking, but his looming presence was a real problem. Going to the market had been a cover for the true reason they'd come into town. Pilar and Tomas had split the gold cuff links taken from Noah Yates and it had been her plan to slip into the home of an old friend of the family who specialized in buying purloined items and leave again with their value in coin, but with the policeman dogging their steps, that was now impossible. One did not bring the police to a friend's door. Her mother needed the money, had been counting on it really in order to pay the ever-increasing taxes the crown kept imposing, but now? She sighed angrily.

They finally reached the small open-air market owned by Carlos Mendez, a widower in his late forties. The policeman followed. "This is all Juan's fault," Pilar snapped and her sister agreed. If her cousin hadn't already been in custody, she'd sail him out into the bay and drop him into deep water for the problems he'd brought down on their heads. The money they'd get for the eggs would be a pittance compared to what they might have received in exchange for the cuff links, but there was nothing they could do about it now, so they led the man on their heels past the penned-in chickens and pigs; the open crates of mangoes, red bananas, and coconuts; and the burlap sacks of yams to the back of the market, where Mendez sat at the rickety table that doubled as his office. His six children could be seen stacking vegetables and opening crates and standing guard to make sure the goods weren't stolen by the gangs of orphans who roamed the streets.

"Good morning, Pilar and Doneta."

"Good morning, Mr. Mendez. We have eggs for you."

The policeman sidled closer, as if he were contemplating buying some of the candy for sale but they were certain he was attempting to eavesdrop on the conversation. They ignored him.

Mendez took the basket of eggs, and after adding theirs to the ones he had for sale, he returned the empty basket and Pilar placed the few pesos he handed her into the pocket of her skirt. "Thank you, Mr. Mendez."

"You're welcome. Give my regards to your lovely mother."

"We will."

As they walked back out to the street, the policeman, now standing over a basket of oranges, pretended disinterest. Pilar almost stopped to ask if he wanted them to wait until he was done looking at the fruit, but decided provoking him was not a good idea. Instead she and her sister walked back the way they'd come. He followed them all the way to the stable where they'd left their wagon, then watched and waited until they drove off before he turned away and headed back to the city's center. Pilar held the reins and shook her head with disgust.

Scattering chickens and a few pigs, Pilar steered the wagon onto their property and pulled the reins to a halt next to the listing wooden barn. Their farm was just outside the city. It originally belonged to their pirate grandfather Benito and his wife, Anitra, who began her life as a slave in Jamaica and lived there until she was stolen away by him during a raid. His ancestors were originally from the Mandingo tribe—tall, strong, and reddish in skin tone, while she was of the Ganga, short and freckled like most of her people. Both Pilar and Doneta had a light dusting of the spots on their upper cheeks, as had their father, Javier.

Their mother, Desa, was seated on the porch. At their approach, she stood and smiled. "How is the city?"

"We couldn't sell the cuff links because we were

followed by the police," Pilar said as she climbed the two broken steps. Like the barn and the house, the porch was a weathered silver. There were numerous slats missing but enough remained to support the old settee and a few chairs so one could sit outside and enjoy the mountain breezes. She handed her mother the few pesos from the eggs. "I'm sorry, Mama."

"That's disappointing. Tell me about this policeman."

So they did.

She sighed with disgust. "This is all Juan's fault. Had he been half as smart as he thought he was he wouldn't be jailed. My poor Ria. She's going to have to go into Santiago and look for work now that Juan can no longer help out."

Pilar was certain the thought of having to hire herself out as a maid or washwoman had likely sent her proud aunt to her bed. Ria was among the best document forgers in Cuba. During slavery, because Santiago held one of the island's largest population of free blacks and free mulattos, escaped slaves flocked to the city's narrow streets and alleys in droves. Their need for forged freedom papers and notes of passage made for a steady income. Now, with slavery on the wane, the demand for her skills had waned as well, and with her son Juan now breaking rocks, the money he'd once made working on the docks would be sorely missed. As Pilar had mused earlier—times were changing. What hadn't changed was her commitment to the rebels, and with that in mind, she needed to prepare the *Alanza* for another run to Santo Domingo for guns.

"I received a letter from my brother in Florida today."

Pilar and Doneta's faces showed surprise. As far as Pilar knew, her mother hadn't received a correspondence from her family in decades. Her Castilian parents pronounced her dead after she ran off on her wedding day to become the wife of Javier Banderas, and one didn't commune with the dead.

"He's invited us to the *rumba* he's having for his birthday in a few weeks. And," she added, "he says he's anxious to renew his ties to me as his sister."

"Is he dying?" Pilar asked.

Doneta snorted.

Her mother laughed, "Not that I know of. No."

"Then why now, after so many years?"

Desa shrugged. "I'm his only sister. With both our parents passed on, maybe he's lonely. I don't know."

Doneta asked, "Are you going?"

"Yes. We're all going."

Pilar stilled.

As if anticipating Pilar's arguments, she stated, "I know you have obligations you deem more important, Pilar, but this is family."

"Mama—"

"Pilar, your father and uncles gave their lives to Cuba, but nothing was more important to them than *familia*. I doubt Antonio Maceo will storm Havana anytime soon."

Pilar studied her and sensed she was holding something back. "There's more, isn't there?"

"Yes. It is my hope that you two will find husbands while we're there."

Doneta's eyes widened with delight.

Pilar's narrowed with suspicion. "I don't want a husband."

"I understand, Pilar, but it is time you started considering it."

"Mama, I'm twenty-five years old. No man will want me as a wife. All I wish to do is help Cuba become a better place."

"Who's to say a husband won't want that, too?"

"I doubt he'll want a wife who smuggles guns."

Her mother smiled indulgently. "True, but you are so much more. Your heart, your great mind, compassion, and dedication are as much a part of you as your fervor for Cuba. A man will value that."

"No, Mama."

"Pilar, I have never put a bridle on you. When you were seven years old and wanted to ride your horse into the mountains alone, I let you go—even though my Javier and I argued about it for days afterwards. When he died, my heart was broken and the very last thing I wanted was for you to go off and fight with the Mambis, too, but again I let you go and prayed for your safe return every day. Do I want you smuggling guns? No. Do I worry each and every moment that you're away?" She laid her hand tenderly against Pilar's cheek. "Again, yes."

There was a seriousness in her mother's eyes that made Pilar gently cover her hand with her own.

"The *three* of us will be going to the *rumba*."

Pilar knew that her mother's mind was made up, and she'd broach no more argument, so after sighing softly in defeat, she leaned over and placed a kiss on her mother's golden cheek. "Yes, Mama."

"Good."

"Tomas and I are taking the ship out tonight. We'll be back in the morning."

"That's fine. When you return we'll make our plans to leave in a few days."

Pilar nodded and went to make her preparations.

After initially hiding the *Alanza* behind the waterfall, she and Tomas made the trek back a few days later to retrieve it, and under a moonless sky sailed it to the Santiago docks and into the small shipyard of a man allied with the rebels. He had the hull painted black and added new sails dyed a deep indigo. The altered schooner now bore little resemble to Yates's *Alanza*, so Pilar rechristened it the *Sirena*.

This night's run would be its maiden voyage and Pilar couldn't wait to feel the waves rolling beneath the hull. Doneta drove her and Tomas to the docks.

"Be careful," Doneta cautioned quietly as Pilar and Tomas climbed down.

"We will," Pilar assured her. "Be back before dawn."

Doneta drove off and Pilar and Tomas moved quickly to meet the shipyard owner. He was a big bulbous man named Gerardo Calvo who loved his cigars and had grown up with General Maceo. He'd be supplying a few of his most trusted workers to round out the crew and the gold for the guns. "You should wait an hour or two before casting off. The navy has changed its schedule. You don't want to run into them the first night out with her."

Pilar didn't like having to delay departure but knew he was right, so two hours before midnight they set sail.

There was a fair wind and they made good time so with the *Sirena* anchored a short distance offshore, Pilar, and two of Calvo's men rowed under the moonless night sky to the rendezvous point on the beach. They were very late for their appointed meeting but it couldn't be helped. She hoped her contact hadn't given up on their arrival, because the rebels dearly needed the guns they could amass.

The wind picked up. A storm was on the way but with any luck she'd be able to conduct her business and return home before the inclement weather took hold.

"Do you think he waited?" One of the men asked.

"I hope so," was all she would say. Voices carried over the water, so the less they conversed the better.

A light flashed in the darkness above the beach. Their signal. The sight filled her with relief. Having risked their lives, she hadn't wanted to return home empty-handed.

"You're late," the smuggler, an old Dominican named Octavio, snapped sharply.

"The Spanish altered their hunting schedule. My apologies."

Even as they spoke she and her crew kept an eye on the water. If the Spanish navy took it upon themselves to suddenly appear, Tomas and the two men on board the *Sirena* would have no choice but to raise anchor and hope to outrun the enemy, leaving behind Pilar and the others on shore. "How many did you bring?" she asked Octavio.

"Ten."

The number was small but it was ten more guns than the rebels had presently.

"There's also gunpowder," Octavio added. He

too kept a keen eye on their surroundings. "Let's finish our business while the moon is still behind the clouds so that we may return home safely."

Pilar agreed and counted out the precious gold given to her by Calvo that he was owed. As he pocketed it and disappeared into the darkness, she and her men loaded the case of guns and powder and rowed back out to the *Sirena*.

Once the contraband was secured, she gave the order to cast off. The anchor was raised and with the *Sirena*'s indigo sails fat with a steady wind, Tomas piloted them west for home.

They were almost there when a flash of lightning broke the silence. An ominous rumble of thunder followed. The wind increased sharply making the sails strain and the schooner began to pitch on an increasingly rough sea. "Tomas!" she yelled urgently over the wind.

"Doing my best!" The rest of the crew scrambled over the deck to adjust the sails and keep the *Sirena* on course. She ran to join them but stopped frozen when another flash of lightning revealed something from a nightmare. The biggest man-of-war she'd ever seen was barreling down on them. "Spanish man-of-war! Tomas! By all that's holy, get out of its path!"

Fat drops of rain began pelting them and soon fell in blinding sheets. She added her muscle to that of the men in an effort to use the wind-filled sails and the sloop's speed to outrun the well-armed battleship. Eerie intermittent flashes of lightning showed the Spanish vessel still on course. "Tomas!"

Her cry melded with an explosion as a cannon-ball found its mark and the concussion flung her high up in the air. She landed in the water just as a second explosion shook the *Sirena*, sending shards of burning wood and spinning metal raining down as if born of the storm. Dazed and disoriented, she instinctively dove beneath the surface of the dark water. Grateful to be wearing the simple cotton pants and blouse favored by the people of her island and not a skirt with a wealth of slips beneath, she swam for her life and hoped her crew was doing the same.

"Pilar! Pilar!"

Pilar could hear her sister Doneta calling from a distance that sounded far away. Struggling out of an encasing fog, Pilar slowly opened her eyes.

"Oh, thank the saints! You're alive," Doneta choked out. "I thought you were dead!"

Pilar realized she was lying on her back on the beach but had no recollection how she'd come to be there. Her thin clothing was soaked through, her head ached tremendously and her limbs were heavy as lead. She closed her eyes again, hoping the pain in her pounding head would cease, and then the retching began. Up came all the seawater she'd swallowed again and again, until her sides ached and her throat burned. Memories of the night rushed back and she went deathly still. "Where are Tomas and the others?" Panicked, she surveyed the beach and then the water. "Did you see them?"

"No. Only you. I've been looking for you since dawn. What happened?"

Pilar scrambled to her feet. Ignoring the question and the pain, she ran to the edge of the water to scan the gray water still churning and angry from last night's storm for any signs of her companions. She looked up and down the beach but may as well have been the only person in the world.

Her sister came to her side and said with quiet urgency, "We need to get home before we're seen. Come."

But Pilar didn't want to leave. If she stayed longer maybe one or all might appear. Suppose they came ashore injured and needed assistance? Worry filled her but she knew Doneta was right. If the Spanish were patrolling nearby she needed to get off the beach.

While Doneta drove the wagon pulled by their old mule, Salazar, Pilar was secreted in the false bottom of the bed. She was exhausted but it was overridden by concern for the crew. Tomas cared for his aging mother, and although she knew nothing about the lives of the others, more than likely they had families that depended on them as well. Everyone tied to the rebellion knew the dangers inherent in their fight, but no one wanted the consequences to come home to roost among their own. Having personally mourned the loss of her father and uncles, Pilar knew such grief couldn't be measured. She prayed the men had reached home safely.

"Halt!"

As the wagon stopped, Pilar stilled. She placed her hand on the hilt of the machete lying by her side.

A male voice demanded, "Your name and where you are bound, senorita?"

"I am Doneta Banderas and on my way home, Captain."

Addressing him by rank was her sister's subtle way of letting Pilar know he was a soldier. "Banderas. Are you kin to Javier Banderas?"

"I'm his daughter."

"Step down please."

"What have I done?"

"Just step down, senorita. We need to search your wagon."

Pilar had no way of knowing how many men there were but that didn't matter. She and her sister were alone and except for the lone machete, unarmed. If the soldiers were intent upon harm, they'd be easily overpowered.

She heard Doneta explain, "There's nothing back there but sacks of meal and fishing poles. I went fishing this morning but caught nothing."

"Either step down or I'll have my men assist you." The threat in his voice was plain.

A few seconds later, Pilar heard footsteps and sounds of the items in the bed above her being moved around. She prayed they wouldn't look further.

The same male voice called out, "Cut those sacks open!"

"No!" her sister screamed angrily.

Pilar imagined the meal flowing out of the sacks and spreading onto the wagon bed or onto ground.

Doneta demanded. "Who's going to compensate my mother for that wasted meal?"

"The families of rebels aren't compensated, but you can always petition the governor," the Spaniard chuckled sarcastically.

Pilar's jaw tightened with anger.

"May I continue on my way?" Doneta snapped.

"Yes, senorita, but be thankful we found nothing. The navy sank a rebel boat off the coast last night. They're pretty sure the crew died, but we'll be keeping a close eye on this area for a while. Would be a pity to hang someone as beautiful as you."

Doneta offered no reply.

Pilar felt the wagon shift as her sister climbed back up to the seat. A few seconds later they were moving again. Pilar was pleased that the soldiers mentioned not having found any of her crewmen.

She hoped that meant the men were safe, but it didn't diminish her worries.

When they reached the farm, Doneta helped the shivering and pale Pilar to the ground and their mother came running. "Oh thank God, you're alive. Come, let's get you into the house."

After stripping away her sodden clothes, drying herself and slipping into an old nightshirt, she climbed into bed and managed to tell her mother the story, to which Desa replied, "There's no guarantee they won't find out who was involved. We need to leave the island as soon as possible. Pilar, you sleep. Doneta and I will get us ready."

The next night, with the help of the local rebels, the Banderas women boarded a boat and set sail for sanctuary with Desa's brother in Florida.

Chapter 6

With his mother's birthday party underway and the house and grounds filled to capacity with relatives and neighbors, Noah found all the celebrating a welcome distraction to his brooding over his stolen ship. Dozens of different scenarios had been running through his mind about what the woman and her gang might be doing. Having served with Simmons, he knew all manner of illegalities could come into play: opium, slaves, children. He prayed they weren't engaging in any of that, but he had no way of knowing. Noah had never approached a woman violently, but the pirate woman he wanted to hurt. In truth, the moment he found her, he planned to turn her over to the authorities, but it didn't stop his mind from fantasizing about feeding her headfirst to a shark.

"If looks could kill."

He turned to find Drew at his side. They were outdoors on the crowded patio, waiting for their mother's birthday cake to be brought out while laughter and their sangria-drinking friends and relatives flowed around them. "Thinking about my ship," he said in explanation.

"And the woman?"

"And the woman."

"You can't kill her, you know."

"I do, but that doesn't mean I can't think about it though."

Drew raised his glass of wine in a salute. "What will you do when you find her?"

"Reclaim the *Alanza* and turn her over to the authorities. Hopefully I'll get some satisfaction from whatever punishment the courts mete out."

"And if you don't find her?"

"Oh I will. That I'm certain of." There were no doubts in Noah's mind that he'd find her. Someone knew who she was and he'd find that person, as well.

"Do you still plan to leave right after the wedding?"

"Yes."

"Then try and have a good time while you're here. You look like you could use some fun in your life."

"Is it that obvious?"

"Extremely."

His brothers knew him well.

Drew's tone softened. "Talking about what happened to you back then might help, Noah."

Noah watched one of the old aunts attempting to teach Tonio to dance. "I'm fine, Drew."

"You've been a terrible liar all your life."

A rueful smile curved his lips and he met his brother's seriously set eyes. "If I talk about it, then your heart will break, too, and mine is broken enough for the both of us." That said, he stood silently as the cake was brought out and everyone cheered.

The day of Alanza's wedding dawned bright with blue skies. Attempting to hold on to her excitement was difficult. *I'm getting married!* came her ecstatic inner voice. And to a man who'd claimed her heart like none other before.

"You look gorgeous, Mama," Mariah gushed as Alanza did a slow turn to show off her new gold gown. Her daughters-in-law were to be her attendants and they were dressed very elegantly as well.

"Gorgeous and happy," Billie added.

"I am both. I want to pinch myself just to make sure I'm not dreaming."

"No dream," Billie said. "In just a little while, you're going to be Mrs. Maxwell Rudd."

"Yes, I am. I have butterflies in my stomach. I can't remember ever being so nervous."

"You'll be fine once everything gets underway."

"Is the padre here?"

"Yes," Mariah said with assurance. "Your cousins are with him downstairs. Are you ready to go?"

Alanza took in deep calming breath. "Yes."

Billie said, "I'll alert everyone that you're on your way and shoo them outside. I'll meet you and 'Riah when you come down."

"Thank you, Billie."

After her departure, Alanza took in the happy face of her first daughter-in-law. "Thank you for this beautiful gown."

"It was my pleasure, and thank you for being the best mother-in-law a girl could ever wish for."

They shared a strong hug so filled with meaning that Mariah had to use her fingertips to staunch the tears threatening to spill from her golden eyes.

"Okay," Alanza declared confidently. "Let's go. I have a man to dazzle."

Mariah lifted the gown's flowing train and Alanza led them from the room.

The wedding was lovely. While Max stood beneath the flower-laden bower with his two groomsmen, the padre, and the teary-eyed Billie and Mariah, Alanza was escorted in by her impeccably dressed sons: Logan in front, Drew on her right, and Noah on her left. The black eyes and split lips were still apparent and caused more than a few titters, but most of the guests were focused on the lovely Alanza and her stunning gold gown.

After the sons delivered her to the groom's side, they stepped away.

Alanza looked up into Max's serious eyes and knew she was making the right decision. As an adolescent, she'd thought herself in love with Abraham, but that hadn't been love. The soaring in her heart caused by the incredible man beside her was the real thing, so as the padre began the words and asked that she repeat the vows, she did so with a firm, strong voice. And when he pronounced them man and wife, and they sealed the ceremony with a kiss, she didn't hear the thunderous applause or the raucous cheers of her sons; all that mattered was Max, and Max alone, until death did them part.

The newlyweds spent the rest of the afternoon reigning over the wedding feast (that encompassed three trestle tables) and receiving the well wishes of family and friends. As the sun made its way across the sky and began to sink towards the evening, Max pulled her aside. "Are you ready to go?"

"Go where?"

"With me."

The mischief in his eyes made her ask over a laugh, "What are you up to now, Maxwell Rudd?"

"Come with me and see."

"Is this an adventure?"

"The first of many, I'm hoping."

She glanced around at the milling guests.

"Don't worry about them, there's still plenty for them to eat and drink, they'll be fine. And I already talked to the boys to let them know we're leaving."

The Alanza of the past would've immediately bristled at the idea of embarking on something so unknown and spontaneous, and she certainly wouldn't've been happy leaving behind a slew of untended guests, but with Max she had the opportunity to be someone new, so she grabbed the brass ring and held on. "I'm ready."

Delight filled his face. He grabbed her hand, she used her free one to hike up her gown, and off they ran.

It was nearly full dark by the time they reached his hunting cabin. He stopped the wagon, set the brake and hopped down. Under the mountain breeze he came around and held up his arms for her, and with one swoop slowly brought her to the ground before him. For a moment they stood silently, feasting on the sight of each other. There was a muted hunger in his eyes that touched her in all the places he'd been gently wooing all summer.

"Nervous?" he asked.

"A little."

"Then we're even."

When he scooped her up into his arms, she barked a laugh that was cut short by the long hard kiss he placed on her lips before continuing the journey to the cabin. He kicked the door open, and once they were inside, carried her through the dark into a room at the back. He set her on her feet.

"Let me light a lamp."

The spark of a match was immediately followed by a small glow that soon grew and filled the room. Alanza stared around, surprised. "When did you build a bedroom?"

"Started working on it last year. Figured my new

wife wouldn't want to sleep in a bedroll on the floor."

"Last year? Pretty confident, weren't you?"

"Yes."

She shook her head at the boast and the smile that accompanied it. They'd used the cabin as their hunting base for years and she had indeed slept on the floor in a bedroll. The new room showed why his carpentry skills were so highly sought after. Polished log walls and a pitched roof held the huge new bed he'd talked about building. "This is the bed you made for us?"

"Yes, as I said, we weren't having our wedding night in the bed you inherited from your mother."

When she married Abe, there'd been no wedding night. He'd slept on the floor in the front room. She found herself quietly looking forward to this one.

"What's wrong?" he asked softly.

She shook her head. "Nothing." She didn't wish to spoil the night by talking about the past.

The new bed was topped with linens and pillows that he couldn't possibly have picked out alone. "Have my girls been up here?" There were curtains and two upholstered sitting chairs and a large fireplace built from boulders and stones.

"Yes," he confessed unashamedly. "Billie picked out the sheets and quilts and that big rug under the bed. Mariah made the curtains."

"All without me knowing a thing."

"See how wonderful being in the dark can be?"

She walked over and put her arms around his waist. "I love you, Max Rudd."

"I love you, too, Lanz Rudd."

She met his eyes. "We're going to be happy."

"As otters playing in water."

That caused her to laugh again and she fit herself against him and rested her cheek against his strong chest. His arms tightened around her and she savored the peace she found in his embrace.

"Let's make a fire and get out of these wedding clothes," he said above her. "This tie is strangling me."

She stepped back so he could rid himself of the formal tie, but she was unsure what she was supposed to do next.

"I need to bring some things in from the wagon. Have a seat and relax. Been a long day."

While he was gone she marveled again at the room mostly to take her mind off how nervous she'd suddenly become. The talk she'd had with Billie a few weeks back about the ins and outs of bed play had been shocking to say the least. The last thing she wanted was to disappoint Max with her lack of knowledge. Abe had been gentle with her in bed but she hadn't actively participated because he hadn't encouraged it and she didn't know she was supposed to. Max gave her the sense that intimacies between the two of them would be different and as a result she was as nervous as a long-tailed cat in a room of rockers.

He returned carrying a small trunk and a covered basket. He set them on the floor near the fireplace and silently lit the logs stacked inside. He looked over at her.

"You okay?"

"Not sure."

He gave her a gentle smile before reaching for the poker to even out the logs. Once he seemed satisfied that the fire was well on its way, he stood and held her eyes. "Your girls sent along some sangria, the boys thought you'd prefer tequila, so I brought both. Which would you prefer?"

"Tequila."

"It's in the basket. Grab it and I'll bring a chair over here by the fire."

She found a bottle of her favorite tequila along with two glasses and said thanks for having raised such wonderful sons. When she turned to join Max by the fire, he was already seated. "Where's my chair?"

He patted his lap.

She dropped her head and then raised it to show her smile. Tequila and glasses in hand, she walked over, settled herself on his lap, and poured them both a small portion. He took the bottle from her and set it on the floor. Glass in hand, he raised it and said, "To otters."

Laughing at how silly he was, she raised hers, too. "To otters."

They both took sips and he eased her closer and kissed the top of her hair. "No fighting boys, no guests, no babies breaking out of jail. I may never take you back."

She agreed "I know. This is nice. Thanks for the rescue."

"Anytime."

They finished their drinks and he placed the glasses on the floor beside the bottle. In the silence only the crackling fire could be heard. He gently raised her chin and gifted her with a slow series of kisses that set her heart to pounding. "I've waited for this for so long, Lanz."

He increased the intensity and soon she was kissing him back with the same fervor, learning, tasting, savoring. He teased the corners of her lips with the tip of his tongue and they parted gently, willingly. They'd shared kisses before, but these were different; these were compelling and possessive—joining, mating, and when he slowly withdrew, she was left dazzled and breathless and wanting more.

Kisses were then brushed over her bared skin above the neckline of her gown and in response her head dropped back, offering her throat to his lips while his hand slowly began to explore. During their courtship, he'd never done more than kiss her and she'd been content with that, but the sensations of his hand moving over her ensured that she'd never be content with that alone again.

She now understood the passion Billie had tried to explain. It was indeed sweeping and marvelous and when he slid her dress aside, exposed her breast and took it into his mouth, she understood why the girls refused to let her wear a corset beneath her gown. She crooned in response to the scandalous suckling, and all thought fled as a deep-seated heat bloomed everywhere—especially between her thighs. And while his mouth at her breast continued to slowly drive her mad, his touch moved there, first outside her gown and then beneath. Her gown was raised to her knees and his possessive palm moved up the length of her silk stocking, past her frilly lace garter, and she instinctively opened to let him touch her there, too. The reward was so staggering, the feel of him teasing her core so overwhelmingly powerful, that when he slid a finger inside, her legs flew apart and she screamed as her first orgasm exploded with the force of a lit stick of dynamite.

It took her a moment to find herself again, and when she opened her eyes, he kissed her and whispered playfully, "Was that you screaming, Mrs. Rudd?"

She managed to pull body and mind together enough to punch him in the arm, but the glory of the orgasm continued to echo.

Grinning he carried her to the bed.

For the rest of the night, Alanza was treated to more lovemaking than she ever could have imagined. She thought she knew the coupling parts, but found she didn't know that with the right man, her body would hunger for the joining, ripen with the sealing, soar on the sultry rising rhythm and orgasm again and again.

Finally, when they'd had enough of each other, he left her lying in the middle of the bed and returned carrying a package wrapped in brown paper and tied up with gold ribbon and a matching golden bow. She sat up. "What is this?"

"You lost the bet."

She promptly rolled her eyes in response. "So I have to wear what's inside?"

He nodded.

She opened it to find three very sultry nightgowns all of varying design. She smiled. "They won't keep me very warm."

"You won't have them on that long."

Exploding with laughter, she fell back against the bed, looked up into the eyes of the man she loved, and couldn't wait to see what the rest of their life together would bring. "I love you, Max."

He leaned over and kissed her brow. "I love you, too, Lanz."

Chapter 7

Upon his return to Havana, Noah went straight to the office of Admiral Rojas, hoping to hear good news.

"Unfortunately, Mr. Yates. I have nothing new to relay. There've been no sightings or reports of your ship docking at any of our ports. One of our brigs sank a ship of similar size while you were away—a rebel vessel we believe, but there wasn't much of it left to identify."

"Was the crew apprehended?"

"Only one man was found. The police are interrogating him but so far he's sticking to his story about being just a simple fisherman."

"May I speak with him?"

The admiral shook his head. "No, Mr. Yates. If he offers anything concerning your ship, we'll let you know."

Frustrated but grateful for the admiral's time, he had one more question. "Who might I call upon to maybe get information on this woman?"

"I'm not sure what you mean?"

"Who runs the underbelly in Havana?"

The admiral stilled.

"I am willing to pay whatever the price may be."

The admiral surveyed him for a moment longer before offering a name. "Victorio Gordonez." He wrote something on a small piece of paper from his desk. "He lives here. But do not tell him I sent you."

Noah placed the paper in his coat. "Understood. You have my thanks."

"Happy hunting, Mr. Yates."

Inclining his head, Noah departed.

Noah would rather have had access to the man the police had in custody, but with that option unavailable, he hoped the name given him by the admiral would be helpful. First, he needed to speak to someone who possibly knew Gordonez to determine the best way to approach him. It was doubtful he could simply show up on the man's doorstep and ask for a meeting, so he had his hired coach take him to the home of Bernita Mendoza. Her father, Paulo, was a low-level diplomat. There was no guarantee Mendoza knew him but Noah had to pursue every avenue if his quest to find the pirate woman was to be a success.

The servant at the door ushered him into Mendoza's study. At Noah's entrance the short man stood with a puzzled look on his mustached face. "Noah? I thought you'd gone back to California."

"I did, but I've returned and am in need of some advice."

"Of course." He dismissed the servant with a nod, and gestured Noah to one of the chairs. "Sit. Sit. How might I be helpful?"

Noah told him the tale and at the end, Mendoza's eyes went wide. "This gang abducted you outside my home? My God, what is this world coming to? Is that where you got that eye?"

For a moment Noah was confused, then he shook his head. "No, this was from a tussle with my brothers."

"Oh, okay. I was concerned that the ruffians harmed you."

"Just my ego. I'm trying to find the woman who headed up the gang and get my boat back."

"You've been to the police?"

"Yes, and Admiral Rojas at the navy offices has been very forthcoming, but there's been no movement in the case."

"I'm sorry to hear that. How might I help?"

"Do you know a man named Victorio Gordonez?"

Mendoza went still and like the admiral studied Noah for a long moment before replying, "Yes. Why do you ask?"

"I was told he knows the illicit side of Havana. I'm hoping he might be helpful in identifying this woman, but I need someone to broker a meeting between us."

"I've met him on social occasions, but he's a very dangerous man."

"Too dangerous for you to introduce me to him?"

"No. He has an image to maintain, so his dealings with those of us in Havana society are kept as pristine as possible. He pretends to be a lamb and we pretend as well."

"I see."

"Let me send a note around to his home to see if and when he might be available."

So the note was sent and while they waited, they chatted about his mother's recent wedding and in an effort to be nice, Noah asked after Mendoza's daughter Bernita.

"She is well. I had high hopes that the two of you would enjoy each other."

"She's a nice girl, but I'd not make a good husband to her or anyone else for that matter. I'm married to the sea."

Mendoza appeared resigned and nodded understandingly.

The servant returned a short while later. Gordonez was at home and would see Noah at his earliest convenience. "Finally some good news," Noah gushed. "I'd like to see him straightaway, so my apologies for leaving so hastily."

"None needed. I hope he can give you the information you seek."

"I do as well. Thank you, Mr. Mendoza."

"Good luck."

When Noah arrived, a house servant led him around to the gated patio, where a portly man in a white shirt sat at a table covered with dishes of food. "Senor Gordonez?"

"You must be Yates?"

"I am."

"You're American."

"Yes."

"Have a seat. Would you like something to eat?"

"No, thank you. My apologies for disturbing your meal."

"Cuban food not to your liking?"

Noah observed him, especially noting the white powder on his face. "I enjoy the food. I'm Spanish on my mother's side. I was raised well enough not to interrupt a person's meal though. I can return at another time, if you prefer."

He waved a fat hand dismissively. "Just testing you to see if you were prejudiced against the food here because many of you Americans are. Please, have a seat."

Noah complied.

Gordonez looked to the servant standing like a sentinel near the table. "Get Mr. Yates some wine. Surely you won't turn that down."

"I'll have a small portion. Thank you." A partially filled goblet was placed beside him and Noah inclined his head in thanks.

"So, how are you acquainted with Paulo Mendoza?"

"Our families are distantly related."

"Ah. Did he wave that beautiful daughter of his beneath your nose like a fragrant piece of meat?"

Noah didn't answer.

"Never mind. If he did, you know she's as empty-headed as an eggshell without its egg." He then speared Noah with his little pig eyes. "Why are you here?"

"I'm in need of information. I was told you might be of help. I'm looking for a woman."

"I'm not a pimp, Mr. Yates."

Noah figured he undoubtedly was but kept the speculation unspoken. "This is a woman who wears a black cloak and commands a gang that's responsible for the theft of my ship."

Gordonez didn't glance up from the chicken and rice he was consuming. "Why come to me?" he asked around the food in his mouth.

"I'm told you may have access to knowledge the police don't."

"By whom?"

"A nameless individual."

"Respectful and discreet. You were raised well. Why do you think I would help you find this mysterious woman?"

"Because I'm willing to pay whatever price you quote for her name."

Gordonez stopped eating, sat back, and picked up his wine. As he took a few sips he assessed Noah silently above the glass before setting it down again. "You've piqued my interest, Mr. Yates, so tell me about this woman and her gang."

When Noah was done, Gordonez once again took him under review. Noah sensed he was trying to determine just how much to ask for. "I believe I know who she is. In fact, I'm quite positive."

"And your price?"

"A thousand. American."

Steep but attainable.

"You didn't blink, Mr. Yates. Maybe I should have asked for more."

"You've set your price. How would you like to proceed?"

"Once I've confirmed the funds are in my bank, I'll send you her name."

"Are you certain about her identity?"

"I am. I've known her family for many years. What are your plans for her?"

"I'll keep that to myself if you don't mind."

"Were I you, I'd turn her over to the authorities first thing. And since her family owes me, I will tell you where she lives for no additional cost."

Noah nodded in gratitude but wondered what the man's history with the family might be. Were they criminal rivals? He seemed eager to offer up the woman's head, and that gave Noah pause, but in the scheme of things, whatever lay between them didn't matter, because the pirate woman owed him now as well. "You've been of immense help, Senor Gordonez. I'll let you get back to your meal."

Gordonez gave him a nod and the servant escorted Noah back to his carriage.

Two days later, Noah answered a knock on the

door of his hotel room. When he opened it a man handed him a folded piece of paper. "From Senor Gordonez."

Noah tipped the messenger and closed the door. When he unfolded the note he read: Pilar Banderas. Santiago.

Pleased, Noah hurried to pack.

A hired boat took him to the Santiago docks that afternoon.

As soon as he left the boat he began asking after her but couldn't find anyone who would admit to knowing the family. A man at one of the small shipyards who gave his name as Calvo looked Noah up and down in response to his request for information.

"Why do you wish to find this Banderas woman?"

"I gave her some property that I wish to retrieve."

"I don't know the name." And he walked away.

Noah knew he was lying but with no means to force him or the others he'd approached to provide the answers he needed, he tersely walked over to a man seated on a coach for hire. "Take me to the city."

That evening as he stood on the verandah looking out at the sun descending like a ball of fire into the bay, he wondered where and when this quest would end. Santiago was the island's second largest city and she could be anywhere—in the city—in the mountains. He had no way of knowing if Gordonez had given him her true name or if he'd simply been fleeced. A knock on his door interrupted his reverie. He opened it to find a man he'd questioned earlier down at the dock.

"You still looking for the Banderas family?" The man asked nervously, looking back and forth.

"Yes."

"You willing to pay?"

Noah paused. "I am."

"Can I come in? I don't want anyone to see us."

Noah stepped back and the man entered.

"You know Pilar Banderas?"

He nodded. "She lives on a farm outside the city. No one said anything down at the docks because she's tied to the rebels, just like everyone else here."

Noah understood now. "How much do you want for your assistance?"

The sum he quoted was a pittance in the scheme of things, but to a man as poor as he undoubtedly was it was large. "I'll pay you when we reach the farm."

"Sure. We should go at first light. Before everyone gets up. I don't want our business known."

Noah agreed.

He came for Noah at dawn. They journeyed on his listing wagon pulled by an old horse out of the city and into the mountainous region that surrounded it. "Cimarrons lived out here in the old days," the man informed him by way of conversation. Noah knew the word referred to fugitive slaves. "They and their descendants have been in these mountains for hundreds of years. This is the area where General Maceo recruited many of the Mambis."

They drove for a short while longer and the man, who'd never volunteered his name, steered the old horse onto a property set back a ways from the road. The weathered home was in serious disrepair, as was its accompanying barn. It was eerily silent. "Doesn't look like anyone's here," his guide remarked.

Noah agreed, but got down anyway and stepped up onto the porch. Mindful of the many missing slats, he made his way to the door and knocked. No one answered. He repeated the action a few more times with the same results. He left the porch and walked around to the back. There were a few broken-down animal pens but they held no occupants. He spotted a well-tended garden set a few yards away, but there were no signs of life on the property anywhere. Sighing with frustration, he returned to the wagon. "Does she have relatives?"

"Yes, but I don't know where they live."

"How do you know her?"

"I grew up here."

Noah passed him the money he was owed. "Take me back to the city."

Back in his hotel room, Noah wanted to punch something. Instead he packed. He'd leave for Florida in the morning. He wanted to meet with his old friend Miguel Ventura about his brothers' interest in investing in the tobacco company and once that was done, he'd figure out what to do next about the missing Pilar Banderas.

Chapter 8

Pilar glanced around the bedroom she and her sister were sharing. It was by all accounts a beautiful room. The bedding and draperies were made of fine fabrics and there was a soft carpet on the floor. The elegantly furnished home owned by her Uncle Miguel Ventura and his family was a castle compared to the humble Banderas abode back in Cuba. They'd been visiting almost two weeks now, and Pilar was ready to return home. Her sister adored the new surroundings and found everything, from the luxurious bath equipped with its inside water to the fine dishes on the tables at mealtime, to the elegant gardens packed with sweet-smelling blooms, much to her liking. When their mother took them shopping for new clothes, the first new things they'd owned since their father's death, Doneta cried. Pilar, more comfortable in the thin cotton trousers and plain shirtlike blouse of her homeland, tried to convince her mother that a ball gown for the birthday *rumba* wasn't necessary, but that fell on deaf ears and she was forced to try on what seemed like an endless stream of gowns until a choice was made—a long, full-skirted one that was mint green in color. The thin straps were anchored to the bodice with a delicate rosette.

"What are you doing up here, Pilar? You're supposed to be downstairs with the dance master."

"I already know how to dance, Tia Simona."

"No you don't. When the dancing begins at the party, it won't be those indecent country dances you're used to back home. This will be waltzing and you need to learn."

Simona was Tio Miguel's wife—a plain-faced shrew of a woman. From the moment the Banderases entered her home, she'd made plain her dislike. Pilar's mother said part of the reason had to do with them being poor—apparently Simona came from an extremely wealthy family who didn't tolerate those who weren't, and the other part had to do with Simona's two daughters, Mari and Anya. She and Tio Miguel were having difficulty finding husbands for their daughters, who closely resembled their mother, and Simona was concerned that having Pilar and the ravishing Doneta under her roof would only make the quest more difficult. "Have you seen my mother?"

"She's out with my husband. They're looking at property. She's thinking of settling here permanently."

Pilar froze.

"Now, downstairs with you."

Stunned, Pilar did as she was told.

After dinner, as Pilar, Doneta, and their mother sat outside on the verandah, Pilar asked about the property. "Are you really thinking of staying in America?"

"Yes, Pilar, I am. I want a fresh start in life and this seems the perfect time."

"But what about our home?"

"We'll make a new home, Pilar. We've struggled and done without for so long. My brother let me know that my parents left me a sizeable sum of money in their will—out of guilt or love, we aren't certain, but it's more than enough for us to live comfortably as long as we stay within our means."

"Then why can't we take that money back to Cuba?"

"Because Miguel has the funds in an American bank. I don't want to take it back and have Spain whittle it away with their taxes and assessments until there's nothing left."

Pilar mulled that over while taking in the beauty of the gardens. "And if I choose to return?"

"You are old enough to make your own way, Pilar. I'll not stand in your way."

Pilar tried to imagine life without her mother and sister because she knew without asking that Doneta would be content to stay. She glanced between the two women who held her heart. "I'll let you know after the party."

"That's fine," her mother replied softly.

Lying in bed in the dark, Pilar knew her sister was awake. "Would you really prefer to live here, 'Neta?"

"I would. I'm tired of having to work so hard for so little reward. Maybe once the country changes, things for people like us will be better, but right now . . . I know you probably think I'm flighty to be impressed by the way our uncle lives, but to have a full belly each night before I sleep, to not have to get up each morning and wear the same clothes. Do you realize we've never had anything new since Papa died? Mama has been doing the best she can to provide for us and we've both worked hard to help her, but for once, I'd like to paint something that I can keep or spend a portion of the day reading instead of trying to come up with yet another way to cheat someone just so we can eat."

Pilar let those words sink in.

"And as I said the other day, maybe I can find someone who will love me. I know you don't care about such things, Pilar, but I do."

She was right, Pilar didn't care about love but didn't begrudge her sister the pursuit of it.

Doneta said, "I do wish you'd consider staying, too. What would I do without you? Who would I confide in or roll my eyes with?"

Pilar smiled. "This new husband you're seeking."

"Husbands don't roll their eyes—or at least I don't think so. The point is. We've been breathing for each other since the day I was born. I don't want a life that doesn't include you."

"Are you trying to guilt me into staying, Doneta?"

"No, Pilar, but I am speaking from my heart."

Pilar got out of bed and walked over to her bed and sat on the edge. "Whatever decision I make, I'll tell you first."

They embraced.

"You promise," Doneta whispered holding on tightly.

Her love for her sister and the idea of losing her put tears in her eyes. "Yes, I promise."

Pilar and Doneta enjoyed the company of their cousins, in spite of their sour mother. They'd helped Pilar and Doneta learn the layout of the house, talked with them about the joys of living in Florida and did their best to relieve the stings of some their mother's barbs. They were not as beautiful as their Banderas cousins but both were smart, kind, and had a great sense of humor. On the night of the ball the four young women got dressed together in Mari's bedroom, which was the size of their house back home. She was three years older than her sister and a year old than Doneta.

"You both look so lovely," she said to Pilar and Doneta.

Anya said, "Mama's going to have a fit."

Mari cracked, "Then she's going to parade us around like prize heifers hoping someone will make a bid."

They all giggled but swallowed their laughter quickly when Simona walked into the room. "Are you ready?"

Desa walked in behind her and Pilar almost didn't recognize her, she was so beautiful. Pilar considered Doneta to be the prettiest of the Banderas sisters but even she paled in comparison to their mother in her striking emerald gown. Her hair was up and her face bore just the faintest application of paint. Simona, in a dress far too snug with far too many drapings for her ample figure, couldn't hold a candle to her sister-in-law.

Simona looked at her daughters. "You both look gorgeous."

And Pilar agreed.

"But the two of you," she declared to Pilar and Doneta, "pull up those necklines so you won't be mistaken for strumpets."

"Excuse me!" Desa snapped.

Simona's lips tightened. "Just remember, Mari and Anya are the ones seeking husbands, not your two."

And she swept from the room.

Anya turned to Pilar and Doneta. "I'm sorry."

Pilar patted her arm. "It's all right."

Desa added. "No apologies needed. We all look absolutely beautiful, so let's go down and see how many men we can bring to their knees."

Laughing, they left the room and as they did, Desa said quietly to Pilar and Doneta, "Remember, we are here from Santo Domingo. We've no idea who might be in attendance."

They nodded.

Pilar was very uncomfortable in her beautiful new gown because she'd never worn anything with a neckline that bared her throat and shoulders and skimmed the tops of her breasts before. Even though it was tastefully designed, she kept wanting to drag the bodice up around her chin. The short heels on her shoes made striding the way she was accustomed to much more difficult than when wearing her army boots or rope sandals but she kept smiling as she wove her way through the party. Doneta was across the room surrounded by a bevy of men buzzing around her like bees at a flower. She appeared to be enjoying the attention and Pilar was happy for her. None of the young men appeared to be showing any interest in their cousins Mari and Anya and Tia Simona was undoubtedly furious, but Doneta couldn't change her facial features any more than the plain faced Ventura girls could theirs. It was a grand affair though, with food and desserts and a small band of musicians. Whenever her uncle or mother brought someone over for her to meet, she forced herself to smile and be pleasant, but she dearly wished to be elsewhere, preferably back at home. Her mother appeared to be happy though, and Pilar supposed her personal discomfort meant nothing in comparison. She hadn't seen her mother sparkle so since before their father's death.

All the doors and windows of the grand home were open to let in the evening breeze, but with the press of bodies the room was still very warm, so she made her way to the refreshments table to get an ice with the hope it might cool her off. As she glanced towards the archway where newly arrived guests were entering, she froze and her eyes widened at the sight of Noah Yates! Her heart pounded and it took all she had not to succumb to the weakness in her knees. She quickly turned her back and slipped into the cover of the mob by the table. As she took the cup of punch from the servant, her hand shook so badly it was necessary to take in a deep calming breath to keep the liquid from splashing over the rim and onto her gown. What was he doing at her uncle's birthday party! Hazarding a quick look back, she watched him being approached by her smiling uncle. In his dark evening clothes, Yates looked even more striking than she remembered and more than a few ladies openly stared with unveiled interest. She glanced over at her sister. The look on her face must've shown her distress because Doneta smiled politely at her circle of admirers and made her way to Pilar's side. "What's wrong?"

"Come out onto the verandah with me for a moment."

Outside, there were a few people enjoying conversation and being away from the noise and heat, so she led her sister to a spot that was unoccupied.

Concern on her face and in her voice, Doneta said, "You look like you've seen a ghost."

"Close. Noah Yates just arrived."

Doneta's jaw dropped. "The man who owned the boat you stole?"

Pilar nodded.

Doneta spun her eyes back to the gathering as if needing to see him before settling her attention on Pilar once more. "What in the world is he doing here?"

"I don't know but I almost fainted when he walked into the room."

Doneta studied the worry on Pilar's face and then smiled. "It's okay though. Weren't you disguised?"

"I was."

"Then he can't put two and two together and come up with you. Can he?"

Pilar mulled that over for a moment and exhaled with relief. "You're right. He can't. Oh thank you for helping me think this through."

"If he approaches, all you need do is act as if you've never met. Simple."

To Pilar it sounded very simple, but there was a nagging something inside that left her still wary. She had been well disguised that night, she reminded herself.

Doneta asked, "Better?"

"Much."

"May I go back to my swains now?"

Pilar chuckled, "Yes, you may."

"Good, because I'm having a marvelous time and some of them are very handsome."

"Make sure the one you settle on is wealthy."

"Of course," she said over a laugh. "You stay vigilant. Yates can't possibly recognize you, but come and point him out so we can both keep an eye on him."

They walked back inside and there he stood, still engaged with her uncle. "That's him."

Doneta said, "Oh my. He's very handsome. The scar makes him look deliciously wicked and dangerous."

Confused, Pilar turned. "What?"

"He looks like I picture some of the men in the romantic novels Mama and I read."

Pilar had no idea what she was talking about and decided she was better off not knowing. "You go back to your bees, and I'll try and stay out of his sight."

"You'll be fine."

Pilar watched him bowing over the hand of her near swooning cousin Mari, and prayed Doneta was right.

Noah wondered why he'd agreed to attend this madness. Due to the crush, he could barely raise an arm to avail himself of the wine being offered by the slow-moving fleet of tray-bearing servants.

It appeared as if every person of Spanish extraction in Florida was in attendance. He'd accepted the invitation because of his friendship with Miguel. They'd first met on the streets of Key West, where Miguel was selling his cigars from a stall on the streets. Noah and King found the cigars so much to their liking they asked if they could sell them to some of the shopkeepers they did business with in Texas, New Orleans, and overseas in places like London and Spain. Miguel agreed and the rest as they say was history. The cigars sold so well, Miguel was forced to increase production and with the financial assistance of Noah and King, a warehouse was purchased and additional workers hired. Ventura was an outstanding businessman and one of the nicest men Noah knew. In truth, Noah was honored to be invited. Not finding the Banderas woman in Santiago still left a bitter taste in his mouth, but he reminded himself of Drew's advice to have some fun, so this would serve as a distraction. Tomorrow he'd meet with Miguel about the business, and then plan his next move against the pirate. At the moment though, he had none. Where had she gone? Had Gordonez somehow tipped her off that he was closing in? Noah had no way of knowing.

"Noah Yates. I want you to meet my sister, Desa Banderas."

Upon hearing her surname, Noah froze.

Miguel added, "Desa is visiting from Santo Domingo."

He bowed over her hand. "My pleasure, senora. Are you kin to the Banderases of Santiago, Cuba?"

"No."

He noticed the slight tremor in her hand and the hint of unease in her gaze. Scenting prey, the tiger inside Noah smiled.

Miguel said to her, "Noah is one of my business partners. We've been friends for years."

"Have we met before?" he asked innocently.

"No," she replied again, adding a hasty shake of denial. He saw no evidence of the telltale scar on the back of her hand, but he found her reaction to him interesting. Was she really from Santo Domingo?

"Did you come to Florida alone, senora?" he asked.

Miguel responded, "No, she's here with her lovely daughters, Doneta and Pilar."

Noah kept his features schooled. Of course there were undoubtedly more than one Pilar Banderas in the world and what were the odds that the daughter would be the one he'd been seeking, but something inside told him she was. *Finally!* The mother watched him closely. He smoothly turned back to Ventura. "If they're as lovely as their mother, I'd be honored to meet them whenever you find the time."

Her eyes narrowed slightly. He sensed she was

uncertain as to whether he was a threat or not and he planned to keep that uncertainty intact for the moment. He bowed to her with all the grace he'd learned from his own mother. "I hope you and your daughters enjoy your visit."

"Thank you."

His elation masked, he left them and moved into the crowd to get something to eat. Drew was correct. Having fun was fun.

Noah occupied himself with his small plate and with trying to guess which of the women in attendance would turn out to be the one he was hunting. There were quite a few to pick from. He eliminated the tall ones, like the lovely in the white gown standing nearby, whose smile let him know she was interested. He found her interesting as well, but not enough to make him veer from the path he'd set. Moving through the mob, he changed positions and took up a spot near the doors leading out to the verandah. Another beauty, this one in a rose-colored gown and surrounded by a gaggle of cow-eyed young men had the short stature he was in search of. When his gaze brushed hers, the furtive response in her eyes gave him pause. She nodded a cursory greeting before returning her attention to the men, but there was a distinct tenseness in her neck and shoulders that made him wait and watch. He'd been keeping a discreet eye on Desa Banderas as well, and so far she hadn't approached either of her chicks. He wondered if her avoidance was due to the extraordinary number of people packed into the ballroom or her way of throwing him off the scent to keep them safe. Time would tell.

Pilar watched Yates watching Doneta and cast a quick gaze around the crowd to find her mother eyeing him as well. Pilar wanted to hear her mother's take on how being introduced to him had gone, but she held off, hoping he'd soon leave. She kept reminding herself that he had no idea what she looked like, but believing it was difficult.

To further complicate matters, her uncle approached. "Ah, Pilar. There you are." He took her hand. "There's a gentleman I want you to meet."

Instinctively, she knew who he meant. "I—was on my way to get some cake."

"This'll only take a moment."

So she let herself be led through the room and over to Noah Yates.

"Noah. Someone here I want you to meet. This is my niece Pilar, Desa's eldest daughter."

His dark eyes met hers and she swore she was going to shake apart. Yates took her small hand in his large one and bowed over it. He seemed to hesitate for a second before bringing it slowly to his lips. The touch burned and sent a shaft of heat up her arm so strong she almost yanked her hand from his. Instead, she forced herself to say, "My pleasure. Are you enjoying yourself?"

"I am. I hope you are as well." She noted that he still held her hand and that there appeared to be a muted humor in his strong gaze.

"Oh, yes," he responded. "Since I don't know anyone else here besides your uncle, may I impose on you to stay and talk awhile. I hear you're from Santo Domingo. I have family there and was wondering if the country is really as unstable as the newspapers are reporting."

Her uncle looked across the room. "Ah, my wife is waving me over. You two talk and I'll go see what she wants."

Pilar wanted to beg that he stay but reminded herself of Doneta's words. Yates didn't know what she looked like, so she relaxed. "Where's your home, Mr. Yates?"

"California."

"What's it like there?"

"Warm, but sometimes cold in winter."

"Ah."

"Have we met before?"

She tensed. "I don't believe so."

"Are you sure?"

"Positive. It's said everyone has a twin some- where. Maybe you met a woman that I remind you of."

"That's indeed possible."

The musicians struck up the first music of the evening, a waltz.

"Would you care to dance?"

Pilar, wanted to scream, "No!" but having always been known for her bravery, she reminded herself of that and met his eyes fearlessly. "Thank you. Yes, I would."

And so, she found herself out among the dancers with one hand captured in his while his other hand burned her waist through the fabric of her new mint green gown. As they moved in time with the music, the heat of his body wafted over her in a way that was dizzying. He was graceful and well trained. She on the other hand had to concentrate on her steps because in spite of her brave front, she was shaking inside.

"You dance well," he told her.

"Thank you."

Looking up at him was akin to looking into the face of a tiger, and an amused one at that. It was almost as if he knew . . . Startled, her eyes shot to his.

As if having read her thoughts, he turned her to the music and said, "Yes, my little pirate. We meet again."

And Pilar did the only thing she could think to do. She ran!

Forcing her way through the crowd in an effort to flee, Pilar must've said "Excuse me" a hundred times. Dancers were pushed aside, diners' drinks splashed, plates were jostled, guests yelled in outrage. She drew the shocked attention of everyone in the room, but she didn't care. She had to get away. A quick look over her shoulder showed him striding determinedly in her wake while smiling, of all things. She had no idea what his intentions were, but she didn't want to find out. When she reached the wide open foyer, there were only a handful of people about, so she hiked up her gown and ran as fast as her heels would allow. She debated heading outside but didn't want to be lost in the unfamiliar streets, so she flew up the wide staircase that led to the living quarters with the hopes of maybe locking herself in a room until she could think of a way out of this catastrophe. He was right behind her, following her with an easy, almost leisurely stride she found absolutely infuriating. That he'd toyed with her on the dance floor added to her rising temper. Running down the hallway, she passed her uncle's sitting room. Upon seeing the crossed rapiers hanging above the mantel inside, she ran in. She snatched one free, turned, and found Yates standing in the doorway. He folded his arms and leaned against the jamb.

"Swords, is it?" he asked.

Remembering her grandfather's training sessions, Pilar kept her back straight, her eyes on him and the rapier extended, raised and at the ready.

"Then I guess the answer is yes." He approached and she warily took a few steps back.

To her surprise he took down the other rapier. While testing its weight and heft, he spoke. "One of the things my very Spanish mother insisted upon was that my brothers and I learn the art of fencing. Not because she expected us to defend ourselves, but because it's what all well brought up Spanish sons were expected to master."

By then her uncle, mother, sisters, and a large group of guests were lined up behind him.

"Noah, what is this?" Ventura demanded.

Yates took a moment to remove his jacket. "A private affair and I insist you stay out of the way."

"Pilar!" her uncle snapped. "Put down that sword!"

"I can't."

The two combatants were slowly circling each other.

"So, you know *Destreza*?" Yates asked her, sounding impressed. In Spanish the word meant "skill" and was applied to that country's version of swordplay.

"*La Verdadera Destreza*," she countered. The True Art. Unlike the linear swordfights taught in places like Italy, Destreza was conducted on an imaginary circle.

"Noah! I demand an explanation."

"Miguel, unless you want your niece handed over to the authorities, I suggest you let the two of us handle this. Piracy is against the law, isn't it, Pilar?"

Miguel croaked, "Piracy?"

His wife, Simona, swooned and fainted in a heap at his feet.

Out of the corner of her eye, Pilar saw her sister and mother. Both looked horrified. Her mother called out, "Mr. Yates!"

He turned and Pilar attacked so swiftly, her blade cut his chin and would've done more damage had he not instantly brought his own blade up to block her next attempt.

He touched his fingers to the wound and the sight of the blood staining his fingers made him look at her with a mixture of admiration and surprise. "Well, well. You do know how to use that, don't you? I thought it was just a prop when we first met, but you have my attention now. Very unfair of your mother to try and distract me, however."

"You're bigger and stronger. I need all the advantages I can get."

They resumed the circular dance: parried, feinted, crossed blades, withdrew, attacked, and repeated the dance again and again until the sharp sound of metal against metal created its own song.

As they crossed swords again, instead of Pilar retreating, she whirled like a dervish, slashed low, and almost caught him off guard again, but he was faster.

"You are very, very good, *chiquita*, but another unfair move."

She circled and tossed back, "You may have been trained by fancy Spaniard teachers, but I was trained by a pirate." And she attacked again, putting all her weight into her parries, but as she'd noted, he was bigger and stronger and had no trouble holding her off.

"You want unfair?"

His lightning-fast rapier severed the band of fabric across her left shoulder and the edge of her gown fell forward to reveal the white strapless corset beneath. Caught off guard, her mouth dropped open. She grabbed her dress to keep herself covered. Her eyes shot fury.

"Being the gentleman that I am, I didn't cut your blade side. Do you yield?"

"No." And to drive the point home, she slashed the other strap, not caring about her scandalous appearance. "I'll save you the trouble." She continued to circle.

He laughed as if he were having the time of his life. "Ah, my little pirate. You're a woman after my own heart."

"I'll take it on the point of my sword."

"I think not. You and I have things to discuss, so let's end this."

He attacked. Pilar did her best to hold her ground, but his skill and power exceeded her own. She held him off for as long as she was able but eventually, her arm ached with her efforts to parry his unrelenting strikes. The sound of the battle filled the room. She was forced to retreat farther and farther until the wall was at her back and she had nowhere else to go. Shedding tears of fury and frustration, she tossed her rapier aside and turned away so she wouldn't see the triumph that she assumed he'd show.

Instead, he whispered, "*Reina guerreras* shouldn't cry," and gently cleared a tear from her cheek.

Startled, hearing herself called a warrior queen, she turned to him and the depth in his eyes captured her like a powerful stormy sea.

"You fought well," he told her. "Hold your head high. You've nothing to be ashamed of."

He left her for a moment to retrieve his jacket and draped it over her shoulders. Holding her gaze, he said, "Miguel, send your guests home. I need to speak with you and her mother."

Her uncle finally found his voice. "Yes. We can use my study."

And to Pilar's surprise Yates picked her up and carried her past the wide-eyed spectators and out of the room.

Chapter 9

Noah would be the first to admit that he had no idea what he was about. What he did know was that battling her left him feeling more alive than he had in years. Her spirit and sheer fearlessness opened up a window in the black recesses of his soul to let in a light so intoxicating and freeing, he craved more, and because of that she'd become the woman he wanted in his life.

"You can put me down now," she directed coolly when they reached the silent book-lined study. Instead, he took a moment to feast on her features, the still damp eyes, the tensely set brown jaw, the pridefully raised chin. The night they'd first met, he had no idea the hooded cloak concealed such a beautiful gaminlike face. Her dark curly hair, its texture resembling his own, was cut short like a youth's, thus setting her apart from most of the fashionable women of the era, yet the style seemed to suit her unconventional nature perfectly. She faced him like an angry prize of war, a true warrior queen—bested but not conquered.

"As you wish." He set her on her feet and watched her pull his jacket closed over her exposed corset. She reached into his pocket and withdrew a handkerchief. Handing it to him she said, "Your chin's bleeding."

He took it with a ghost of a smile and pressed it against the nick.

"I won't apologize for that."

"I don't expect you to."

Her mother entered with the young woman in the rose-colored gown he'd noticed earlier. Based on the strong resemblance to both Desa and Pilar, she had to be the other daughter. Both women shot him impatient glares and went to her side.

"I'm fine," she assured them and sent him a blaze-filled look that left him quietly exhilarated.

Miguel Ventura entered next with his wife. Concern filling his face, he looked first to his niece and upon finding her alive and in once piece, asked Noah, "Now what is this about piracy?"

Noah's gaze shifted back to the woman in his coat. "Pilar, do you wish to tell the story?"

"I'm sure you can tell it better than I."

He inclined his head and gave her uncle a truthful but abbreviated version of both his abduction and the theft of the *Alanza*. When he concluded, Miguel appeared to be speechless. His wife wasn't.

"I knew we shouldn't have taken them in! Soldiers could come knocking on our door at any moment. I'll not lose everything we have because of your sister and her trash!"

Miguel snapped, "Be quiet or leave us! My apologies, Desa."

The blaze in Desa Banderas's eyes mimicked her

daughter's. "Accepted." She then warned Simona, "Do not slur my girls again."

"Or what?" she sneered.

Desa's powerful slap sent her sister-in-law reeling. "That's what! Now, shut your foul mouth!"

Simona was so stunned, it apparently took a moment to register what had just occurred. Hand to her face, tears flooded her eyes. "Miguel!"

He gritted out, "Go put some cold water on your face, Simona."

"That's all you have to say?"

"Yes. Leave us!"

With a wail, she hurried from the room.

The still seething Desa spun to Noah. "So, what do you want in compensation?"

"Permission to marry your daughter."

The room went still as a tomb.

Ventura offered an uncomfortable-sounding chuckle. "Surely, you're joking."

"No. Would you rather she be turned over to the authorities?" he asked, viewing Pilar's shocked face.

"Of—of course not," he stammered. "But—Noah, you don't even know her."

"True, but I would like to, and I think we would suit. If you'd prefer a courting period, I'd agree to say, a month, two at the most." He knew he couldn't just carry her off like he wished, and being well raised, he'd conform to the necessary protocols, but within his parameters. "I'd like to get back to California as soon as I can to resurrect my business, with my wife."

Her mother finally found speech. "And if you don't suit?"

"As I said, I believe we will." He glanced Pilar's way. She was staring at him as if he'd suddenly grown two heads. "Not what you were expecting?" he asked her.

"No." It came out a whisper.

"Neither was I." His eyes lingered on her for a long moment before he turned his attention back to Miguel and her mother. "Discuss my proposal and let me know what you decide. I'll be out on the patio."

And he exited.

In the silence that followed his departure, Pilar was still so stunned, speech refused to come. She looked to her mother, who appeared equally as outdone.

Doneta asked her uncle, "Tio, do you think he would really give her over to the authorities?"

He shrugged. "I've never known him to be anything but honorable and a man of his word. If what he told us was true he has more than ample grounds on which to bring charges."

"But I don't wish to be courted or marry, Mama!" Pilar stated wildly.

"I understand that, Pilar, but do you wish to be imprisoned?" she was asked.

"Of course not."

"And we don't wish for you to be either."

Her uncle mused aloud, "Maybe if we offer to get the boat back to him—"

Her mother confessed: "It was sunk by the Spanish navy. And Miguel, as much as I hate to agree with Simona, there is a chance that the government may seek her out." She told him about Pilar's run-in with the navy.

He threw up his hands. "*Dios*! This gets better and better. Desa, what kind of child have you raised?"

"A fervent but reckless one sometimes." There was sadness in the smile she sent Pilar's way.

Pilar didn't mind her mother's description but had no intentions of spending her remaining years being described as the wife of Noah Yates. She'd never been courted by a man in her life.

Her mother asked her uncle, "What do you know of him?"

"That he's very wealthy and from an old and venerable Spanish family in California. She could do worse."

"I'd think a man of that stature would have his pick of any woman he fancies."

He shrugged again. "Apparently he's taken a fancy to your daughter."

Doneta said, "Tio, maybe if you talk to him he will see reason."

Pilar shook her head. She had come to a decision. "No. If anyone talks to him it should be me."

"Are you certain?" her uncle asked.

"Yes." But it was lie. She wasn't certain at all. In fact, having to broach this madness with Yates filled her with dread.

Her uncle said, "You've done him a great wrong, Pilar. That ship was his livelihood and my livelihood is tied to his as well. He could've easily gone straight to the American authorities; instead he's offered you something you just might want to consider."

Properly chastised, Pilar knew he was telling her the truth but it was not what she wanted to hear. "Yes, Tio." She felt as if the world had suddenly turned on its axis and now more than ever she wished she had listened to Tomas and chosen another target. Marriage? To him? She had to find a way to talk him out of it without being jailed.

"Let's repair your dress first," her mother suggested.

Needle and thread were found and after a few well-placed stitches, Pilar departed.

As she wound her way through the house, a part of her hoped he'd changed his mind and gone away, but she knew that was just wishful thinking. Walking outside into the torch-lit darkness, she heard off in the distance the faint buzz of the guests making their departure. The gossips were going to have a field day. She was truly sorry for turning her uncle's birthday *rumba* into a debacle but there was no help for that now. The swordplay was something people would be whispering about behind their hands and relating to others for months, if not years, to come.

The scandal aside, it was an idyllic night. The moon was high, casting light along the stone path she was following and the air was sweet with the scent of flowers in bloom. Too bad her nerves weren't as peaceful or serene.

He was sitting in a chair on the patio when she walked up. A lone, lit candle inside of a glass globe sat in the middle of the table and sent wavering flickers of light over his presence. He stood gallantly at her approach.

"I've been expecting you. Join me, please."

She handed him his coat and as he helped her with her chair, she swallowed her nervousness. For a few moments she studied him silently and tried to decide the right tack to take. "From what my uncle tells me, you are wealthy enough to have any woman in the world, so why me?"

"Because you're the only one who can wield a rapier."

She didn't believe that.

"It's what a woman with your spirit and fire deserves."

That made her heart pound. She'd never had a man say anything so potent to her before. "You can't possibly care for me."

"No, but I hope to in time, and that you will come to care for me as well."

His soft-toned reply set off more inner havoc, even as she wondered if he had some sort of mind sickness. "I don't understand."

"Neither do I but I'd like to try and sort it out. Would you prefer to be my mistress instead?"

"Of course not."

"I didn't think so."

She thought she saw a faint smile as the light played over his scarred face and she wished for full day so she could see him better. "For the sake of argument suppose we do marry. As my husband you can do whatever you wish to me. Are you doing this so you can take your revenge on me for stealing your ship?"

"No, Pilar. I may appear to be a barbarian on the outside, but I am a gentleman underneath. As my wife, you'll have all the advantages a woman of my set has: a nice home, servants if you choose, money of your own. Whatever your heart desires, within reason, I will move heaven and earth to set at your feet."

Her heart stopped and she stared. Once again rendered speechless, she finally managed to say, "This doesn't make sense."

"We are in agreement. Have you ever been courted?"

She wanted to lie and say *Dozens of times,* but . . . "No."

His voice was soft. "Have you given your heart to anyone?"

This was the most unnerving situation she'd ever faced. In spite of his quiet tone and manner she found him so overwhelming, she wanted to hike up her skirts and flee again. "No."

"Then let me court you, *chiquita*. Let me show you what it means to be with a man who finds you intriguing and yes, desires you. I promise, we'll go slow."

Pilar's heart was pounding; her breathing heightened, her senses spinning.

"Say, yes, *mi pequeño pirata* . . ."

Pilar couldn't've said her name.

"If you're worried about being so far from your family, my mother will be as fiercely protective of you as your own. You'll have two sisters-in-law who will help you along, and should anything untoward happen to me, my brothers will care for you as if you were their own blood."

"But I don't wish to marry you."

"Understood, but many couples in arranged marriages have managed to find their way."

"Not always. My mother left her *novio* at the altar to run away with my father."

"Is that where you get your determination?"

She'd hope to throw him off pace with that example; instead he'd responded with hushed-voice praise that once again set her senses spinning. "Suppose I offer to pay you for your ship?"

He evaluated her silently for a moment. "You

offered to pay for it, but not return it. Why is that?"

She hesitated so long he coaxed, "Pilar?"

She finally confessed, "It was sunk. Cannon fire from the Spanish navy."

"Were you on board?"

"Yes."

"Were you hurt?"

"Bumps and bruises. Swallowed a large amount of seawater . . ." Her voice trailed off.

"And my *Alanza* was being used for . . . ?"

"Gunrunning."

He chuckled softly, sat back, and folded his arms. "For the rebels?"

She nodded and hoped her answer would scare him off. As she'd noted to her mother, no man wanted a wife who smuggled guns.

"Is the government searching for you?"

"Possibly."

"As the wife of an American citizen you may be offered some measure of protection should they come hunting. Yet another plus for saying yes."

But who would protect her from him? came the thought.

His next question brought her back. "How long have you been with the rebels?"

"Since my father's death in 'seventy-seven."

"And you were how old?"

"Fifteen." She'd begged her mother to let her join the Revolutionary Army, but because she was deemed too small to fight, she'd been attached to the Mambi women who ran the support columns.

"How did he die?"

"Spain hung him for treason."

He went still. "My condolences."

"Thank you." Her father's death broke her heart. She'd loved him so much. He'd taken up the cause for his lost brothers, and she'd done the same for him. Now she was being forced to live for herself and she wasn't certain she knew how. "I can sail a ship and shoot a gun. I can walk a hundred miles silently through a jungle on little food and no sleep. I can start a smokeless fire, feed myself on what I can forage, treat wounds, and sharpen a machete until it gleams. I know nothing about being a wife."

"And I know nothing about being a husband. That makes us even. Once you and I have worked through our initial clash of wills, I will send for your mother and sister with the hope that they'll consent to visit."

"I doubt this will go as easily as you envision."

"I'm envisioning a hard-fought battle, Pilar. Nothing worth having comes easy, especially not a woman so beautiful and fearless."

Once again she was swept away, but managed to say. "As long as you understand."

"I do."

And with that she stood, and she was admittedly shaking inside, not out of fear of him or for her safety but of something unnamed: something that called to a portion of herself that was as intrigued by him as he claimed to be by her, even though the thinking rest of herself didn't wish to be.

"You still haven't given me an answer," he reminded her softly. "Do you wish to be courted?"

"You don't leave much choice, do you? Yes, you may court me. I'll see you in the morning."

She distinctly saw him smile that time. "This isn't funny."

"No, but battling you will be fun. There's a difference."

Exasperated, Pilar shook her head and left him.

As she disappeared into the darkness, Noah mined his own thoughts. He was now certain he'd lost his mind, but the parts of him that were drawn to her didn't care. As he'd noted, she was as lovely as she was fierce; even though it was readily apparent she'd never crossed swords on the field of courtship. He couldn't wait to begin his quest to win her. The memory of the rapier battle resurfaced, bringing with it the glorious surge of joy he'd felt during the encounter. To experience that again even occasionally was worth more than gold. He'd been wearing the dark horror of the island like a lead-lined mantle for over a decade. Never once had it fully lifted—until tonight. And even now, as it slowly descended again, the knowledge that it could be banished even temporarily gave him hope that over time he might escape it permanently. She held the key, the first he'd ever found, and just thinking about her seemed to ease the pain. Because of her he knew that hidden beneath his inner darkness lay something still alive, and he wanted to feed it so it could rise and grow. And as it did, and he and his recalcitrant warrior queen feinted and parried their way to a mutual understanding, maybe, just maybe he'd get to experience the joy his brothers seemed to have found with their wives, and that gave him hope as well. He was so elated by the evening's turn of events he wanted to wire Drew and let him know, he was finally having fun.

Pilar's mother and sister were waiting in the bedroom the sisters shared when she returned.

"How did you fare?" her mother asked.

Pilar sank into a chair. "He refuses to change his mind." She thought back on the overwhelming encounter and fought to ignore the lingering effects on her senses. "I asked if this was his way of extracting his revenge."

"And his reply?"

"No."

"Then why do this?" Doneta wanted to know.

Instead of revealing he'd spoken of desire, she hedged. "He said it's because I'm the only woman he knows who can wield a rapier." She rolled her eyes at that, and added truthfully, "He also said that I would have a fine home, money of my own, servants. Whatever I desired he'd move heaven and earth to place at my feet."

Her mother stilled with surprise.

Doneta said over a laugh. "Oh my. If you don't want him, Pilar, I'll take him."

They all laughed, and Pilar wondered how she'd survive in California without Doneta's wonderful sense of humor. She held the gazes of the two people she loved most in the world. "He wants the two of you to come to California to visit once he and I are settled. I told him it wasn't going to be that easy. He can't possibly believe he'll win me over in two months."

"Does he frighten you?" her mother asked quietly.

She shook her head. "He assured me I won't come to any harm and truthfully, I believe him. I just don't understand why he's so set on doing this."

"Maybe he's in love with you," Doneta said and shrugged. "Tio said he's honorable. You could do a lot worse."

"But I don't want to do at all." She thought back to the night she ordered him to the rowboat. "He said he'd find me, and he has." The confusion on her mother's face made her explain what she was referencing.

"He's very driven then," her mother concluded.

"Apparently." She quieted and thought back on his potent encounter once more. "I don't know anything about being courted, Mama."

"I do," Doneta said dreamily. "In the books, the man takes his *novia* walking, brings her flowers and chocolates, and sometimes when the duenna isn't looking, he'll steal a kiss."

The thought of Noah Yates kissing her made Pilar go weak. "I won't be kissing him, Doneta." Would he really try and kiss her? She guessed he would. Saints help her!

Her mother was eyeing her keenly.

"Yes, Mama?"

"Nothing. I'm just listening to your silly sister. Did he say anything about when he'd return?"

"No, but I told him I would see him tomorrow."

"Did you agree to be courted?"

"I don't have much choice."

"Maybe this will work out better than you think."

"I doubt that."

"Just keep an open mind."

Pilar didn't want to do or think about anything that might bring her closer to the man she'd left sitting on the patio. "I'm ready for bed."

"I believe we all are. It's been quite the evening." Her mother gave her a kiss on the cheek. "Rest well."

"You too, Mama." But Pilar doubted she'd be able to, knowing she'd be facing Noah Yates for battle in the morning.

Chapter 10

Pilar assumed Yates would make an appearance first thing, but as the morning slid into afternoon and he'd not shown up by lunchtime, she relaxed. She hoped he'd decided that a woman who smuggled guns was indeed unworthy of further pursuit and would never bedevil her again, but she knew that to be wishful thinking. More than likely he'd been waylaid by a business matter of some sort and would visit tomorrow. In an attempt to put him out of her mind she spent the afternoon sitting in the garden having her portrait done. Doneta thought a painting of her would be an excellent keepsake when she moved to California.

"Pilar, stop moving," Doneta pleaded. "Each time you do, it throws things off."

"Sorry." This was Pilar's first time as a model and having to sit as still as a rock was difficult for a woman unaccustomed to doing so. "How much longer?"

"If you keep moving about, we'll be here until Christmas."

Pilar sighed.

Her mother appeared. "Pilar."

Glad for the reprieve, she broke her pose and heard her sister's frustrated groan, which she smilingly ignored. "Yes, Mama?"

"Do you remember meeting a man last night named Luis Garcia?"

"No." Pilar didn't remember anything about the evening that didn't involve Noah Yates.

"Apparently, Senor Garcia remembers you. He's here and has asked me if he might sit with you in the parlor for a few moments."

Pilar was confused. "Why?"

"I think he's interested in courting you."

She sighed. She'd lived her entire life without any male interest and now they were lining up at the door. Granted there were only two, but that was two more suitors than she'd ever had before. "So what did you tell him?"

"I told him yes. If you are so opposed to Mr. Yates, maybe if you show an interest in another he'll bow out."

Pilar seriously doubted that but before she could express it, Doneta asked, "What does Senor Garcia look like?"

"Looks are not always a true measure of a man, Doneta."

"That means he's overweight and has a glass eye, Pilar."

Their mother shot her a quelling look. Doneta pretended to fiddle with her paints and their mother turned back to Pilar. "Go upstairs and change into the blue day gown we bought for you—"

Pilar opened her mouth.

"Do as I asked, please, unless you prefer to go to California?"

Pilar left without another word.

When she entered the parlor, the man she assumed to be Senor Garcia stood. He was no taller than she and appeared to be quite a few years older. There was a balding patch on the crown of his head and he sported an enormous broomlike mustache that caused her to wonder if he'd cultivated it to make up for the baldness and his short stature. He took her hand and bowed respectfully. "I am honored to see you again, Senorita Banderas."

Even though she still didn't remember being introduced to him, she replied, "I am honored as well." His hand was sweaty, so much so she had to force herself not to drag her palm over the skirt of her dress to rid it of the clammy moisture. Instead, as she sat down, she discreetly used the arm of the settee instead. At her age, she didn't need a duenna but her mother played the role anyway because Garcia was a stranger, and her forced grin matched Pilar's.

His smile showed a few rotting teeth. "And how old are you?"

Thinking that an odd way to begin the conversation, she eyed him for a moment. "Twenty-five."

He appeared surprised. "You look much younger."

"Thank you." She supposed that was the correct response. In truth, she wanted to get to her feet and leave Senor Sweaty Hands where he sat. She gave her mother a glance and saw *Be Nice* displayed on her face, so she drew in a deep breath and reset her false smile.

"And how often do you attend mass?"

Pilar believed in the Savior but her family had never attended worship regularly. "Easter and Christmas."

His eyebrows rose. "That is all?"

"Yes."

"I see."

Pilar wondered how long it had taken him to grow that elaborate mustache. It seemed to originate somewhere within his nostrils and looked to weigh almost as much as he.

"Senorita Banderas, I asked you if you've been baptized?"

She'd been so intent on the hair she hadn't heard his question. "My apologies. Yes, I've been baptized."

"At birth," her mother added, sounding proud.

"The woman I marry will be expected to attend mass each Sunday."

"I'm sure she'd find that agreeable."

He scanned her with mild disapproval.

She waited.

"I am a wealthy man."

"That's very nice." Again, she had no idea how to respond properly.

"And your expectations of a husband?"

"The senorita would expect her husband to have a boat."

Pilar froze in response to the familiar male voice, turned and saw Noah Yates standing in the doorway. His arms were filled with flowers. How long he'd been there was anyone's guess.

"A boat?" Garcia echoed, sounding baffled.

"Yes. You know those vessels that move on water. The senorita likes to sail."

Yates bowed before her mother and presented her with a large bouquet of stemmed red roses. "Senora, I tried to find blooms as beautiful as you, but the florist said that was impossible."

Her chuckling mother shook her head at his outrageousness. "Thank you, Mr. Yates."

He then crossed to Pilar and handed her an even larger bouquet of yellow roses. "Pilar."

"Thank you," she replied coolly. Doneta's words of last night rose tauntingly. *He brings his novia . . . flowers . . .*

"Who are you?" Garcia demanded.

"Noah Yates. Miguel Ventura's business partner." He then asked her mother in an innocent tone, "May I join the family for dinner, senora?"

Sitting there with a huge pile of gorgeous roses in her arms, she gave him the only obvious answer. "Of course."

"Thank you." He moved his attention to Pilar. He bowed her way, straightened, shot her a smile and exited.

She sighed. He'd caught her so off guard that had she been on a true battlefield, she'd be severely wounded or dead. First blood. Noah Yates.

Senor Garcia looked to the hallway Yates disappeared into and then back to her. "You like to sail?" He eyed her as if she were something he'd never seen before.

"Yes."

"And your uncle sails with you?"

"No."

"Then with whom do you go?"

"Friends. Sometimes alone. My grandfather taught me."

"You let her sail alone, senora?"

"I do. She's very knowledgeable about the sea and boats."

Pilar asked him, "Do you sail, Senor Garcia?"

"I'm a tailor. What reason would I have to be on a boat? My wife won't have any reason to be on one either. Especially unaccompanied."

Pilar kept her smile in place as she turned to her mother. "I'd like to put these in water, Mama. May I be excused?"

Her mother stood. "I think that would be wise. Thank you for your visit, Senor Garcia."

He appeared taken aback by the sudden dismissal. "You're—welcome."

"Let me see you out," her mother offered encouragingly.

He bowed stiffly to Pilar. "Good-bye, senorita."

"Good-bye, Senor Garcia."

Picking up the hat beside him, he followed her mother's lead, and once they were out of sight, Pilar exhaled an audible sigh of relief.

"Seemed like a nice fellow," Yates said, magically appearing again. "We've both probably caught fish larger than he is. Mustache was very formidable though."

She swore she'd swallow a fish hook if she laughed. "Go away."

"Do you think people mistakenly step on him in the dark? He'd be in real danger at my family's ranch. My brothers and I are fairly tall."

Pilar wanted to run him through with her sword even though she was grateful that his entrance helped set in motion Senor Garcia's departure.

The intensity in Yates's eyes as he gazed down at her suspended time. His voice softened. "Do you like the roses?"

She glanced at their beauty in her arms and couldn't lie. "Yes."

"Doneta said no one has ever given you roses before—or flowers of any kind, for that matter. I'm enjoying being your first."

Her senses took flight again because she knew he was talking about more than flowers. "I—I need to find a vase." Why he had the ability to make her stammer when she'd never stammered before—ever—was beyond her ken. She wondered if her mother would mind if she killed her sister.

"You find your vase. I'll see you at dinner." And he took his leave.

One of the servants found her a vase and offered to arrange the roses for her, but Pilar declined. Even though she knew nothing about doing the task properly, for some reason she wanted to try. Taking both the flowers and the vase up to her bedroom she sat on the floor with them beside her.

Doneta came in. "See, I was right. The *novio* brings flowers."

Pilar rolled her eyes. "Why are you helping him?"

"Because my, I've—never—read—a—love novel—sister, that is my role."

Pilar stared.

"The younger sister is always on the hero's side."

Pilar shook her head.

"Besides, I'm hoping he has brothers."

"He does. Two. Both married."

"Oh," she replied dejectedly.

Doneta watched Pilar trying to put the roses in the vase in a fashionable order. "You first need to cut some of the stems so you have a few shorter ones. Then place them in front of the taller ones."

"How do you know that?"

"I'm a painter and that's how you do it in a painting. Tall blooms in the back. Short in the front." Doneta found a pair of scissors. "Here."

Following her sister's instructions, Pilar ended up with a beautifully arranged vase of roses.

Doneta said, "You have to admit, they are lovely."

"True, but you are not to tell Yates anything else about me. Nothing."

"Pilar. I'm helping you."

"No, you're not."

"Yes, I am, because you need it. If this were left up to you that gorgeous man would walk away from here and wind up being some other girl's brother-in-law, and I'm not going to allow that to happen. Besides, he loves you."

"No, he doesn't."

Doneta sighed. "Fine. Be dense. When you love him so much you want to eat his shoes, don't say I didn't warn you."

"What!"

"I've nothing else to say."

"Eat his shoes? Women eat men's shoes in those silly books you read?"

"It's just an expression, Pilar."

"Said by whom?"

"Never mind."

"You're making me concerned about you, 'Neta."

"You just mind your pole and don't let this big fish get away."

Pilar sighed and shook her head. First eating shoes and now, allusions to fishing poles. Noah Yates had driven her sister insane.

• • •

Noah was enjoying dinner with Miguel Ventura and the Banderas women if only for the opportunity to view Pilar at his leisure. She was wearing the same blue day gown she'd had on earlier. It was plain, high necked, and had long sleeves. The line of buttons up the front, in tandem with the bodice's snug cut, emphasized her curves. There were simple hoops in her ears. She possessed a natural beauty that didn't require a lot of adornment, so their sedateness was just the right touch.

Miguel was the only member of his immediate family present. He explained that his wife and daughters had left early that morning to visit her sister in Yorba City. Although Noah found the daughters pleasant enough, he didn't miss Simona or her judgmental attitudes in the least.

He was seated directly across the table from Pilar, who was doing her best to ignore him but he didn't mind. Each time she did send him a furtive glance, his eyes were waiting and hers would go chasing away. Again, he wanted to carry her off and be done with this courting-ritual nonsense. He could already imagine her soft lips opening under his own and what her nearness would do to him when he finally got the opportunity to slide his hands slowly over the curve of her hips and feel her nipples berry against his palm. Were she able to read his thoughts, she'd undoubtedly grab her sword and behead him there and then.

Senora Banderas asked her brother, "How long will Simona be away?"

He sipped his wine. "She said she won't be returning until you and your daughters have moved into a place of your own."

"Then we shall try and conclude the arrangements as quickly as possible."

"Take your time."

Everyone fought their smile.

"Where is the property you're considering purchasing, senora?" Noah asked.

"Here in the Keys. Most of my countrymen are here."

"Many Cubans have also settled in Yorba City," Miguel added. "But I'd prefer to have my sister and her daughters near me whether Simona agrees with that arrangement or not."

Because Noah had already staked his claim, Miguel would be doing without Pilar's company. "Senora, may I have your permission to tour the gardens with Pilar after we're done here?"

Pilar glanced up. She didn't appear pleased by the request, but he'd expected that and was looking forward to their sparring.

"I'm sure that will be fine, Mr. Yates. Are you agreeable, Pilar?"

She shrugged. "Why not."

"You will conduct yourself as a gentleman?" her mother asked him pointedly.

"Always."

Pilar's tiny eye roll made him smile inwardly.

So after dinner, they went walking. At the outset, she refused to take his arm. "I'm a twenty-five-year-old woman who's been to war, not a simpering girl needing a man's arm to keep from falling down."

"Understood," he replied with light amusement. "Is there anything you might need a man for at your advanced age?"

That earned him a look of disapproval. "Not as far as I know."

"Such innocence."

"Meaning?"

"When we marry, I'll explain."

"Ah, the kissing and the marriage bed, correct? I doubt either will leave me weak-kneed."

They came upon a bench set within a stand of fragrant jasmine as beautiful as he thought her to be. "Shall we sit?"

"If you insist," she said disinterestedly.

He couldn't wait to give that sassy mouth something to do, but that also would come in time. "So, did you enjoy your visit with Senor Shorty?"

"His name is Luis Garcia."

"My apology, but I prefer my name. More apropos, I think. You couldn't possibly be interested in being his wife?"

"I'm not interested in being your wife either, but I'm entertaining it."

"*Touché, mi pequeño pirata,*" he replied, mixing the French with the Spanish.

"And I do wish you wouldn't address me that way."

He was having such a good time with her. "Because . . . ?"

"Because the way you say it, it sounds like . . ." Her words trailed off and she looked away.

He gently turned her face back to him and stared down into her flashing brown eyes. "Like an endearment?"

She nodded.

"Suppose I told you it was." He found the curve of her lips mesmerizing. "Do you really think you're immune to a man's kisses?"

She backed out of his light hold on her chin. "If you suggested this walk so you could kiss me, please do so, so I can return to the house."

He steepled his fingers and studied her silently. What a little hornet she was. Her response proved she had no idea he could remove her stinger in ways that would not only leave her weak-kneed but craving more as well.

"Well?"

"Well, what?"

"Why the hesitation? Are you going to kiss me or not?"

"I think not."

She blinked with surprise. "May I ask your reason?"

The feather-light line he drew down her cheek made her eyes slowly slide shut. The tender tremble of her skin in response to his touch was highly arousing. "You aren't ready, but then again, I could be wrong."

"Being kissed is not going to make me . . ."

His lips gently met hers and the contact made her immediately soften. "Oh my," he heard her sigh.

Under his coaxing invitation, her mouth opened and he teased the ripeness with tiny movements of his tongue. She purred and he husked out, "This is what a man is for." He wanted to drag her onto his lap and savor the warm pressure of her weight against him but that too would come in time. Instead, he contented himself with kisses: teaching her, tasting her, and silently letting her know that he wasn't immune to her either. Leaving her parted lips for a moment, he traveled down to fleetingly sample the thin band of bare skin above her collar, and when he flicked his tongue against it, she whimpered with pleasure. Moving his lips to her ear, he breathed, "You were saying, *chiquita?*"

She responded by bringing her hand up and pulling him closer. He thrilled at that and his manhood awakened. She was the loveliest, sweetest thing he had had in his arms in recent memory and all he wanted to do was show her the full measure of what desire meant. And then, as if she'd suddenly realized just how responsive she'd become, she stiffened. Her eyes popped open and she looked appalled. He watched with silent amusement.

She jumped to her feet. "I—I have to go."

He nodded but kept his laugh to himself.

She stammered, "Good—good-bye."

"Good-bye, Pilar."

She all but ran back in the direction they'd come.

Rattled and outdone, Pilar stood in her bedroom with her back against the closed door and tried to slow her racing heart. How in the world had she lived twenty-five years and not known the power a man's kisses could wield? The instant his lips met hers she'd melted into the stone bench as if she'd been rendered boneless. *This is what a man is for* . . . Hearing that, she'd wanted to throw back a tart, clever rejoinder, but what he was doing to her mouth with his, and to the corners of her lips with the fiery tip of his tongue, left her with the brain of a crustacean. There were no weapons in her bow for this. He'd set her adrift, rudderless, no sails. When his hot lips moved to the trembling skin beneath her jaw, her hand had suddenly grown a mind of its own and drawn him closer. A part of her had found the heat of him against her glorious; his teasing tongue divine, until a voice in her mind woke up and screamed: *What are you doing!* That's when she knew she had to flee.

She drew a still trembling hand over her face. Whatever was she going to do!

Only then did she see her sister across the room seated in front of her easel, brush in hand.

Doneta scanned her for a silent moment before asking "He kissed you, didn't he?"

"No."

"You're lying. From the looks of you, you were either kissed or struck by lightning."

"Hush!"

Doneta smiled knowingly and resumed painting. "Do you wish to talk about it?"

"I'm not speaking to you."

"Suit yourself, but you're doomed now."

"What do you mean?"

"Once the young lady is kissed—all she wants is more of the same."

Pilar moved away from the door and walked to her own bed and sat down. "That's ridiculous."

"Is it?"

"Yes."

"Were I you, I'd end the courtship and go straight to the wedding."

"But you're not me."

"No, I'm not. But if I were, I'd know that hoping for a miracle to make this all go away will not be forthcoming. You're being pursued by a man so delicious he makes most sane women's teeth ache the moment he walks into a room. Just surrender and find some happiness."

Pilar fell back on the bed and cried out in frustration, "But I don't want to marry him."

"That's the rebel gun smuggler speaking. What's the woman in you saying?"

Pilar refused to explore the opinion of the newly awakened part of herself because she wanted her to go away and never be heard from again. She also refused to admit that her sister knew way more about this madness than she'd ever imagined.

"Your answer?"

"I'm not speaking to you, remember."

Doneta put brush to canvas. "That's right. I forgot, but when you're ready to talk about what a great kisser he is, let me know." She smoothly ducked the shoe Pilar aimed at her head.

Chapter 11

The following morning, Noah sipped coffee while standing out on the verandah of his rented room and watched the sunrise. All he could think about was Pilar. He chuckled at the memory of her face just before she took off running and shook his head at her efforts to deny what he already knew. She was a passionate woman—not only in life but in his arms as well and he couldn't wait to show her just how much. Oddly enough, he'd slept the entire night. Usually a few hours was all his body seemed to want, which he took as its way of avoiding the nightmares. They hadn't plagued him recently, but he knew they were there, looming, waiting to pounce and feed on the pain and horror that continued to lurk inside. However, as he'd noted before, being around his little pirate seemed to be an antidote to the island's lingering poison. He had no idea how long it might hold, but he would enjoy her and his life for as long as it lasted.

Still musing on her, he wondered if she'd awakened yet or was still asleep. The idea of waking up beside her at some point in the near future was pleasing to contemplate. Did she snore? Would she hog the bedding while they slept? Would she enjoy making love in the early-morning hours as the first light of dawn streamed through their bedroom windows? All questions he had no answers for, but he looked forward to having them resolved.

In the meantime, he'd be spending the day touring Miguel's warehouse with an eye to learning how the operation could be expanded so they could increase their profits. He'd spent yesterday touring boatyards with the hope of finding a vessel to replace the *Alanza* but what he'd seen had been either too old, too small, or too large. The ship once named for his mother had been perfect in every way and coming across one with similar attributes was going to take a lot longer than he'd initially imagined. He planned to be patient, however, even though it was not one of his virtues.

And because he struggled with patience, he was chafing at the idea of prolonging this courtship. Yesterday's kisses among the jasmine made him crave more; much more. He wondered how Miguel and Desa Banderas would react if he proposed ending it and moving on to the wedding. He could already imagine Pilar's. She'd have to be dragged kicking and screaming to stand before a priest, and getting her to willingly repeat the vows would be about as easy as teaching a dolphin to build a fence. Ideally, his family would be in attendance. Watching him marry no matter the circumstances would ease all the worry they'd been harboring about him these past ten years—

especially his mother—but that was probably impossible, so he put it out of his mind. But Pilar stayed with him. He planned to see her later, and so to precipitate that he finished his coffee and stepped back inside to finish dressing so he could meet Miguel at the warehouse.

The tour Miguel gave him took up most of the morning. They visited the rooms where the leaves of tobacco were stored for curing and he watched with awe as workers expertly hand rolled the leaves into the cigars he'd come to enjoy. After he and Miguel talked logistics, they paused for coffee and sat outside to enjoy the nice day.

"I want to thank you for requesting the hand of my niece."

"You're welcome. I'm enjoying the challenge."

"I worry that were it not for you she'd be a burden to her mother for the rest of her life."

"How so?"

"I doubt any other man here would offer for her. Luis Garcia doesn't count. He's a widower looking for someone to raise his five children and any woman will do."

"I doubt Pilar would have a problem finding suitors."

"You're very kind, Noah, but no sane man would want a woman who fights with a sword and may be wanted by the crown for smuggling guns as his wife. Not that you're insane, of course."

Noah smiled at him over his raised cup. "I find her fascinating."

"I find her wild and untamed."

Noah paused and studied him.

"Don't get me wrong. She is my niece and I would defend her with my life, but I don't approve of the way she was raised—or not raised, depending on how you view it. She was obviously allowed more freedom than was good for her and I lay that not at my sister's feet but at the feet of her late husband Javier. He was not the man my parents planned for her to marry, but Desa had always been headstrong and rebellious and made her own choice by turning her back on her *novio* on her wedding day."

"Pilar and I discussed a bit of the story."

"Then I won't rehash it, only to say I don't wish my daughters to think they too can be wild and untamed."

Noah tried not to be judgmental. "So you'd feel better if Pilar were not around them."

"I don't wish to sound uncharitable, but yes. Call me old-fashioned, but a daughter like Pilar would have put me in my grave long ago. My heart stopped when I saw her with that rapier in her hand and then to discover she actually knew how to use it." He shook his head. "I couldn't believe it."

"Do you wish to amend the courting terms?"

"Frankly, yes. Of course, Desa may not, but I do.

And if the authorities are indeed on my nieces's trail, it would be better for all involved if she were in California and not in my home or her mother's."

Noah wanted to point out the holes in the man's position but didn't. As Miguel stated, he was old-fashioned and had been raised to believe a woman's place didn't involve gun smuggling or rapiers, but having been raised by Alanza the Brave, Noah knew that not all women were meek and content to spend their life being told how that life should be led. He also didn't point out that throughout history, females had participated in the fight for freedom in countries all over the world. "You plan to speak with Senora Banderas about this?"

"I do. The sooner you and Pilar marry, the better it would be—of course I have no idea whether you agree or not, but I sense you might."

In truth, Miguel's angst played right into Noah's hands, but rather than admit he'd marry Pilar in an hour if the arrangements could be made, he replied, "Speak with your sister and if she agrees, we'll discuss how we might move forward."

"Thank you, Noah."

He inclined his head and their talk returned to the business of cigars.

Pilar was in the garden once again, sitting for the portrait, when her mother interrupted them. "Pilar, Gerardo Calvo is here."

Pilar stilled. "Here?"

"Yes. He needs to speak with you right away."

Why would the Cuban shipyard owner suddenly seek her out this way? she wondered. It had to be something of importance. Was it news concerning Tomas and the other men lost that night? Had General Maceo marched on Havana? Dozens of questions competed to be answered and all were underlined with a rising dread.

When she entered the parlor, her mother left them alone.

"It's good to see you, again Senor Calvo," Pilar said.

"I feel the same. I bring you sad news, however. You friend Tomas is dead. He was captured the night the boat was sunk, along with two of my men, and tortured. I've no idea what happened to the third man who sailed with you."

Her heart stopped.

"Our allies tell us that the crown is now searching for you as well. No one knows what information the men may have revealed before their deaths but you would be wise not to return to Cuba."

The rebels knew the dangers inherent in their fight but she felt solely responsible for the deaths. Knowing she'd never see Tomas again left an ache inside too terrible to bear. "Were arrangements made for his burial?"

Calvo shook his head. "I'm told his body along

with the others was thrown into the sea and his mother taken to one of the camps."

"No!" she cried. His elderly mother would never survive the terrible conditions there. The camps were filled with disease, filth, vermin, and starvation. Pilar found it hard to breathe.

"You might want to disappear for a time. Spain may or may not be able to touch you legally here but they do have eyes and ears in the Keys and in Yorba City, and I'd put nothing past them. I plan to vanish for a time as well. Like you, I know too much about the other *arañas* in our webs to risk being taken and tortured."

It was wise advice. "Is there anything else I need to know?"

"Only that our side has put out the rumor that you drowned that night, but whether it will be believed . . . ?" He shrugged.

She understood. "Thank you for coming, senor."

"You've been an asset for many years, Pilar Banderas. It was the least I could do."

"I'm so sorry for the deaths of your men."

"So am I," he whispered before he bowed and exited, leaving her alone.

Pilar dropped into a chair and silently wept for Tomas and his mother. She and her lifelong friend would never sail together or ride into the mountains or share smiles, ever again. The knowledge that he'd suffered so and was denied the decent burial owed every human being added to her despair. She knew he'd not want her to blame herself but she did, and with no idea if she'd ever be able to forgive herself. Spain had taken yet another person from her life and she swore to do everything in her power to keep that from happening again. She hadn't been sure before, but Calvo's visit cemented the fact that she and, more important, her mother and sister were in danger. Momentarily setting aside her grief, she thought about her options and after coming to a decision got to her feet. She knew what had to be done.

"Are you sure this is what you want?" her uncle asked when he came home.

"Yes." She'd already discussed her decision with her mother and sister and although they agreed, they were saddened.

"Okay," he replied somberly, "Noah is due to arrive any moment. When he does, I will send him in to speak with you."

"Thank you, Tio."

Alone in her uncle's study, Pilar looked out of the windows while she waited. Dusk would be descending soon on a day that began with sunshine and blue skies and was now filled with sorrow and sadness. There was no way of knowing where her life might be by the time night fell, but she was determined to face it with resolve. A soft knock on the door interrupted her musings. "Come in."

And there he stood. He viewed her silently and worry filled his face. She knew her eyes were still red from her tears but that couldn't be helped. "Close the door, please."

He complied. "What's happened?"

So she told him of Calvo's visit, Tomas's terrible demise and Calvo's parting advice. When she finished, she vowed, "I will not let Spain take another loved one from my life, so I plan to take the advice and disappear." Even though her next words were necessary, the parts of herself that had stood tall and without fear for so many years wept inside at what she was about to do. "If you will still have me, I'd like to get married as soon as possible."

To his credit, he didn't poke fun at her or do anything else to add to her pain. "Your decision is wise. And yes, I still want you as my wife," he assured her quietly. "I doubt we'll be able to purchase train tickets this late in the day but we can see about that first thing in the morning. Does your uncle know a priest who will conduct the ceremony without the necessary papers?"

Her relief soothed only a portion of her inner conflict. "I spoke with him earlier and he says he does."

"Then have him contact the padre so we can move forward."

"Thank you. If you will wait here, I'll let him know."

She walked to the door and as she came abreast of him he gently caught her hand. "This will work out, Pilar."

"It didn't for Tomas," she replied and exited.

They were married an hour later. At her mother's insistence she wore the mint-green gown she'd worn to her uncle's *rumba*, while Noah remained in the same black suit he'd worn upon arrival. It was necessary for him to donate a large amount of money to the coffers of the priest's church in exchange for the hasty summons and lack of requisite documents. There would be no mass conducted of course but neither of them cared as long as the certificate proving they were man and wife was signed and sealed. Once that was done, the priest departed.

Feeling as if she were encased in stone, Pilar said to him, "Thank you again. I will do my best to be a good wife."

Noah said in kind, "And I shall do my best to be a good husband."

It had already been decided that they would leave right after the ceremony, so she excused herself to go pack.

Up in her room, she placed her small amount of clothing and personal belongings in a case borrowed from her uncle. Her mother and sister looked on sadly.

When she finished, their mother asked Doneta, "Will you leave us a moment please?"

Doneta slipped out and closed the door behind her.

"Do you have any questions about your wedding night, Pilar?"

Embarrassment heated her from the roots of her hair to the soles of her feet, but she nodded.

When her mother concluded, she added, "Some women find the marriage bed pleasing; others don't."

Pilar wanted to ask if she had, but again, embarrassment took hold.

As if having read Pilar's thoughts, she confessed with a fond smile: "Your father and I enjoyed that part of our marriage very much."

There was a knock on the door. It was Pilar's uncle. "The coach is here, Desa. Noah would like for Pilar to join him."

"Thank you. We'll be down in a moment."

He withdrew and her mother pulled her into a tight embrace and placed a kiss on her cheek. "You and your man will do fine. You'll see."

Pilar hoped she was right.

He was waiting for her in the parlor. "Take a few moments to say good-bye. I'll be out in the carriage."

She was grateful for that small kindness. "Thank you."

He bowed to her mother. "I will send for you and Doneta as soon as we reach my home."

After his departure, Doneta embraced her first

and Pilar's heart ached. "Please don't cry," she said, even as tears spilled down her own cheeks.

"But I will miss you so," her sister whispered thickly.

"I'll miss you, too, very much." She leaned back and took a long last look. "You'll take care of Mama."

"Always. Be happy."

Pilar didn't speak to that but instead hugged her sister tightly again and placed a parting kiss on her wet cheek.

Next came her mother, whose smile melded with her tears. Holding Pilar close, she said confidently, "I will see you soon. God keep you safe."

"You too, Mama. I'm sorry."

"No need to apologize. Things happen as they will. I'll keep you and Noah in my prayers."

The love she felt for her mother was unequaled and Pilar had no idea how she'd get through life until she saw her again. Everything that she was and believed in had been bestowed upon her by her parents, and every day since her life had begun, one of the two had been there. Now, her father was among the saints and her mother would be thousands of miles away. Her world was shattered. She stepped into her uncle's wide-open arms. "I'm sorry for the shame I brought to your house, Tio," she whispered.

"No shame. You've made me very famous. Everyone will want to come and buy cigars from the man who had a sword fight at his birthday *rumba*."

She laughed and wiped at her eyes.

"I will look after your mother and sister. Have no worries on that."

"Thank you. Thank you for everything. Give my cousins my love."

"I will. Go with God, my rebel niece. May you find favor."

Picking up her borrowed case, she took a final look at the people she loved, gathered herself and stepped out into the darkness.

Chapter 12

He was waiting by the coach. She was glad the darkness hid the evidence of her tears. She hated showing any form of weakness, so she quickly dashed away the remaining dampness and hoped there would be no traces left when they reached their destination.

"I'll take your bag."

"I can carry it."

"It's called chivalry, Pilar. I help you with your bags and hand you into the coach. Humor me if you would."

She pushed the bag practically into his chest. She thought he cracked a bit of a smile but it was too dark to see clearly.

"Now, your hand please, so I may help you in."

"I've been getting in and out of carriages my entire life."

"Not with a husband, you haven't."

He was right of course, and because she had no ready riposte, she impatiently extended her hand. He took it in his own and the warmth that radiated rippled over her like stones across a pond. As soon as her foot gained the lip of the coach, she broke the contact in order to restore her breathing to something akin to normal.

The interior had only one bench, so she chose to

sit on the far end beneath the window. He followed her inside.

The coachman got them underway and she tried not to think about leaving her mother and sister behind. It was difficult. "Where are we going?"

"To the boardinghouse I'm staying in. As I said, we'll see about the train in the morning."

Another thing she tried not to think about was the wedding night. She was thankful for the information given to her by her mother concerning what she might expect. Pilar didn't reveal that during her time with the Revolutionary Army she'd inadvertently happened upon a few men and women coupling under the cover of darkness but had quickly veered away so she wouldn't be seen. Nor did she reveal that one of the Mambi women had told her that with the right man the marriage bed could be heaven, but with the wrong one, hell. She wondered which he might be and if she'd be able to tell the difference. She hazarded a glance his way and found him watching her. "How long will it take us to get to your home in California?" she asked to cover her nervousness.

"Five days—maybe seven, depending on the tracks, the weather—any number of variables."

"Do your mother and brothers live nearby?"

"We all live on the ranch."

"In the same house?"

"No. My brothers have their own homes. You and I will be staying with my mother in the house where I grew up until we decide where we might want to live."

"Oh." She wondered how his mother would take to her and what he'd been like as a child. Had he gotten the scar back then? More questions without answers, so she sat in the darkness and tried not to wail aloud over this unwanted turn in the direction of her life.

Noah couldn't believe she'd wanted to argue with him over entering the coach and chuckled inwardly. Having her in his life was going to be an ongoing challenge. He'd have to keep reminding himself that she was twenty-five years old and had been making her own way in the world for quite some time. When other fifteen-year-old young ladies had their heads filled with parties, new gowns, and dreams of *novios*, she'd gone off to war. Deferring to a man on such mundane matters as etiquette was undoubtedly something she'd never had to take into consideration before. He cast back to the memory of her standing so stoically in her uncle's study. It had probably killed her inside to ask that he marry her. Under normal circumstances her words would have been music to his ears. Although there was nothing normal about the threats she and her family were possibly facing, he still wanted her as his wife and dared the Spanish or anyone else to try and take her from him.

At that moment the coach's open window caught

the passing light of a streetlamp to reveal the sadness on her face. His heart opened in a way that was as new to him as his rising feelings for her were. It had to be excruciating for her to leave her family behind, especially coupled with the grief she felt as a result of her friend's death. He very much wanted to offer her solace but she'd probably pull a machete out of her bag and hack him into small pieces if he approached her in that way, so he settled back and shared the silence.

It was a bit past ten when they left the carriage and walked to the door of the boardinghouse. The place was dark as befitting the lateness of the hour. The owner, a short, large-breasted Irishwoman named Ira Fitzhugh, didn't issue keys to the front door after eight o'clock, so he had to knock and hope she didn't curse at him for getting her out of bed. Dressed in a robe thrown over her night-clothes, she finally answered the summons, took one look at him and Pilar, and said in an icy tone, "I don't allow men to have women in their rooms, Mr. Yates."

"This is my wife, Pilar, Mrs. Fitzhugh."

Her attitude instantly gentled. "Oh, then come in. Were you married today?"

"Yes."

"And she's such a pretty little thing. Lucky too, eh, Pilar. Not many women are blessed with such a handsome man. I remember my wedding night. I was so afraid, but when my Jamie began—"

At the sight of Pilar's appalled face, Noah cut her off. "We're going to go on up, Mrs. Fitzhugh. My apologies for making you leave your bed to let us in."

She waved him off. "No apologies needed. Have fun." After throwing them a bold wink she padded back down the hallway to her room.

After they climbed the dark stairway to the second floor, Pilar felt as if she was walking to her doom. She stood silently while he fit his key into the lock of one of the doors.

"Stay here a moment and let me light the lamp."

Once it was lit, she entered. The weak light flickered around the small room to reveal a large bed which she quickly averted her eyes from, a writing desk, a few chairs and a screen which she assumed hid the pot. She was more nervous than she'd ever been in her life. She watched as he removed his coat and pulled his tie free.

"You should crawl into bed and get some sleep," he told her. "We've a long day ahead of us."

She went still. Would there be no wedding night?

As if having read her mind, he said quietly. "We'll save the wedding night for the future. I want you to be as ready for me as I am for you. Tonight, you're not."

Although being with him in bed wasn't something she'd been pining for, she was now trying to determine if she should be offended. "You don't want a wedding night?"

"I do, but as I said, you aren't ready."

"And you know this how?"

He walked over to where she stood and placed a finger beneath her chin to gently raise her eyes to his. "Because you aren't. Shall I show you?"

Pilar trembled under his intense gaze but not wanting to admit defeat, she nodded.

"You're certain now?"

"Yes," she all but gritted out.

He eased her close and when his mouth claimed hers she was instantly lost. This was a repeat of their interlude in the garden. His kisses ignited a slow heat in her blood like a too potent sangria, leaving her sighing, breathless and brainless.

"Open your mouth, *mi pequeño pirata* . . . let me taste you . . ."

Her lips parted of their own accord. He slipped his tongue inside and she moaned from the sweet feel.

"When you're ready, you'll want me to do this." Lips as hot as his tone blazed a lazy trail down the edge of her neck and then journeyed back up again to reclaim her mouth, while his hand cupped her breast and bold fingers teased the nipple through the layers of her thin gown and chemise. She fought to breathe as kisses singed the flesh at the base of her throat. When he dragged down the bodice of her dress, taking the edge of the chemise with it and fed himself on the hard nipple that came free, the intensity crackled over her like lightning striking the sea. She cried out, pushed him away and covered herself. The air was thick with the sounds of their accelerated breathing and Pilar's blood pounded in her ears.

"Now do you understand?" he asked quietly.

Every inch of her being was aflame and pulsating. A part of her wanted to hike up her skirts and flee from this overpowering man who'd given her his name, while another wanted to throw open her gown and let him feast. Saints help her.

"Go to bed, Pilar. When you're ready we'll play again."

That said, he moved to the French doors that led out to the verandah and left her inside alone. Pilar sank to the bed and fell back against the mattress. Looking up at the shadowy ceiling, she lay there throbbing. Her gown was still askew, her nipple damp and pebbled and the feel of it in his mouth reverberated in her memory again and again. She sat up and put her head in her hands. Nothing in her life had prepared her for such sensual upheaval. Across the shadowy room lay the doors he'd used to exit. Had the brief encounter affected him as much, or was he too experienced to be moved by his virgin wife? Another question with no answer, so she dragged herself to her feet and changed into her nightclothes. Beneath the crisp clean sheets, she wondered if he planned to stay outside for the rest of the night and what it might be like to sleep beside him. Deciding she'd asked herself more than enough unanswerable questions, she drifted into sleep.

Outside, Noah wondered if she was asleep or awake thinking of him the way he was thinking of her. *Dios*, he was hard—harder than he remembered being in quite some time. He'd wanted to carry her to the bed, strip the gown from her, and take her with a sweet, bed-rocking ferocity that had been almost too powerful to control. But control himself he had, much to the disappointment of his still throbbing manhood. He shifted in the chair. He'd been wanting to taste and touch her without restraint from the moment she fled from him at Miguel's birthday party. Twice now he'd kissed her and each time he'd tasted a virgin's reluctance and then a passion he knew could be stoked to the fullest when the time came, but that time was not now, so he willed his body to calm and sat and waited for the sun to rise.

As always, Pilar awakened with the pink and gray skies of dawn. She glanced around the room and finding herself alone, wondered where Yates might be. Leaving the bed, she took care of her morning needs and pulled a skirt and blouse from her carpet bag. Once dressed, she dragged on her stockings and garters, stuck her feet into a pair of worn leather slippers and walked through the silent room to the doors that led to the verandah. And that's where she found him, fully laid out on the floorboards, asleep with his face atop his folded coat. He was snoring softly. Why he'd chosen to sleep out of doors only he knew. The scarred side of his face was hidden against his coat and she took a moment to evaluate his unblemished profile. There was no denying he was a handsome man. Lost in sleep, he looked peaceful—as if the world held no worries or challenges. He certainly bore no resemblance to the man who'd overwhelmed her with passion, or made her melt by calling her his little pirate. This Noah Yates seemed younger, almost innocent, but she knew better, so she left him and went back inside to await his awakening.

She didn't have to wait long. When he entered she was seated in one of the chairs.

"Good morning," he said. Even rumpled from sleep his powerful presence filled the small room.

"Good morning."

"I didn't mean to keep you waiting."

"You seemed to be sleeping so peacefully—I didn't want to wake you."

Last night's encounter rose again and the memory of his fervent kisses and warm mouth on her nipples made them harden beneath her cotton shift and blouse. "I'll—wait out on the verandah so you can take care of your needs." Without waiting for a reply, she slipped past him and stepped through the opened doors.

Noah thought about her as he dressed. What sort of challenges would she bring today? She looked none the worse for wear from their fiery predawn episode, and he hardened thinking about her satiny soft skin and soft gasps of passion. Dragging his mind back to the present, he searched through his lone bag of luggage for a fresh shirt and suit. Once dressed, he stepped out to join her. "Are you hungry?"

"A bit, yes."

"Mrs. Fitzhugh offers a good breakfast. Shall we go down?"

She nodded and joined him inside.

"Let me get the door."

"Another chivalry rule?"

"Yes."

She rolled her eyes.

He smiled and pulled the door open. "After you."

Seated at their table in the small dining room, he watched her scan the eggs, grits, bacon, and toast on her plate. "Something wrong?"

"Not what I'm accustomed to. What is this?" she asked.

"Grits."

He saw no recognition in her eyes. "It's hominy. A grain."

She used her fork to taste a bit of it and made a slight face.

"Most people use butter and salt and pepper to flavor it. Here in this part of the country it's sometimes served with shrimp as well."

She glanced around quickly. "There's shrimp here?"

He found this very endearing. "No, Pilar. I'm sorry."

"Oh," she said plainly disappointed. "And these strips are what?"

"Pork. It's called bacon."

"Why is it flat like this? We eat pork at home, but it doesn't resemble belt leather. How do you eat it?"

"Just pick it up with your fingers and bite." He watched her taste it.

"Very dry and salty," she noted.

"Americans eat it for breakfast. What do you customarily have?"

"*Mangú*—which is mashed plantains, eggs, salami, peppers, onions . . ." Her words trailed off.

"When we get home you might find the food more familiar, but until then, it will be mostly American food."

Again, disappointment, but she began to eat her eggs.

"Ah, Mr. Yates. I see you are still with us."

He looked up to find Senor and Senora DeValle and their sixteen-year-old daughter, Caralina, standing beside the table. He'd met them on the premises a few days ago. It was the wife who'd greeted him. "Good morning," he offered in a polite response. "How are you?"

"We're fine, aren't we, Caralina?"

"Yes, we are." The daughter viewed him as if he were a dessert she wanted to try. It was yet another case of a mama looking to wrangle a mate for her unmarried daughter.

Pilar viewed them coolly. He was about to introduce her when Senora DeValle asked, "And what are your plans for today, Mr. Yates? Caralina is very anxious to visit the gardens here. Maybe the two of you—"

"*Querido*?" Pilar inquired softly, "Would you like more coffee?"

Noah, who'd just taken a sip from his cup, choked upon hearing himself referred to as her *darling*. There was a distinct stormy devilment in her dark eyes and he couldn't suppress his smile. "No, *querida*, I'm fine for now." He turned to the DeValles. "I'd like you to meet my wife, Pilar."

The shocked mama's eyes widened. The daughter shot daggers at Pilar, who raised her cup mockingly in response. The father dropped his head with abject disappointment.

"When did you marry?" Senora DeValle asked, looking quickly between them.

"Yesterday," Pilar answered. "It's been nice meeting you."

That earned her a glare, but having been effectively dismissed, there was nothing for the family to do but move on. They did so and sat at a table on the far side of the room.

Noah studied her.

"I am your wife. We may not have a love match, but I'll not tolerate calf-eyed girls or their mothers slavering over you, at least not in my presence."

He raised his cup. "Noted."

"Good."

An amused Noah went back to the food on his plate.

"Do you have a mistress?"

He paused and looked up. Her face was unreadable. "Not officially, no."

"So that means there is a woman or women in your life?"

Rather than dance around what felt like a trap, he offered the truth. "There is a woman I sometimes keep company with when I'm in San Francisco." Her name was Lavinia Douglas. Her father, Walter, owned a small shipyard."

"And now that you are married?"

"The men in my family honor their wives, Pilar. There are no outside women."

"Thank you. I just wanted to know."

"And for the record, I'll not have calf-eyed men slavering over you in my presence, either."

That earned him a raised chin. "Noted," she replied.

He saw Senora DeValle watching them. She didn't appear pleased, but Noah was very pleased with this first shared meal with his new wife. However, there was something he'd been meaning to ask. "This may spoil the morning, but what happened to my belongings on the *Alanza*?"

She slowly put down her coffee cup. "I sold them."

He cocked his head.

"Did you expect me to box them up and store them away?"

He didn't know what to expect—but: "Did they fetch a good price?"

"They did, but I may have gotten a better one had I not had to sell them so quickly."

He was almost afraid to ask. "Meaning?"

"We needed to pay the boatman who took us to Florida, and I didn't have the luxury of haggling, so I sold him your gun and holster. The painting went to someone on the dock. He wanted to give it to his mother for her birthday."

He choked on another swallow of coffee. Picking up his napkin, he wiped his mouth and once recovered, asked quietly, "The one that was hanging in my quarters?"

"Yes. Did you paint it?"

"Yes," he said, knocked for a loop by her disclosure.

"I thought you might have. Doneta said you have a talent."

"I saw her painting. She paints well, too."

"Yes, she does. She's the family's art forger."

His eyes widened and he looked around to make certain no one was eavesdropping. "Art forger?"

She nodded. "Some of her work is hanging in museums. Of course they don't know they're forgeries. We switched hers with the true versions."

Noah was so stunned and confused he didn't know what to ask next. "Have you finished eating, because we need to continue this conversation in private."

"Yes, I have."

Still staring at her as if she'd turned herself into a mermaid, he left the money for the meal on the table and they went back up to their room.

"Now, begin again," he said to her once they were settled in the chairs.

"I'm from a family of forgers, counterfeiters, and thieves, for lack of a more refined description."

"And your specialty—besides stealing boats?"

She cut him a look, which he ignored. "I steal things."

"Such as?"

"When I was very young, I was trained to steal small items from homes."

"By whom?"

"My father and uncles."

"So, where some families trade in, say, carpentry or sailmaking, yours trades in theft."

"The sarcasm is not appreciated, but yes."

He found this utterly appalling yet fascinating. "How would you go about it?"

"They would boost me through a window after

dark and I'd take whatever I could find. Silver, small statues, jewelry if it was left out on a nightstand or dresser."

"You'd enter bedrooms?"

"Yes. I was very quiet and quick."

"Were you ever discovered?"

"Once. I was about seven years old and a man came upon me as I was leaving. When he asked me what I was doing in his home, I began to cry and told him I was looking for my mother and that she was a maid and hadn't come home, but I couldn't seem to find the right house."

"And he fell for that?"

"Yes. In fact, I was so convincing, and he was so concerned, he wanted to accompany me to the other homes nearby to aid my search."

Noah chuckled with disbelief. "And the forged paintings?"

"Sometimes we'd switch Doneta's forgeries with the ones we found in homes, but a few times, we went for paintings hanging in museums. My father had contacts in Havana who'd sell the real ones to Americans or Europeans. Many wealthy people have no idea whether their paintings are real or not. I'd hire in as a maid, bring the forgery in at night, give the true one to my father waiting outside, and the owners were none the wiser. I'd leave their employ a week or so later and move to the next job."

"I'm impressed."

"I've a question for you. How did you know I'd be at my uncle's home?"

"I didn't. I was there because of our partnership and I showed up that night for the party only because I'd been invited. When I didn't find you at your home in Santiago, I had no idea where to search next."

She went still. "You went to our home?"

"Yes."

"How'd you find out where I lived?"

"I paid a man named Gordonez for the information."

"That bastard."

He studied the anger on her face. "How well do you know him?"

"He was the *novio* my mother left at the altar. He hated my father as a result."

"He seemed to be holding a grudge against your family, but I didn't want to ask about it."

"His lie to the Spanish authorities that my father was a high-level rebel leader is what led to his death. None of us will ever forgive him."

Now, he understood the acrimony he sensed in the man that day. He wondered how much joy Gordonez felt knowing Noah was hunting Desa's daughter. "And the rest of my belongings, like my clothing, did you sell them as well?"

She quieted for a moment as if thinking. "Tomas took your clothing. Not sure what he did with it." Her face saddened.

"I'm sorry. I didn't mean to bring back your grief."

"I will miss him terribly."

Her tone made him wonder if the man had held her heart, but he didn't ask because he didn't want the answer to be yes.

"As for the rest of your things, I gave your paints and easel to Doneta. We also found sheets of music. Did you write them?"

He nodded. "I did. Did you sell them as well?"

"No, I put them back in your desk."

"Which is now at the bottom of the sea?"

Her reply was a quietly spoken, "Yes."

That was the greatest loss as far as he was concerned. His gun, the clothing, even the painting could be replaced, but he'd been composing that requiem on and off for a number of years. Now he'd have to try and recreate it from scratch.

"As your wife now, I suppose I should apologize."

"Only if it's genuinely offered."

"My apology—genuinely given."

"Thank you," he said, hoping it didn't come out as curtly as he felt.

The way her eyes flashed, he knew that it had. "What instrument do you play?"

"Piano."

"Had I the opportunity to do it all again, I would have chosen another target that night."

"I'm sure you would've, but there's no changing

the outcome now. Shall we go see about the train tickets?"

She nodded.

When they reached the door he asked, "Will my mother have to hide the silver when we get home?" he asked.

"Are you deliberately being insulting?"

"Just an honest question in search of an honest answer."

"I don't steal from family."

"Good to know."

"You were the one who initially wanted this marriage, remember?"

"And last night, so did you."

She looked away. "This isn't easy for me."

"I understand. Knowing you've been stealing since you were little isn't an easy thing for me either."

He opened the door and she silently led him out.

As they made their way to see about tickets for the train, Noah was still bowled over by her revelations. A family of thieves? He knew Pilar wasn't the average woman but to find out the totality of that . . . And sweet Doneta, who'd fed him information on her sister—an art forger? He wondered what role their mother Desa played, and decided he didn't want to know. Surely Miguel wasn't a party to their roguery? He looked down at her walking so silently by his side. They'd gone from having a leisurely breakfast to snapping at each other, but he felt justified in asking the question that he had about the silver. Were he to bring a thief into his mother's home and something came up missing, she'd take a shotgun to them both. Earlier, he'd wondered what challenges his new wife would bring to his day. He had his answer.

Chapter 13

"The ferry to the mainland leaves tomorrow morning at four sharp. Train at five," the depot agent told them as he handed over the tickets. "You'll be going to Birmingham, Alabama, and then north for the train to St. Louis. This being the South you'll have to ride separately."

Pilar had no idea what that meant, but the ice that entered Noah's eyes left her concerned.

"Sorry, sir," the man offered. "I don't believe in the practice, but I'm not the president of the railroad."

"Understood," Noah replied tersely, "Smoking car or stock car?"

"Smoking, sir, but with any luck the conductor in St. Louis will be a good man and you and the little lady won't have any problems getting to Denver."

She watched Noah place the tickets inside his coat. "Thank you for your help and honesty," he offered.

"You're welcome. Next person."

As she and Noah left the depot, she noted that his cold manner remained.

"We have to ride the train separately? Men can't ride with women?" she asked.

"No. Here the races are separated by law. On

some trains, people like us are relegated to the smoking car, and on others it's the stock car with whatever animals are being transported."

"We may have to ride across the country with pigs or goats?"

"Or horses or cattle," he said bitterly. "What would you like to do for the rest of the day?" He appeared so incredibly angry his scar seemed to throb.

"If you prefer to return to the boardinghouse, that would be fine."

"No. I need to do something to rid me of this mood. When I took the train home for my mother's wedding I went through Texas and there was no discrimination, but being here reminds me why I usually avoid traveling by rail whenever possible. I detest how humiliating it's designed to be."

There was discrimination in Cuba, and it was one of the things men like General Maceo railed against. If and when the railroads came to her country she hoped such ideas wouldn't be instituted.

"Pilar, is there something you'd like to do?" he asked again cutting into her musings.

"My apologies. I was thinking of home. Yes, there is something. I'd like to walk on the beach and say good-bye."

"To whom?"

"My Cuba, the sky, the ocean."

"There's ocean in California."

"But these are the waters of *my* ocean. I was born on them." She looked up to see how he might be taking her request. "You think I'm just a silly woman from the countryside, don't you?"

"No," and he added, "Never."

She looked away. She was already homesick. "Just for a short while is all I ask."

"We can stay for the rest of the day if you like."

His words to her on the night of the sword fight returned. *Whatever you desire . . . I will lay at your feet.* She compared him to the man who'd been so curt with her back at the room and wondered if she'd ever know the true Noah Yates. "I'd like that."

"Then shall we? I doubt the Spanish will sail up and attempt to take you from me on American soil in broad daylight."

They found a stretch of beach a short distance away. The wind was rising and there were a few people watching the curling waves, but she and Noah continued on until they found a deserted spot. For a few moments they stood and just looked out at the blue water. There was a small boat out near the horizon. Pilar filled her lungs with the tangy air and let the wind bring solace to the sadness in her soul. "I will miss this," she said quietly and looked up to meet his eyes. She had no idea what he might be thinking, but the intensity was familiar. Memories of being in his arms resurfaced and she hastily turned her mind to something else, something she felt needed to be made clear. "I'm very grateful for what you've done for me. To pay you back by stealing from your family isn't something I'd ever do."

"I'll take you at your word, so let's not speak of this again."

She nodded and focused again on the waves. "Will you buy another boat?"

"Yes. Unless you'd care to steal me another."

She was about to take offense until she saw the whisper of his smile. "When did you first go to sea?"

When he didn't reply she saw that the smile had been replaced by an emotionless mask, as if the question had triggered something unpleasant. "My apologies. I didn't mean to pry. I'm going down to the water."

Noah watched her walking away. He supposed she was owed an answer, but he'd held on to that event so closely, he didn't know where to begin, how much to reveal, or if he should reveal any of it at all. If he'd been unable to share the experience with his brother, Drew, someone he'd known and loved his entire life, how was he expected to do so with a wife of one day? Her choice to come to the beach was a good one, though. He missed being on the water. It was his balm, his companion, his life, and he, too, needed to say good-bye.

He walked down to join her at the water's edge,

and for a moment stood silently at her side. "I was shanghaied at the age of eighteen."

She didn't hide her surprise. "That's akin to impressment, isn't it?"

"Yes, and at the time perfectly legal in America."

"How can it be legal to steal someone away? Sounds like slavery. This is a very strange country."

"I agree, but when the backers of the practice are in the government they write the laws in their favor."

She turned and stared.

So he told her a bit about the abductors, known as *crimps,* and the boarding masters who employed the crimps. "The crimps are paid for each abducted man turned over to the ship captains. The more men supplied, the more blood money they earn, as it's called. Once you're abducted, they make you sign a contract called the articles, and by law you had to serve a year on board, sometimes two, or risk prison."

"And some of these crimps were in the government?"

"Yes. At one time two men, Joseph Franklin and George Lewis, were elected to our state's legislature. Both were well-known crimps."

"Where were you abducted?"

"From a San Francisco tavern, where I was celebrating my birthday with some friends."

"Were your friends taken, too?"

"No, they managed to escape during the melee."

"Did your mother and brothers know about this?"

He shook his head. "No."

"How long were you away from your family?"

"Almost two years."

She turned her eyes back to the water. "That's a very sad story."

"Yes," he agreed. "The only good that came out of it was learning to love the sea."

She was quiet for a few moments before asking, "You don't talk about this often, do you?"

"No. How'd you know?"

She shrugged. "Just a guess."

"It's a good guess."

There was a large, water-weathered log behind them and she walked over to it and sat down. When she folded back her skirt and exposed her legs, his eyes widened, then widened further at the sight of her removing her dark stockings. "What are you doing?"

"Taking these things off, so I can put my feet in."

He scanned the surroundings.

"No one's nearby. I hate stockings almost as much as I do skirts and dresses. They're hot and clammy and useless really."

She snatched off the offending hosiery, rolled them up and set them beside her. She righted her skirt but the remembered sight of her bared legs drove off all thoughts of being shanghaied, and his manhood tightened in appreciation.

"Are you going to join me?"

He shook his head. "No."

"Oh come on. No one's going to see you. We're going to be riding on the train with pigs for saints' sake, you should at least have a bit of fun, first."

She was as alluring as a sea sprite, but the fun Noah wished to have with her had nothing to do with pigs or getting his feet wet. "You go ahead."

"I think you need more fun in your life, Mr. Yates."

"I've heard that."

"You should take it to heart."

He didn't reply. He was too busy basking in her smile and the joy she seemed to find in life. His joy had been stolen and the thought made the dark memories return. He cursed himself for allowing them to resurface and wished he could go back to a time a few days ago when she'd been all he could think about.

"Are you unwell?"

Her concern brought him back. "No. I'm fine."

She didn't appear convinced, so to keep her from attempting to delve deeper into his feelings, he sat and pulled off his boots.

"You're going to join me?"

"I am." With the hopes that his mind would be free again. His socks came next and he took a moment to roll up the legs of his trousers.

Finished, he stood. "Now, show me how to have fun."

She punched him in the arm. Hard. "You're it!" And she took off down the beach.

Mouth open at her audacity, he barked a laugh and ran after her. She was fast. With her skirt held high, and her laughter rising, she led him on a merry chase. As he closed the distance between them, she looked back, screamed with mock fright and ran faster. She headed out into the surf and he followed. Two strides later, he grabbed her and swung her up into his arms and began to spin around, all the while miming tossing her in. "Don't you dare!" She laughed, throwing her arms around his neck.

"Then I claim a boon." A moment ago he'd been under the black clouds of his past and now he felt like he was being bathed in sunlight.

"Crazy American! Put me down!"

Instead he spun them around a few more times and each time pretended to toss her away. Their laughs melded and rose. Finally, so overwhelmed he ached with the sweetness of it, he slowed and stopped. He wanted to visually feast on her for the rest of his life.

She asked quietly, "What do you claim as your boon?"

"Two things."

"Two!"

He tossed her high up in the air and she was

still screaming with laughter when he caught her again.

"Okay, two! What do you want?"

"One, that you address me by my given name." She quieted.

"You've been addressing me as Mr. Yates—although I did enjoy being your *querido* this morning."

"And the second, Greedy Noah from California."

"A kiss."

"Now?"

"Yes." He watched her roll her eyes. "Think of it as practice," he chuckled softly.

"I think you're taking advantage of me."

"And I think you're trying to wiggle out of your debt."

She leaned up and placed a quick kiss on his cheek. "There. Debt paid."

"You call that a kiss?"

"Yes."

"No." Still holding her he walked out of the water and back towards the beach.

"Where are we going?"

"To sit so we can discuss this. And I am having fun, by the way."

She gave him another roll of her eyes.

He sat on the log. She made a move to leave his lap. "You're fine where you are."

But in Pilar's mind, she wasn't fine. Their intimate positioning made her very aware of him and the closeness of their bodies exuded a heat that began playing havoc with her breathing and her ability to maintain the aloofness she thought necessary.

"So, about that poor excuse for a kiss."

"It wasn't poor."

He nodded. "So poorly done that I think you should try again."

"You are truly overstepping your bounds."

He brushed his lips fleetingly over her cheek, and her eyes slid closed.

"You think so?" he murmured.

"I know so," she somehow managed to reply. Soft lingering kisses burned over her jaw and the shell of her ear. "You're not playing fair, American."

"This is how the game is played, *querida* . . ."

His mouth moved to hers, inviting, seducing, inflaming, and soon, because she had no will, she began to respond. She heard him sigh with pleasure and felt his warm palm roaming lazily over her spine. He enticed her mouth to open and his tongue teased and cajoled. She was eased closer until his hard chest was flush against her breasts and the intensity sent her senses soaring like a kite caught in the wind. Last night, she'd been caught off guard by passion's overwhelming power and in truth she was a novice still, but she reveled in the way he made her feel.

He finally pulled away, and a moment later she

opened her eyes. He ran a worshipping finger over her tingling bottom lip, then raised her mouth for yet another. When he reluctantly withdrew again his burning gaze held her in thrall.

"Is my debt paid?" she asked hoping being flippant would help her find herself again.

"For now." He kissed the faint brown freckles dusting the crowns of her cheeks. "I like your spots."

"Hated them growing up."

"Why?"

"Because no one outside of our family had them. The children at school called Doneta and me the Leper Twins."

"They're not that prominent. They look like tiny shavings of cinnamon bark."

"In my mind they were large as coconuts."

He brushed his lips over them again. "I think they're sweet."

Pilar didn't know if she was supposed to thank him, but her heart was beating so fast, she doubted she'd've been able to form the words anyway.

"Thank you for the fun, today."

"You're welcome." Her eyes strayed to his mouth. "Is this the way with all husbands and wives?"

"Not always, but with the right husband and the right wife it can be."

"Do your brothers have the right wives?"

He nodded. "They're all madly in love."

Pilar doubted the two of them would ever fit that description yet wondered what it might be like to be madly in love. She supposed maybe she should've read a few of the books her sister took such pleasure in instead of trying to help win a war. "Why did you really want to marry me? And none of that hokum about my handling a sword."

"Didn't care for that explanation?"

"Nor did I believe it."

"You should, because it was partly true. Crossing swords with you made me feel more alive than anything has in quite some time—years in fact."

Although he'd replied with what sounded like sincerity she wasn't sure it was the truth.

"Doubts?" he asked as if having read her mind.

"Yes, but only because I don't know you well enough to be able to know what's truth and what's not."

"I spoke truly. No woman has ever challenged me with a sword before and I found it . . . invigorating."

"You're very odd."

He laughed softly. "And you say that, why?"

"Blood sport isn't meant to invigorate."

"But it did. In fact, I can't wait for you to get angry enough at me again to want my heart on the point of your sword."

She shook her head, unable to fathom the very strange American she was now wife to. "You're safe then. My mother made me leave my grandfather's behind when we left Cuba, and there was no room in my bag for Tio Miguel's."

"When we get home, we'll find you another."

That surprised her.

"And I can give you lessons."

"I don't need lessons. My grandfather taught me well enough."

"No. Your stance was too open and you let your emotions rule your strikes."

"So, you can teach me well enough to beat you?"

"Not on your life, but I can teach you to be better than you are now."

"Then I suppose I shall have to be satisfied with that." Pilar didn't want to like him but he had a way about him that made it hard to maintain her distance, and she didn't even want to think about what his kisses were doing to the barriers she'd been trying to keep intact.

"So, what would you like to do now?"

"I've no idea, but later I'd like to find someone who can cook me a good Cuban meal before I'm relegated to pork belt leather for the rest of my existence."

"American food is not that bad."

"That's only because you don't know any better. Have you ever had *frijoles negros*?"

"Of course. Everyone traveling to your country has black bean soup and I enjoy it."

"What about black beans with rice and *maduros*?"

"No."

"*Ropa vieja?*"

"No. Which is?"

"Shredded beef over rice."

"Ah."

"How about *sancocho?*"

He shook his head.

"Your stomach has been so deprived. Hopefully one day you'll be able to eat like a Cuban, and you'll never be content with pork belt leather again."

He kissed her brow. "As I said, invigorating. Now, up with you. Let's walk. My legs have gone to sleep."

"I didn't ask to sit here," she reminded him.

"I know, but husbands enjoy having their wives on their laps. The kisses have been fun as well."

She wouldn't meet his eyes. They had been fun but he didn't need to know how she felt.

He gently turned her chin around. "Did you not like the kisses?"

She didn't reply.

"Refusing to answer means, yes you know."

"It does not."

He drew his finger slowly over the shape of her lips, leaving behind a trail of heat. "Sure it does." He repeated the lazy tracing. Her eyes slid closed and she wondered if this was what Doneta meant about him being deliciously wicked—or had it been wickedly delicious? Pilar couldn't recall. In fact, she was having difficulty recalling anything at the moment.

He placed his lips lightly against hers, then sensually increased the pressure until her defenses slowly crumbled and she began answering him measure for measure.

Moving to the shell of her ear, he husked out, "Did you like my kisses, *querida*?"

Hearing him whisper the word so seductively turned her insides into warm honey and she was ready to tell him whatever he wished to hear.

"You know that lying is a sin."

Pilar couldn't breathe, couldn't see, couldn't do anything that constituted the strong, fearless woman she knew herself to be. Seated on his lap and being treated to the spell of his deliciously wicked kisses made her as boneless as a jellyfish washed up on the beach. And in reality, she didn't care.

He circled a finger around her nipple and she drew in a soft shuddering breath. Most of her adult life, she'd never given her breasts much thought—they'd simply been another part of her anatomy, but his touches made them bloom and hunger in a way she'd never thought possible and she found herself wanting to strip away her blouse so his hands could caress her flesh.

"If I take you in my mouth again, will you say yes . . ."

Pilar whimpered.

"Shall I, Pilar?"

Bold hands were undoing the buttons on her blouse, bolder kisses were moving over the bared skin above her exposed chemise. He tugged it down and took the freed breast into his mouth to feast, to tempt, and make her groan aloud from the exquisite sensation. "Noah."

"Say yes, *reina guerrera.*"

He treated the other breast to the same dazzling conquering, then worked his way back and forth, until she thought she'd go insane. "Yes," she gushed. "*Dios*, yes!"

In his wildest dreams Noah never imagined wanting a woman so much. His desire for her filled him like the opening notes of a beautiful sonata. He wanted to kiss her, touch her, taste her, suckle her sweetness until he was old and gray. "God, you're sweet," he whispered and left her breasts to take her lips again while his hands kept up their ardent play.

He looked up to find a small boy watching them with wide eyes. At the boy's side stood a brown-and-white spotted dog. Noah paused. Pilar noticed the child, too, and quickly turned against his chest to cover herself.

"Go away!" Noah growled, and the boy took off at a run with the dog close on his heels.

He glanced down at her. "My apologies for not keeping better watch."

"You were a bit busy."

He chuckled and pressed his lips to her forehead. "I was indeed."

She used the moment to right her clothing.

"I'll keep better watch next time."

"There will be no next time."

He sighed. "You do know you're destined to be proven wrong."

"I know nothing of the sort."

He slid a finger over her now covered nipple and she playfully slapped at his hand. "Stop that!"

"You're the one insisting I need more fun in my life, and as soon as I find an outlet you want to change your tune."

"You are incorrigible."

"You don't know the half of it," he declared meaningfully, enjoying the play. "Up with you. Let's get our stockings and shoes and go back to the room. Later we'll see if we can find you some Cuban food for your last meal. And who knows, maybe we'll take one last stroll down here after we're done."

"Only if you promise not to undress me."

"My mother taught me to never make promises I can't keep."

"Crazy American."

On the way back, they stopped at the telegraph office so he could send a message to his mother to let her know he was on his way back to California with a bride.

Chapter 14

After they returned to the room, an uncharacteristic shyness filled Pilar again. Being in the small space made her all the more aware of him, leaving her unsure where to settle her eyes even though he was all she could see. "I should probably wash off the salt and sand before we venture out again," she told him.

"Shall I have water brought up?"

"If it isn't too much trouble."

He exited and she let out an unconsciously held breath. Just like last night his caresses today on the beach left her body shimmering. Her lips were kiss swollen, her nipples yearning for more, and no matter how much she tried to ignore her response, the sensual power he wielded would not let her be. He'd awakened something inside herself that now hungered to be fed and she was left wondering how to make it cease. Surely well brought up women didn't let their husbands bare them in public and not care about being seen. Yet she'd done both and that secretive, awakened portion of herself eagerly anticipated further encounters. Shocked by the thoughts, she cast the yearnings aside and prayed the old, disciplined Pilar Banderas would somehow stand up and reassert herself. This new Pilar Yates was a woman she didn't know, recognize, or seemingly control.

He returned with a servant girl bearing water. Once the buckets were set inside the screen, the girl departed.

"I'll wait out on the verandah to give you some privacy."

"Thank you."

Once she finished and put on fresh clothing, she joined him on the verandah.

"Better?" he asked.

"Yes."

"Good. Give me a moment to clean up and I have a surprise for you."

"What is it?"

"If I tell you it won't be much of a surprise now, will it?"

"No, I suppose not," she said eyeing him with a bit of skepticism.

"It will be something you will enjoy, I promise."

While she waited, she wondered about the surprise, but decided she'd know soon enough, so she reviewed the day. She thought he'd taken the information she'd shared about her family's background as well as could be expected. After all it wasn't every day that a person from a family as esteemed as his found themselves married to someone like her. But as she'd stated, she'd never steal so much as a pea off a plate from his family, and she hoped he believed her. She was still dazzled by his kisses, but no matter the attraction, there would have to be more to their marriage. What would become of her when they reached California? There'd be no call for rebels, and certainly no reason to be smuggling guns. What role was she expected to play in his life, and more important, in her own? She doubted she'd be content to spend her days shopping and ordering the servants around like her aunt Simona. So what would she do? It was a subject she needed to discuss with him and it was her hope he'd have an answer she could embrace.

She heard movement inside the room and went to investigate. The sight of a strange man and woman setting a table with dishes from a stacked cart stopped her in her tracks. When she looked over at Noah he smiled. "Your surprise."

Once the woman left, he gestured. "Shall we dine?"

She sat, he helped her with her chair, and took a seat opposite her.

When he began removing the covers from the food she was truly surprised. Cuban food!

"Where'd this come from?" she asked eagerly, eyeing the familiar sights and savoring the heady aromas.

"When I went down to make arrangements for the water, I asked Mrs. Fitzhugh if she knew anyone who did good Cuban food, and the answer was yes. She has a good friend who owns a boardinghouse close by and the cook there is from your country."

"I love her!"

The appetizer was still warm *chatinas*, and she munched the fried green plantains with glee. The main dish, *pollo asado*, a Cuban version of roast chicken highlighted by a sweet tomato sauce known as *salsa crillo*, was so good and tasted so much like her grandmother's it brought tears to her eyes. Along with the chicken was *Moros y Cristianos*, a side dish of black beans and rice.

"'Moors and Christians'?" he asked, doing the translation.

She nodded. "The black beans are the Moors, the white rice is the Christians. In Cuba though, it's the Africans and the Spanish."

Dessert was *flan Cubano*, a rich caramel delight made with milk and eggs. Once she finished her serving, Pilar was so stuffed she couldn't eat another bite. "Thank you, Noah. Everything was outstanding."

"You're welcome."

"I wish we could take the cook with us on our journey to your home," she said. "Although it might be a challenge to prepare *flan Cubano* while traveling with goats and pigs."

"True. I'm glad you enjoyed your surprise."

"I did. You have my permission to surprise me anytime."

"I'll keep that in mind for the future."

Something passed between them and she wondered why this man affected her so.

"Is your mother a good cook?" he asked.

"Not really, she grew up with servants when she was young, so when she married my father she didn't even know how to boil beans. But my grandmother—she could cook a wooden crate and we'd all line up for more."

"And you?"

"I did most of the cooking at home, when I was there. Your mother's Spanish—weren't you raised on food like this?"

"No. There are flans for special occasions but we eat mostly American food—steaks, potatoes, some rice."

"Belt leather pork?"

He chuckled. "Yes, lots and lots of bacon."

She made a face. "Do you think your mother would mind if I cooked every now and then?"

"She has a cook. An Irishwoman named Bonnie, but I doubt she'd mind, especially if this is what you'll be putting on the table. Once we get our own place, you can cook as often as you want."

"Good. What's your mother like?"

"Fearless, stubborn, and when I left home last, very much in love." He went on to explain about his mother's newly wedded status and the story that went with it.

"Have you ever been in love?" she asked.

"No."

"Neither have I but my mother truly loved my father. Doneta wants that kind of love, too."

"And you?"

She shrugged. "I don't know. Being with someone who doesn't mind that I smuggled guns and began stealing almost as soon as I could walk is enough for me. It doesn't have to be a love match."

He met her eyes.

"I don't expect you to love me, Noah."

"Suppose we do wind up loving each other?"

She scoffed, "Don't be silly."

"Why is that silly?"

"Because it just is. Can I ask you something serious?" She wanted to change the subject.

He didn't call her out about it though. He sipped at his wine and said, "Of course."

"What will I do as your wife? Do your brothers' wives work at anything?"

"Logan's wife, Mariah, is a seamstress, not sure what Drew's wife, Billie, does. What would you like to do?"

She shrugged her shoulders. "I don't know but I'd like to do something. Do you have people who take care of your animals?"

On his side of the table, Noah almost laughed but realized she was serious. "Yes, the ranch employs men to do that." He couldn't believe she was asking to be a ranch hand. "My mother does some charity work through her church. Maybe you'd like to help with that."

"Maybe. I'm good with a machete. Do you have brush that needs to be cut back or trees to clear?"

"Pilar, you're not going to be a field hand."

"Why not?"

"Because you're my wife."

"So I'm not supposed to earn my place."

"No."

"Why not?"

"It isn't necessary."

"Does money grow on trees in California?"

"Of course not."

"Then I need to contribute."

He sensed he was not going to win this, so he said, "How about we discuss this again when we get home?"

"Fine, but I'm not going to sit around like a hothouse flower while others wait on me."

"Understood."

"Good."

She was the most driven, unbelievable woman he'd ever met. "Would you like more wine?"

"Yes, please."

He poured more into her glass. She could also hold her spirits, he noted. They'd consumed most of the bottle he'd had brought in with their meal, but then her roots were Spanish, too, and she had probably been drinking wine as a matter of course her entire life, just as he had. He raised his glass to her. "To the future."

She lifted hers in response. "To the future."

Dusk was falling and the wind could be heard in the trees. "Would you like to take your wine outside? We could sit for a while before bed."

"I'd enjoy that."

They stood, but instead of moving to the door, he held his position before her and she found herself captured once more by his commanding presence. All evening, she'd managed to set aside the heat being with him caused, and now that they were alone in the close confines of the room, her gaze quickly fled lest her desire resurrect the woman she couldn't control.

"What's wrong?"

She debated telling him the truth. She didn't wish to be laughed at or thought weak or evoke any other reaction from him that might make her feel silly or naïve by revealing her inner feelings, but she desperately wanted to go back to being who she'd been before he entered her life. "Since I was a little girl, my father and grandfather instilled in me the importance of discipline, and those lessons have served me well throughout my life. It helped me be an efficient thief and gave me the strength I needed to be with the Mambi Army. Now?"

He gave her a ghost of a smile.

"This isn't funny."

"I'm not laughing at you, *querida*, just watching you fight against something there's no known antidote for."

Certain he had no idea what she was referencing, she challenged, "And that is what?"

"Desire. Passion. Need. Want. Whatever you wish to call it."

"How could you possibly know that's what I'm feeling?"

"Weren't you the woman on my lap at the beach?"

Not wishing to answer, she said instead, "I shouldn't be wanting you to . . ." Her words faded.

"Wanting me to what?" he coaxed gently.

She faltered for a moment, then plunged ahead. "Kiss me—or touch me."

"Why not?"

Her mind scrambled for a reply. "Because it can't be proper."

"No one can judge what's proper between a wife and her husband except the man and woman involved."

"Then how does one make it cease or go away, for saints' sake?"

"You can't. I mean there are ways to attain temporary relief but once it settles in there's no way to make it cease permanently."

He used the tip of his finger to draw a soft line down her cheek. "As your husband I find your desire very thrilling, Pilar, there's nothing wrong with it. No man wants a wife who responds like a rock."

"I don't like feeling rudderless."

"If it's any consolation you play havoc with my rudder as well."

Once again she had no way of measuring the truthfulness of his words.

"Do you want me to offer you a measure of relief?"

Pilar sensed that agreeing would change her life but the alternative was to walk around with this unquenched heat inside herself and being ruled by it. "Yes," she replied firmly.

"My fearless warrior queen." He placed his lips against her brow. "All right, relief it shall be, but it may make things worse—just so you'll know."

Her eyes narrowed.

His smile was indulgent as he loosely draped his arms around her waist.

"You're teasing me," she stated.

"No, Pilar. I am not." He kissed her gently, letting her become accustomed to him once again, then eased her closer when the intensity rose to ensnare them both.

"I want to have our wedding night," she stated, whispered while she fought to hold on to herself.

"Do you?" he husked out against her ear and trailed his kisses down the edge of her throat.

"Yes." She wanted to *know*.

"Are you certain?" He nibbled her bottom lip, then teased it with the tip of his tongue.

She trembled in response. "Yes."

And soon, because he was so skillful and

masterful, Pilar was without rudder or anything else to guide her course. His kisses became her stars, his warm exploring hands her sails. Her sighs were soft as moonlight and her heightened senses roiled like storm-tossed seas. While the current of desire threatened to sweep her away, he anchored her, steered her, and splendidly showed her just how powerful a son of the Haitian goddess *Yemaya*—the mother of all waters—could be.

Her dress was unbuttoned to her waist, her shift unbuttoned as well, and his lips on her breasts seared her flesh like sensual lightning. When he bit her gently, she sucked in a breath. A yearning took hold between her thighs and her hips moved unconsciously to an ancient rhythmic drumbeat.

"Let's get you out of this dress."

Through the haze shimmering around her, she mindlessly stepped out of it, and stood pulsing in the fading light wearing her drawers, stockings, and opened shift while he placed it neatly over a chair. His return brought more kisses and slow tours of his hands until she thought she might melt from the heat. His touch inside her drawers made her startle and then croon as his expert fingers played in the damp darkness hidden there. The sensations sent her spiraling so high, her hand went to her mouth to keep her cry of delight contained. She was certain she was destined for hell for indulging in such decadent pleasure but she greedily wanted more and shamelessly widened her stance.

Watching her body rise to his play as she flowed over his fingers almost made Noah come then and there. Damn, he was hard and he wished she weren't an innocent so he could love her as fiercely as he craved. The tension had him strung tight as a bow but he held on. He could tell by the increased cadence of her breathing and the sultry movements of her hips that she was almost ready to peak and the male in him wanted to watch her explode from his pleasuring. Seconds later the orgasm shattered her, making her shudder and cry out hoarsely while he feasted with glowing eyes and kept up his play. She was slick and wet; her body bowed and he leaned down and licked a pebble-hard nipple before closing his mouth around it and tugging at it with lust gentled teeth.

"Oh, stop!" she begged and quickly backed away.

The tiger enjoyed his mate's beautiful distress but he was so engorged he found it difficult to breathe. If she couldn't handle more he'd abide by her decision but he prayed she'd agree to see the act through because he hadn't gotten nearly enough of her lushness, and truly needed the sweet relief only she could provide. "You wanted the wedding night, *querida*. Shall we continue?"

He sensed she was having second thoughts but knew the desire flaring inside was making it difficult for her usually sharp mind to hold sway. Much to his delight, she finally whispered, "Yes." He held out a hand and led her to the bed.

Once there he prepared with all the care necessary for such a precious moment, taking time to bring her to the heights again, savoring her gasps of passion and the moans of delight that slipped from her parted lips. She was twisting and wet and open when the time came to join their bodies, so he pushed in gently. "The first time may be painful, *querida*, forgive me."

She was so tight and warm, he wanted to storm his way through.

"Oh, wait, please Noah."

He forced himself to comply. Holding himself above her he closed his eyes and drew in a deep breath while he throbbed within her sheath.

He could feel how tense she'd become. Desire had been replaced by apprehension and undoubtedly a measure of fear. He kissed her reassuringly. The last thing he wanted was for her to rue this night and be put off lovemaking for the rest of their married life. "I'll go slow. I promise." He sensed her nod, and so fitting actions to words, advanced as gently as he could, then pulled out and slowly repeated the move again and again until she began to return the rhythm. A few moments later, they were moving as one. His tight hold on his discipline broke and he increased the pace, hoping he wasn't being too rough, but unable to stop if a gun was put to his head. She cried out as the orgasm grabbed her, and he roared as his own tore him apart and flung him up to the stars.

Later, he came back to life holding her in his arms. He could almost see her face in the darkness. "Did I hurt you?"

"At first, but then, I enjoyed it."

He chuckled softly. "That's good to know. I enjoyed it as well, so much so that were you more seasoned, I'd start again."

"Again?"

"Until sunrise."

He sensed her shock and traced a finger over her parted lips. "You're a very passionate woman, *querida*. I'm looking forward to many more nights like this, but in the morning you'll probably be sore, so let's get some sleep. We've a ferry to the mainland to catch at dawn."

"I suppose we won't be able to do this amongst the pigs and chickens."

"No, we won't."

"A pity."

He laughed and eased her closer.

Later, as they slept, his nightmare returned. In the dream it was once again his first night on the island and the Englishman Barton Felix and his henchmen had come for him. Upon realizing what Felix was after, Noah and Kingston fought like demons, but were outnumbered and easily over-powered. A crowd gathered and cheered as both men were forced onto their stomachs, held down, and their trousers stripped away. As always, his own screams tore him from the dream and he was thrust back into the present, covered with fear-fed sweat and trembling. Only this time, Pilar was beside him.

"Noah, you're shaking. Were you having a bad—"

He thrust her hand away and left the bed. "Go back to sleep."

Her stunned silence was like a cut through his heart, but he walked out onto the verandah and drank in the night air until he regained a measure of calm. *Dios*, he hated the memories. Since that horrid night they'd plagued every step of his life and seemed intent upon accompanying him to his grave. How naïve he'd been to think a mere slip of woman could rid him of the degradation and yes, the shame. While with her, he'd somehow been able to keep his demons at bay, only to have them return as they always did when he was most vulnerable. By not offering Pilar an explanation for his rude behavior, he could only imagine what might be going through her mind. They'd had a perfect time together, made love, and now? How did one explain such a vile experience, especially to one's innocent wife? He closed his eyes to rid himself of the lingering visions in his head.

"Noah?"

He didn't move. "My apologies for being so

callous, but please go back to bed. I'll see you in the morning."

For a moment there was silence before she quietly responded, "As you wish."

He heard the sounds of her whispered retreat and slammed his fist on the iron railing. He would've howled like a beast had he thought it would help. Instead, he looked out into the night and waited for the sunrise.

Chapter 15

The next morning, Pilar awakened to thunder, rain, and the wind screaming like something alive. Late August often brought hurricanes, so she hoped there wasn't one bearing down on them. Sitting up, she looked around the room and found herself alone. She wondered where Noah might be. His behavior last night still stung. They'd gone from making love to him suddenly kicking her away as if she were a cur on the street. It hurt. What hurt more was his lack of explanation. A part of her hoped he'd headed off to California alone, thus affording her the opportunity to resume her own life, but at that moment, he entered the room carrying a tray supporting covered dishes. He hesitated for a moment at the sight of her. She ignored him. Leaving the bed she saw the small show of blood on the mussed sheets. Ignoring that as well, she walked behind the screen to handle her morning needs.

When she came out, she dug through her bag for a skirt and blouse, and not caring if he watched, got dressed.

"I brought you breakfast."

"Thank you." She pushed her feet into her worn slippers. She was grateful for the meal but had nothing more to say.

They ate in silence. A mask over his features hid the man whose company she'd begun to enjoy. Gone was the teasing, the fun, and the passion. That hurt as well. Deciding she'd not wallow or speculate any longer about the reasons for his abrupt change in manner, she finished her meal and waited for him to relay what they were doing next.

"I'll take the tray back down to Mrs. Fitzhugh and we can depart when I return."

She nodded.

Noah knew he'd hurt her, but no amount of apologizing would soften the flinty frostiness in her eyes, at least not one that wasn't tied to an explanation. Since he had none to offer, he picked up the tray and made his exit.

It was pouring rain outside. By the time they ran from the doorway to the waiting hack they were both drenched. He at least had a coat; she had a thin shawl. He took his coat off and handed it to her. "Here, put this around you before you catch a chill."

"I'm fine. I've been wet before."

"Pilar—"

Tight-lipped, she took the coat from his hand and draped it over her shoulders. Had she her rapier they'd probably be circling each other in the dance of *Destreza*. He almost wished they were; she'd at least have to look at him. His eyes lingered over her averted profile. What a beauty she was. From her unconventional close-cropped hair and gamine face to her proud chin, any man would be honored to have her in his life, but he was afraid of how she'd perceive him should he tell her the truth, and therein lay the rub. It was a dilemma he had no idea how to broach and although it potentially doomed them to spend their lives going through the motions like strangers staring at each other over the divide, she was in his blood and he refused to give her up.

After a rocky ride on the ferry, the train was there and waiting when they reached the depot. Noah paid the hack and he and Pilar hurried to the covered platform to escape the deluge. There was a small crowd of people of varying races in line. The agent they'd spoken with yesterday raised his voice. "All coloreds to the smoking car."

Noah saw his own frustration mirrored in the faces of those the announcement applied to. He told himself at least they weren't being relegated to the cattle car, but it was a small consolation considering everyone was paying the same fare.

Inside the smoking car, men grabbed chairs to sit in on the start of various card games, while others sidled up to the bar to buy spirits. A man at the piano began a lively tune and two fiddlers jumped in, sawing away. Outside the rain pelted the windows in sheets and the wind howled shrilly. He hoped they wouldn't be delayed by the weather. Train tracks were notorious for being washed out by downpours like the one they were experiencing. All he wanted was to get home.

Pilar wished to go home as well, but not to California. The pangs in her heart from missing Cuba, her mother, and her sister rose with each passing moment. She'd never begged for anything in her life, yet she dearly wished to be elsewhere, but knew the wish would not be granted.

Many of the segregated travelers were families with small children and they took up positions on the floor against the far wall.

"Would you like a seat at one of the tables?" he asked.

Not wanting to be around the cigar-smoking gamblers or the heavily made-up ladies of the night offering false smiles, she said. "No. I'll sit with the families." And she walked off and found a space on the floor a bit away from the fray. To her surprise he dragged a couple of chairs over to where she was seated. "You might prefer this to the floor."

She saw some of the women eyeing their exchange, so rather than draw more attention she sat in one and he took the other. "You can go join the tables if you like, I'll be fine," she told him.

"Thank you, but I don't want any of the men to get the mistaken impression that you're traveling alone."

It hadn't occurred to her that she could be in danger but in reality knew he was correct. She assumed she wouldn't be accosted by the men seated with their families, but the fancy types with their flashy suits and pomaded hair were another story. "Then I thank you for the company."

"You're welcome."

Silence rose between them in spite of the music and noise that filled the air.

"Pilar?"

Cool eyed, she faced him.

"About last night. I was rude and boorish. I'm sorry."

To mask her hurt she kept her features unreadable.

"I have nightmares sometimes and . . ." His voice trailed off. He began again. "They don't come often but this one caught me unawares. I treated you badly."

She searched his scarred face and wanted to ask about the nature of the dreams, but held off. His discomfort with the explanation was plain. Maybe in time, he'd offer more.

"Should it occur again, I'll do my best to react differently."

"Thank you. If I can help—"

He shook his head. "I'll be fine. I just wanted to assure you that it wasn't anything you did or said."

That he was in pain was also apparent. Wanting to assuage it somehow welled up inside of her with such force she was taken aback by the strength. She was coming to care for him far more than she realized and wondered if doing so was wise.

"I did enjoy yesterday," he said, interrupting her musings.

She thought back on their time together by the water and their lovemaking and admitted truthfully, "I did as well."

"Can we start again? That I need more fun in my life is readily apparent."

She hesitated. Once burned, twice shy. Could she trust him? She didn't know but a part of her wanted to, so she nodded. "I'd like that."

He took her hands gently in his and gave the fingertips a fleeting kiss. "Thank you for your graciousness."

"Thank you for the apology." He'd seemed so sincere and repentant, it would be incredibly mean-spirited of her to deny his request for a truce but she planned to be less open in the future and remain on guard.

"Would you like a cup of tea or something to warm up so you don't catch a chill from the rain?"

"That would be nice."

"I'll be right back."

Still wrestling with her uncertainty, Pilar watched him go.

Noah crossed the crowded room and savored her grace. Her wariness had been plain and, frankly, expected. He'd ambushed her, taken the good will she'd tried to bring to their unconventional marriage and run a sword through it, thus his attempt to explain. No, he hadn't told her the full extent of the demons riding him, mostly because he had no desire to plunge her into hell with him, but in truth she was already. Going forward he had no idea what to do except take each day and moment as it came and hope the future offered a solution that would free them both.

As night fell, mothers gathered their children and the families unrolled thin pallets from their packs and bedded down. Lamps were lit for those still at the gaming tables and the drinks and music continued to flow.

Pilar and Noah left their chairs and sat side by side on the floor. He eased an arm around her waist and held her close. Since neither had enjoyed a full night's sleep last night they were both sleepy. She placed her head on his chest. He kissed her brow. "Try and get some sleep."

Nodding, she closed her eyes.

Noah was still awake at sunrise.

Due to the inclement weather, the journey to Birmingham, Alabama, took longer than expected. At one point the conductor entered the car to inform everyone that they were indeed feeling the effects of a hurricane making its way into the Gulf and apologized for the slow going. Pilar prayed that the people she knew at home were safe, and once again her mind turned to her friend Tomas and his untimely death.

• • •

Back in Cuba Pilar had ridden in wagons carrying livestock to the market, but never in her life had she had to sleep with them or spend each waking moment gagging on the stench of their bodies and dung. Thus was the journey from Birmingham to St. Louis, where every person of color was forced to endure the horrid conditions of the stock car. Were she being petty she would've laid the appalling set of circumstances at the feet of her husband, but it wasn't his fault. He was equally furious, and they passed the two-day journey in companionable anger.

When they got off the train, the first thing she wanted was a bath. "Is there someplace I can wash?"

"Yes. There are bathhouses not too far away."

"Are they segregated, too?" she asked as they left the station.

"Yes, but there are a number to choose from. Afterwards, new shoes and a few new changes of clothing are in order. We both reek."

She sadly agreed. Her slippers were crusted and stained with the leavings of the animals and her skirt was smelly and stained. She wanted to take everything off and dump both shoes and garments into the nearest waste receptacle, but walking naked through the streets would probably shock the citizenry.

"Hopefully, we'll be treated equally on the ride to Denver."

She hoped so as well.

After the bathhouse and a change into clothing from their valises they made their way to shops recommended by the owner of the bathhouse.

As they walked, Pilar asked, "How far are we from Florida?"

"Over a thousand miles, I'm guessing."

"I had no idea America was so large."

"We've many more thousands to go before we reach San Francisco."

For a woman raised in the countryside, the idea that she'd eventually be thousands of miles from home was very daunting. The streets were congested with carriages and coaches. There were crowds of people on the walks and she found it hard not to stare around in wonder at the young boys hawking newspapers, the men in hats and spiffy suits accompanied by women in costly costumes and carrying small parasols.

"Not what you're accustomed to?" he asked.

"No. I've never seen so many buildings." They were made of bricks and wood. Many looked to have been thrown up on the spot, unlike Cuba's old Spanish architecture. Feeling homesickness beginning to settle in, she turned her mind away from it and kept pace at his side.

When they entered the clothier's, a short dark-skinned man greeted them and introduced himself as the proprietor, Claude Dell.

"Welcome. Never seen you folks before."

"We're on our way to Denver. I was told you offer an assortment of readymade goods."

"That I do. Take a look around and when you're ready to pay just come on back."

The place wasn't very large or busy, but it was clean and the items for sale were neatly stacked on tables and displayed on dress forms. While Pilar wandered over to the women's area, Noah picked out a suit, a couple of shirts, socks, and a few other items. Pleased with his selections, he walked to the counter. A few moments later, Pilar joined him with her choices: an ugly, shapeless brown gingham decorated with bows and ruffles, a shirtwaist, two skirts and a pair of men's boots. In reply to the confusion that must've shown on his face, she explained, "These boots will do me just fine and keep my feet dry."

"But don't you want something a bit more . . . ladylike?"

"I'll not subject any more ladylike shoes to animal dung."

He supposed that made sense, but . . . he decided not to argue, but the dress warranted discussion. "Are you sure about this dress?"

Mr. Dell broke in apologetically. "Sorry we don't have anything more fashionable for the little lady."

"That's quite all right," she said to him. "Being fashionable is not a concern."

Eyeing the god-awful dress, Noah readily agreed, but kept that to himself. He had two very fashion-minded sisters-in-law. It was his hope that once they reached the ranch, Mariah and Billie would take Pilar under their wings. She was far too beautiful to be walking around in something so ghastly.

Noah paid for the purchases and they exited to search out the boardinghouse that the bathhouse owner also suggested. It took them a while to hail a hack that would ferry people of color, but once they did, they settled in for the ride. The train to Denver wouldn't be leaving until tomorrow so they'd be needing a place to sleep for the night. They hadn't slept in a bed since leaving Mrs. Fitzhugh's. Although Pilar hadn't whined or complained about the poor accommodations on the train, he knew she'd enjoy laying her head somewhere besides a fouled floor. The thought of sharing a bed with her sent his mind back to their lovemaking and the disastrous aftermath. Although his desire for her was still high, the last thing he wanted was to subject her to another round of his nightmares, so he'd let her have the bed and make do with a chair or whatever else the room had to offer so she could rest peacefully. It wasn't his first choice, but undoubtedly the wisest.

It was so wonderful being clean again, Pilar wanted to sing. The stench of the stock car on her skin had been replaced by the subtle sweet fragrance in the soap she'd used and she felt human again. As the driver, a kindly older gentleman who'd introduced himself as Oscar, drove them to their destination, she glanced Noah's way and found him watching her. He leaned over, brushed his lips against her brow and said, softly, "You smell good, *querida*."

This was their first intimate contact in days. Having been at odds when they left Florida and then being subjected to the cattle car, there had been no opportunity for closeness, but the feel of his lips let her know that in spite of pledging to guard her feelings, she missed his touch. Cognizant of the driver in front of them, she leaned close and whispered. "I've missed your kisses."

He stilled and smiled. "Really?"

She nodded.

He kept his voice low. "Then I'll be sure to remedy that as soon as possible."

She snuggled close and he draped an arm over her shoulder. "Good."

When they reached the boardinghouse, Oscar promised to return the next day to drive them back to the train station. After receiving his fare and a generous tip, he drove away and Pilar and Noah went inside the large, green gingerbread-trimmed house.

The owner, a mulatto woman named Andora Pennington, greeted them as Noah closed the door. "Welcome."

"Thank you. I'm Noah Yates. My wife Pilar. We were told you rent rooms?"

"I do. There's only two other boarders here right now, so you have your pick of three regular rooms or the big room on the top floor. I charge more for it, however."

"May we see it first?" Noah asked.

"Of course, but the rate is set. There'll be no bargaining."

"Understood."

"The two of you really married?"

"Yes, ma'am."

"Good. I don't allow any sinners here."

Noah and Pilar shared a speaking look and hid their grins as they followed Mrs. Pennington to the stairs.

She ushered them into what was a well-appointed and spacious room. "There's an attached bathing room with a tub. If you want to pay extra you can eat in here rather than down in the common room. There's also a sitting porch through that door."

"How much?"

The price she quoted made Pilar stare in shock.

"We'll take it," he said.

Pilar turned her stare his way and it earned her an amused wink.

"We'll be staying just one night and we prefer to eat privately."

"Fine. Pay in advance." She held out her hand.

He placed the bills on her palm. "Thank you, Mrs. Pennington."

"You're welcome." And she departed.

Pilar said, "She's quite the businesswoman."

"That she is. Does the room meet with your approval?"

She took in the fine upholstered chairs and settee, the grate, the large wardrobe and the cream-colored walls. "It's a fine room. I choked when she quoted the price, however. You sure it isn't too costly?"

He walked over and draped his arms loosely around her waist. "For you, I'd willingly pay for a room in the Taj Mahal."

"What's the Taj Mahal?"

"I consider it to be one of the wonders of the world. An Indian king built it as a tribute to his late wife and it's constructed of beautiful white marble. Maybe one day we can journey to India and see it."

"I'd like that."

"Now, about the kisses you've been missing."

She lowered her amused eyes then raised them again. His held an intensity she'd come to know well in the short time they'd been together and in spite of everything, her senses sparked and flared. When his mouth met hers, she immediately melted in sweet response. The kiss was an invitation, a beckoning, an acknowledgment of a passion they both shared and she offered an invitation of her own by parting her lips and letting him seek out the tender corners with the searing tip of his tongue. Her body, now familiar with desire's dance, came alive and bloomed. He moved his mouth down the edge of her throat then meandered up to the shell of her ear, leaving behind a trail of heat.

Expert fingers conquered the line of buttons on her blouse and soon his lips were searing the bare skin above her corset and chemise. He flicked his tongue lazily against the trembling hollow of her throat, making her arch and purr.

Noah had missed her kisses, too. He'd missed the silkiness of her skin, her soft moans of pleasure, and the feel of her nipples grazing his palms. When the freed halves fell away, he slid his hand inside and filled it with warm velvety flesh. He took the candy-hard nipple into his mouth. As he ardently relished first one and then its twin, his manhood stretched lustfully. Wanting more, he undid the button on the waistband of her skirt and tugged it down until the garment pooled at her feet. Filling his hands with the rich curves of her hips, he eased her closer and recaptured her lips while his hands circled and explored.

Within the haze surrounding Pilar, she was aware of her ragged breathing and racing heart. Her nipples were ripe and damp, her legs parted, and the heat between her thighs begged for his touch. When his fingers found her, she drew in a shaky breath and closed her eyes against the bliss.

"I could make love to you for a lifetime,

querida," he whispered thickly, still dallying in the humid *vee* of her thighs. It never occurred to her that lovemaking could be done during the day with the sunlight pouring in through the windows, but she found the setting as decadent as his hands. Her drawers were drawn down and off, and there she stood in her opened corset and stockings while throbbing in response to his continuing expert touch. The heat in his eyes burned like flames. The play of his fingers instilled their own version of flame and the orgasm, like a storm in the distance, began to rise.

She watched with steamy eyes as he began to undress. When he was done, she visually feasted. He was gorgeously made. She hadn't touched him the night she lost her virginity but passion made her bold enough to slide a palm down his chest and over the soft pelt of hair and then lower to take him in her hand. His eyes closed and his head arched back. He felt like strength overlaid with warmth. "Show me what to do . . ."

He covered her hand and guided her in a slow sultry rhythm.

After a few brazen moments, he backed away. Breathing harshly, his eyes were lit by his wicked smile. "Aren't you the bold one?"

"Is that not allowed?"

"Allowed and encouraged. And you get a prize."

He slid a thumb across her nipple, bent to take one in his mouth again and she groaned. As his tongue teased and tantalized, she asked languidly, "What kind of prize?"

"Hold on. Be right back."

"Noah . . ." she whined softly when he left her. She watched the bold play of his legs and hips as he disappeared into the adjoining bath. He came back into view immediately with a towel slung over his shoulder. When he reached her, he placed the towel around her waist and used it to draw her close enough to kiss, and then led her across the room. He placed the towel over the settee and took a seat on top of it.

"I want you to kneel over me. Place one knee here and the other here," he said indicating the settee cushions.

She followed his instructions but asked, "Why?"

"So I can do this . . ."

Feeling him fill her gently but so fully made her croon with lusty delight. He began to move, she began to follow. "Do you like?" he asked, guiding her, kissing her.

"Very much."

And she did. It was shocking but oh so satisfying to be moved up and down on such hard male splendor. The friction rekindled her desire like kindling being added to a fire and the distant storm of the orgasm drew nearer. The next few moments were a carnal blur filled with kisses, heat, touches, and licks. He touched her, she touched him, and their breathing filled the quiet of the sunlit room.

Noah couldn't have asked for a more passionate student and Pilar panted over her scandalous teacher. When he reached between their rising bodies and teased his finger over the bud that defined her as a woman, the storm broke and her orgasm tore his name from her lips. As she twisted and shuddered in the rictus of her completion, the sight coupled with the tight clutching of her sheath made him grab her hips, pump uninhibitedly, and explode with a shout of erotic joy.

As they came back to earth, she said to him, "I never knew you could do this—this way."

He slid a hand up her damp back before gifting her with a soft kiss. "There are many, many ways and we have a lifetime to explore them all."

She drew back and eyed him. "All of them?"

"Until we get too old."

She fit herself against him again and said, "I hope we never get too old."

"I agree. In fact," he said feeling himself coming to life again within her. "I think we deserve another round."

"Do you now?"

"I do."

"I think I'm married to a very scandalous man."

"And I have an equally scandalous wife."

And so, they began again and this time when the intensity peaked Pilar knew what to expect. She rode him hard and he played counterpoint with blazing abandon and they kept at it until they were sated and too weak to move. Afterwards he carried her to the bed and they slept.

Chapter 16

Standing out on her verandah watching the moon rise, Alanza was enjoying being Mrs. Maxwell Rudd, especially at night. She was now more experienced in the sensual arts of marriage and just thinking about some of the paces they'd taken each other through was enough to make her blush. It was the end of another day and all was well in her world. The ranch continued to prosper, her sons and their wives were happy, as were her two grandchildren. The only missing piece of the puzzle was Noah. She worried about him and had done so since the day he'd returned from being shanghaied all those years ago. Something had obviously happened during the time he was away to change him from the bright artistic boy she'd raised to the brooding silent shadow he'd become, but she had no idea what it might be. At first, she'd pressed him to talk about it, but getting no response, she'd given up.

Earlier, she'd received a telegram from him that read:

Found pirate.
Married.
Traveling by train.
Home soon.

The news threw her for a loop. Whom had he

married—the pirate? She dearly wished he'd been more forthcoming, but there was nothing for her to do but wait until he arrived.

Max came up behind her, put his arms around her waist and grazed his lips softly against her neck. She loved him so much.

"You coming to bed?"

"Yes, my impatient *querido*."

"Still brooding over the telegram from Noah?"

She turned to him and nodded.

"You'll get the full story when he gets back."

"Do you think he married the pirate who took his boat?"

"Who knows, but Logan married a rock thrower, Drew married a lady of the evening and now, your youngest may have married a lady pirate. Have to admit, your boys have got them some real interesting wives."

She agreed.

"But I have the most interesting one, so how about you come to bed and let me show you."

"You are so scandalous."

"You wouldn't want me any other way."

He was right of course and because he was, she wrapped her arm around his waist and they went inside.

The train to Denver did not segregate the races, so Pilar had a chance to actually see the countryside from her seat by a window. She was again awed by the sheer size and scope of America. They passed wide-open areas—Noah called them prairies—and there was nothing like them in her old home of Cuba. Her thoughts went back to her family and she wondered how her mother and sister Doneta were faring and if they were missing her as much as she missed them. She hoped they would be able to take the train out to visit her in her new home on Noah's ranch as soon as possible, because she dearly wished to see them again. For her own part, she was happier than she had ever imagined she would be when Noah Yates demanded her hand. Back then she had no idea how charming he could be. Since their truce on the train ride he'd been attentive, concerned, and delightful to be with—not to mention extraordinary in bed. Maybe, just maybe their marriage would be a success. Her monthly courses came the day they left St. Louis, so there was no baby on the way and she had mixed feelings about that. On one hand, she did want a child but on the other, not too soon. She wanted to learn the ins and outs of Noah first before turning her attention to a baby. As far as she knew, he'd not been visited by the nightmares that were at the root of their initial rift but she couldn't help wondering just what the dreams were about. Rather than pester him about it though, she kept her questions unasked, with the hope the matter would resolve itself in a manner that satisfied them both.

"Penny for your thoughts," he asked her as the train chugged them towards Denver.

"Just marveling over how large this country is. You could probably fit a hundred Cubas just in the land we've passed in the last day."

"It is a big place and once we get to Denver, we have two more days of travel before we reach San Francisco."

"I'm enjoying the sights but tired of traveling."

"So am I." He rubbed a gentle hand over her back. "How are you feeling?"

"I'll be better once my courses are done, but I'm not too uncomfortable." She'd had no idea the subject was something women discussed with their husbands, but since first becoming aware of her condition he'd been nothing but concerned and attentive, going so far as to ask her if there was anything he could do or provide to help her along. His regard was endearing. "What's the first thing you want to do when you get home?"

"Besides make love to my wife?"

She shook her head at his ribald ways. "Yes, besides that."

"Sleep off all this travel, then go to San Francisco and see about a new boat."

Guilt swept over her. "I'm sorry about the *Alanza*."

"Water under the bridge. Besides had that not happened, we'd not be man and wife."

She was grateful for his generous attitude. "What kind of boat are you wanting?"

"I'm undecided."

For the next little while they discussed the advantages and disadvantages of sloops over cutters, and how ships fed by steam were making those powered by the wind-fed sails all but obsolete.

Their conversation was interrupted by the appearance of the conductor, who announced, "We'll be stopping to take on water for the boiler in about thirty minutes. You folks can get off and stretch your legs if you like. Lady has a stand that sells sandwiches at the depot, too."

He moved on to the next car.

"Are you hungry?" Noah asked her.

"I am."

"When we stop, we'll get something to eat."

The stop didn't last very long but it was enough time for them to buy two fat sandwiches stuffed with ham that they washed down with tumblers of sweet chilled lemonade. By the time they retook their seats, they were refreshed and ready for the remaining journey to Denver.

The first thing Pilar noticed when they stepped off the train at the Denver depot was the chill in the air. "Why is it so cold?"

He laughed. "It isn't cold."

"Yes it is. I'm shivering."

"You're Cuban."

"You're my husband. Do something," she said, hugging herself.

"Let's see if there's a place nearby that sells coats."

"Thank you."

She had to settle for a cloak, but it helped. The train for San Francisco wouldn't depart until the next morning, so they found a boardinghouse and after dinner, the exhausted Pilar crawled into bed. "I'm sorry we can't make love."

"Nothing to apologize for, *querida*. You just rest. I'll come join you in a bit."

She nodded, covered herself with the blankets and drifted off.

While she slept, Noah took a seat in the small room's lone chair. He was exhausted as well. The past month had taken him from the ranch to Cuba to Florida, and now back to California in the company of a small spitfire by the name of Pilar. He adored everything about her, from her lyrical Spanish-tinged English to her beauty, to the way she'd accepted his apology for hurting her so badly after their wedding night. Although she hadn't said anything about it since, he could tell the incident still lingered. He'd looked up a couple of times during their journey to find her watching him as if trying to determine his true measure. And until yesterday in the cab, the open playfulness that he'd found so endearing had not been on display. It was as if she was keeping parts of herself locked away and out of his reach and he didn't blame her, but he could no longer imagine his life without her presence in it. For the past decade he'd sailed the world, mostly in an attempt to escape it. Fueled by the memories of the island's horror, he'd eschewed ties to everything save his music, family, and the solitude to be found on the deck of a ship. And now, a different Noah Yates was taking shape, one who could envision raising a family and all it entailed, one who didn't have to separate himself from happiness or joy, one who could look forward to the future instead of being mired in the past, if he could just find a way to rid himself of it permanently. He owed her that.

And because he did, he also needed to figure out what he wanted his immediate future with her to be. He doubted he'd ever give up his ties to the sea, but having a wife meant he could no longer justify spending months and months aboard a ship thousands of miles from home. Although finding a vessel to replace the sunken *Alanza* was a priority, sailing it as a way of life wasn't, and that admission surprised him because it wasn't something he'd ever thought about before. It never occurred to him that he might willingly come to such a conclusion. Since being shanghaied all he'd ever wanted was to be on the sea. He glanced over at her, sleeping in the shadows on the far side of the room. From the moment they'd crossed swords he knew she could change his life, and she had, not in large ways but in ways as small and as powerful as she.

Rising from the chair, he stretched in response to the weariness of the past few days. He then undressed and doused the lamps. Carefully, so as not to wake her, he slid beneath the bedding. She roused for a moment to voice a sleepy good night. He pulled her close, placed a tender kiss on the top of her hair and closed his eyes.

An hour out of Denver the train was winding its way through the mountains when Pilar asked, "What is that white color on top of those peaks?"

"Snow."

Her mouth dropped and she quickly turned back to the window.

Noah chuckled softly. "You've never seen snow, I take it."

"No, it doesn't snow in Cuba. Does it snow in California?"

"Where we're going, only occasionally, but places north of us get quite a bit." He found her reactions captivating.

"So what do you do when it does happen?"

"We throw extra wood on the fire and dress warmly."

"*Dios*," she whispered.

"I'll keep you warm. I promise."

"Snow, riding with animals, belt leather pork. What am I doing here? I vote we go back to Florida."

"Too late. The votes have already been counted."

She playfully elbowed him in the ribs and returned to the sights outside her window, while Noah went back to the newspaper he'd picked up at the Denver depot that morning. One of the most interesting items was an article about German inventor Karl Benz and his unveiling of something called the Benz Patent Motorwagon. It was billed as the first gas-burning automobile designed to generate its own power. The report went on to speculate that in the years to come the new engine could be applied to all modes of transportation, thus making coal- and steam-fueled engines on trains and sailing vessels a thing of the past. Noah wasn't sure he believed that, but planned to keep an eye out for further articles in the future. Another article had to do with the army and their futile attempts to capture the Apache chief Geronimo, who reigned as the last major Indian leader not penned in a reservation. Noah hoped the wily old chief continued to make them chase their tails.

"Any news in there about Cuba?" she asked him.

He glanced through the pages ahead. "Not so far. Oh, wait. As a matter of fact there is. It seems Spain is considering outlawing slavery there."

"It's about time. Cuba and Brazil are the only two places left in the world that still practice it, but I won't believe them until it happens. Anything about General Maceo or the rebels?"

He read the article. "No."

"Okay. Thank you."

Her sadness touched his heart, but since he had no way of making her feel better short of letting her return to the island so she could take up arms against Spain, he solemnly went back to his newspaper.

Pilar's sense of homesickness returned tenfold. Cuba was going on without her and she wasn't sure how to reconcile that fact. Since the age of fifteen, fighting for her country's future had been her entire life and now she was in a land several thousand miles away where snow fell, for saints' sake, unable to offer her aid. Learning that Spain might be considering abolishing slavery was good news though, and although it was unwise for her to return, she dearly wished she were there.

As if reading her mind, he said softly, "I'm sorry, Pilar."

She turned and lied, "It's okay, Noah," but added truthfully, "my life is with you now. Hopefully I'll learn to love your home as much as I loved my own."

"I'll do my best to make sure you do."

"I'm holding you to that."

By the time, they reached San Francisco, Pilar didn't want to see another train for at least five years. Her back hurt not only from the prolonged sitting but from having to sleep in her seat as well. The food choices had been limited and baths had been out of the question. Her courses were done, however, and that pleased her if nothing else.

"We've one more train to catch, *querida*, then we can both fall over from relief."

They were walking away through the bustling station.

"Is it a long ride?"

"No. Just a few hours."

"Then I'm sure I can survive."

"Noah!"

The feminine scream of joy was followed by a fashionably dressed woman in green who launched herself at Noah like a dog greeting the long-awaited return of its beloved master. Pilar looked on coolly as her husband did his best to disentangle himself from the arms around his neck.

"Hello, Lavinia. What are you doing here?"

"I just arrived from Los Angeles. Where have you been, you naughty man?"

Pilar arched an eyebrow.

"'Vinia, I want you to meet my wife, Pilar. Pilar, this is Lavinia Douglas."

The woman's eyes went so wide, Pilar thought they might pop out and roll around on the floor of the station.

"Your wife?"

"Pleased to meet you," Pilar offered. She could see herself being critically assessed and apparently found lacking.

"Same here," came her indifferent reply before

she immediately returned to Noah and showed a false smile. "Married. What a surprise. How long?"

He draped an arm around Pilar's waist. "Not very. Took us by surprise, I must admit." His smile earned one from her in reply.

"And you met her where?"

"Cuba. I was immediately captured."

Pilar was amused by his play on words.

"I must say, I never expected you to be captured by someone so—foreign, shall we say."

Pilar immediately took offense, but tempered it with the realization that she was Mrs. Noah Yates, and this *vaquilla* in the pert green hat was not. Taking in Noah's tightly set jaw, it was apparent that he hadn't appreciated the verbal slight either, and that further buoyed Pilar's spirits.

"Are you on your way to the ranch?" Lavinia asked.

"Yes. This is Pilar's first time in the States. I'm anxious for her to meet the family."

"I see. Be sure to let me know the next time you're in San Francisco so we can have dinner. Papa would love to meet her as well. And please wear that quaint little dress, Pilar. You'll be all the rage."

Pilar's eyes flashed angrily. Seeing how Lavinia and the other women in the depot were attired, her gingham dress and men's boots made her look like a ragamuffin in comparison. She might need to learn to dress like an American, but Lavinia needed a lesson in manners, so Pilar thought them even.

"Nice seeing you, Noah." And without a word to Pilar she took her leave.

As she walked away, Pilar asked, "That's the *vaquilla* you've been keeping company with?"

He laughed loud and long and tightened his arm around her waist. "Oh, Pilar. You're so wonderful. She'd have a fit hearing herself called a heifer."

"I'm not sure why. It probably wouldn't be the first time."

"Thank you for marrying me."

"I didn't have much choice, as I remember."

"No, you didn't but I'm so pleased."

Still laughing he led her through the station to catch the final train to his home. Pilar was too exhausted to quiz him further about the rude Lavinia Douglas but planned to do so in the near future.

Chapter 17

Pilar swallowed her nervousness as the hired hack passed beneath the arched iron sign that read RANCHO DESTINO. She was moments away from meeting Noah's family and she wasn't sure how she'd be greeted. If they were aware of her stealing his ship, she didn't expect to be welcomed with open arms. Having to spend the rest of her existence among people who couldn't abide her was not her idea of a happy life, especially after traveling so far and having left her own family behind. Deep down inside she wanted them to like her but if that didn't turn out to be the case she supposed she'd manage somehow.

Her nervousness was soon overridden by wonder. The ranch was vast. She knew he was wealthy but the sheer size rivaled some of the large plantations at home. There were acres and acres of land for as far as she could see: cattle, corrals holding horses, orchards, workers. "I had no idea your ranch would be so large."

"My mother has built quite a legacy here."

"Your father's passed on?"

"Yes, when I was very young. She worked herself to the bone to create this. My brothers and I are very proud to be her sons."

Pilar noted the respect and love in his tone. It

was plain that he cared deeply for her and she found that knowledge pleasing.

The sprawling house that came into view was grand as well. Well-kept gardens and wrought-iron verandahs caught her eye. Even the outbuildings were grander than her house at home. What would his mother think of her youngest bringing home a virtual pauper for a bride? Pilar had no answer but drew in a deep breath to try and settle the butterflies in her stomach. "I'm very nervous."

"You shouldn't be. She'll adore you as much as she does my sisters-in-law."

She hoped he was right even though a part of her found that hard to believe. After all, she'd been responsible for the sinking of the ship bearing her name. How could she be happy knowing her son had married the culprit? Pilar prayed this initial meeting went well.

When the hack stopped, Noah helped her out.

"Noah! You're back!"

Pilar turned in the direction of the joyful exclamation and saw a woman in a divided skirt and black boots hurrying down the stairs. His face broke into the widest grin Pilar had ever seen and his arms opened wide. Their strong embrace pulled at Pilar's heart.

"So glad to have you home," she gushed.

"It's good to be home. Mother, may I present my wife, Pilar. Pilar, my mother, Alanza Maria Vallejo—Yates—Rudd.

His mother was stunningly beautiful, and from her golden features and accented English, obviously Spanish. "Welcome to your new home, Pilar."

"Thank you. It's an honor to meet you."

"Noah, she's lovely."

He smiled. "Yes, she is."

Pilar inwardly thanked him for that.

"Now, I have three *nueras*!" Alanza declared in a voice so filled with pride and excitement Pilar couldn't help but smile.

While Noah stepped away to pay the driver and get their bags, Pilar saw his mother viewing her intently, making her wonder if the woman was taking in how badly dressed her new *nuera* was. There was nothing but kindness in her dark eyes, however, and Pilar was certain that would change once she learned of her role in the theft and sinking of her son's ship.

After the coach drove away, the three of them started towards the steps leading to the wide front porch. "Noah, I received your telegram," his mother said, "but it was confusing. The wording made it seem as if you married the pirate."

Pilar froze.

"I did."

Alanza took in Pilar with wide eyes. "Pilar is the pirate?"

"Yes."

"This tiny little thing?"

"This tiny little thing stole my ship, sank it—"

"The Spanish navy sank it," Pilar interrupted, coming to her own defense.

"I stand corrected, but we wound up dancing *La Verdadera Destreza*."

"Swords!"

"She's very good with a rapier, Mama."

Pilar groused, "Plainly not good enough, as I was forced to yield."

His mother looked between the two of them, appeared about to speak, but apparently changed her mind and laughed. "Let's go inside before I fall down."

"I'm glad you insisted we take lessons, otherwise she might have bested me." His eyes teased Pilar.

Alanza exclaimed, "First Mariah, then Billie, and now a swordswoman named Pilar. *Dios*!"

The interior of the house was as beautifully furnished as one would expect. Fine rugs sat atop gleaming wood floors. Lamps with wrought-iron bases anchored well-polished side tables made of lustrous dark wood. There were sumptuous gold-colored drapes and lovely upholstered chairs and sofas. The vases and small statues of saints reminded her so much of home, her heart ached and before she knew it, there were tears in her eyes.

Alanza asked with concern, "*Qué pasa*?" What's the matter?

That Alanza had addressed her in Spanish, a language she thought she'd never hear on a regular basis again, added to her sudden and embarrassing bout of homesickness, so she replied in a rush of Spanish that she was just homesick for Cuba and her family, and missed speaking her native tongue, and how embarrassed she was to be in tears. She dashed away the telling moisture and before she could glance at her husband to gauge his reaction to her uncharacteristic show of weakness, Alanza smiled fondly. "None of my *nueras* speak Spanish and I've secretly longed for one who does. You will be my special joy, Pilar. Has Noah not been speaking Spanish with you?"

"He has but only occasionally. I'm not sure how fluent he is, to be truthful." So far, she'd only heard him use Spanish when speaking endearments.

"He speaks both English and Spanish. Always has. Why does your wife not know you speak Spanish?"

His reply was tinged with amusement. "Pilar, you're in the house two minutes and have already gotten me into trouble."

"My apology, but I didn't know."

"I'll rectify that. I promise."

The heat in his gaze, potent as a caress, caused her nipples to tighten shamelessly and she quickly looked away.

"Where is everyone, Mama?"

"Billie, Mariah, and the babies are out visiting friends, and your brothers are in town."

"And Max?"

"At the sawmill looking over some wood. Everyone will be here for dinner as always. Are you two hungry? I can have Bonnie prepare you something to tide you over."

Pilar knew from Noah that Bonnie was the house cook. She was indeed hungry after the long day.

He spoke for them both: "That would be grand."

"Okay, take my *nuera* upstairs and I'll send Bonnie up shortly. Dinner will be in a few hours." She paused, gently took Pilar's hands and said with sincerity, "Welcome."

Her reply was equally as sincere. "Thank you."

As they made their departure, Alanza watched them go. She was still taken aback by the news that Pilar was the dreaded pirate. The newlyweds had offered no further information on the circumstances surrounding their marriage other than there'd been swordplay. That Noah seemed genuinely taken with the terribly thin and badly dressed Cuban was surprising as well. Alanza assumed the full story would be revealed in time, so for the moment, she was just happy to have her son home.

Walking down hallways and up staircases and past framed paintings of the blessed Virgin, a few saints, and stern-faced men and women she assumed to be ancestors, Pilar accompanied Noah to his rooms, all the while wondering how long it might take her to learn to navigate the home without getting lost.

"My mother grew up in this house," he explained at her side. "Her parents inherited it from their parents and each generation has added to the original building. It's not nearly as much of a maze as it might seem."

Pilar tended to disagree.

He pushed open a carved wooden door accented with leather and hobnail fittings and to her surprise picked her up.

Laughing, she asked, "What are you doing?"

"Carrying you across the threshold."

"What on earth for?"

"In some places it's a tradition for the man to carry his new wife into their home."

Knowing nothing about such a thing, she rested easily in his arms until he placed her gently on her feet. She looked around. Like the rest of the house, the room was large, so large in fact her entire home back in Cuba could have fit comfortably inside with lots of space to spare. One wall held a grate, and spread around were lamps, comfortable-looking chairs and a large sofa. The space also held a magnificent piano.

"This is the sitting room," he told her. "Bedroom is this way."

She followed him, and found it, with its

luxurious draperies and massive four-poster, even larger.

"Bathing room with running water is through that door there. The doors behind you lead outside to the verandah."

"You live well, Noah."

"*We* live well, Pilar," he countered. "This is your home now, too."

The idea of that would take some getting accustomed to, but for the moment, she just wanted to sit, relax, and not think about boarding another train. She dropped into a chair by the windows. "Feels so good to be done traveling."

"I agree." Noah would be the first to admit that having her with him made him feel even better. "Was I right about my mother's reaction to you?"

"Yes, Noah. You were correct. She's very gracious. Your brothers are both married to American women?"

"Yes. Logan's wife, Mariah, is from Philadelphia and Drew's Billie is from San Francisco. I never thought about Mama wanting a Spanish daughter-in-law, but I suppose it does make sense."

"It'll be nice to converse with someone who shares my tongue."

He walked over and sat on the arm of her chair and said to her in Spanish, "I'd like to share your tongue . . ."

She replied in the same language. "Does your mother know how incredibly shameless you are?"

"No, so don't tell her." He traced her lips. "Been wanting to kiss you all day." Fitting action to words, he leaned down and skimmed his lips over hers, wondering if his desire for his soldier wife would ever diminish. "Over the next few days, I'm going to make love to you in every possible way and in every inch of this room . . ." He coaxed her up and she rose to her knees on the chair cushion so they could devour each other more comfortably. ". . . in our bed, on the rugs before the fire, outside on the verandah under the moon."

Her trembling response stretched his manhood lustily. "Then I'm going to take you on top of my piano and paint your nipples with honey . . ."

She drew in a shuddering breath and his desire roared. There was a knock on the door. "Mr. Noah. Your food."

He shot angry eyes towards the interruption. "Be right there, Bonnie." He left her lips reluctantly. "Don't move."

"I wouldn't dream of it."

"Welcome home, Mr. Noah."

"Thank you, Bonnie," he replied, taking the tray from her hands. "My wife, Pilar's lying down. I'll introduce the two of you later."

"That would be fine. Please tell her welcome."

"I shall."

Walking back into the bedroom, he paused upon seeing his wife folded up on the chair fast asleep. Shaking his head a bit disappointedly because he'd planned on making love to her, he set the tray down. Going over, he picked her up gently, placed her on the bed and covered her with a light quilt. She never moved. He stroked a finger down her cheek. They'd come a long way since leaving Florida, and in truth she'd earned some rest. "Welcome home, Pilar. Thank you for your sunlight."

Leaving her, he picked up the tray and carried it out to the sitting room so she could sleep in peace.

Chapter 18

At dinner later that evening, Pilar met the rest of Noah's family members: his brothers, the strongly built Logan who typified how she imagined an American ranchman would look, and Drew whose devastating Spanish handsomeness would've set the hearts of the ladies at the Old World king's court all aflutter. Then there were their wives, the stylish and beautiful Mariah with her golden eyes, and Billie with her warm smile and unblemished chocolate skin. She also met their children, the mostly quiet Little Maria, dressed in trousers of all things, and the rambunctious Antonio, who seemed to take great pleasure in throwing things from the tray of his high chair, until his mother gave him the look that children worldwide knew and feared. Last but not least was Alanza's husband, Max Rudd, who was as handsome as her sons and offered Pilar a kindly nod.

Logan raised his wineglass. "I propose a toast to Noah and Pilar and to a long and happy marriage."

"Hear, hear!" came the boisterous response.

Pilar smiled over her glass. She was pleased that everyone had welcomed her so warmly. She was still a shade nervous but everyone seemed to be going out of their way to put her at ease. She couldn't help but notice how wrenlike she looked in comparison to her two peacock sisters-in-law. Although they weren't overdressed, she, in her plain blouse and cheap skirt, looked like a poor relation. She didn't want to be an embarrassment should they go calling, so she hoped she could convince Noah to fatten up her wardrobe a bit and that Billie and Mariah could help her choose more stylish attire. Her sister Doneta knew all about those kinds of things but she wasn't there. Feeling sadness descending again, she turned her attention back to the myriad conversations flowing around the large table.

Alanza asked, "Pilar, would you mind if we had a small gathering to introduce you to the neighbors?"

Billie said, "Don't let her fool you, Pilar. When she says small you can count on three-quarters of the state being invited."

"Hush, Billie," Alanza said around a smile.

Mariah weighed in, "Billie's right, sister. Mama doesn't know how to do anything by half. Her annual birthday party lasts almost a week."

Pilar blinked and looked to Noah for guidance.

"You may as well say yes and get it over with because she's going to get her way. Always does."

"Rotten children," Alanza groused mockingly.

Drew added, "But in Mama's defense, her affairs are usually a lot of fun."

"Unless you don't care for dancing bears or clowns or jugglers," Logan quipped.

Pilar was now staring. *Dancing bears!*

Max said, "Your mother-in-law is extravagant to a fault but her heart's in the right place."

"Thank you, Max," Alanza said. "I think."

He saluted her with his wineglass.

"So," Alanza asked, "do I have your approval?"

"I suppose so."

"Good."

Mariah said happily, "Which gives us wives an excuse to go shopping."

Billie raised her glass. "Amen!"

Logan eyed his wife. "Just leave us menfolk enough money to pay the hands and the bills, okay?"

Everyone chuckled, including Pilar, who decided she might just enjoy being in this family after all.

Dinner ended a short while later and Noah and his brothers drifted outside to have their cigars. Logan was immediately called away by one of the hands, who rode up to tell him that cows were escaping through a break in the perimeter fence.

Drew said to him, "We'll tell Mariah. You go on. We'll need those cows if the women are going shopping soon."

Laughing, Logan hurried off to retrieve his horse, leaving Noah and Drew behind on the patio.

"So, Noah," Drew said. "Are you happier than when I saw you last, or is it just my imagination?"

Noah struck a match to the end of his cigar and passed the flame over to his brother, who did the same. Noah exhaled slowly. "It's not your imagination."

"Tell me first about this pirate. Your cryptic telegram had us all confused. What happened to her?"

"Like I told Mama earlier, I married her."

Drew began choking. Strangled by the smoke, he said between coughs, "Pilar is the pirate?"

Noah smiled while his brother tried to clear his lungs. "Yes." He then told him the story, giving him the details about the initial abduction, his search to find her, the sword fight, and the subsequent marriage. "The moment I crossed swords with her it was as if my whole world opened up."

"So you asked for her hand?"

"I did, but in the end, she asked for mine." And he explained.

"She's a rebel gun smuggler, possibly wanted by the Spanish? That's quite the story, baby brother. Our family has always needed a female revolutionary. Now, we're complete."

Noah laughed. "Revolutionary or not, I had to have her, Drew."

Drew stared his way in wonder. "Are you sure you're Noah Yates?"

"I had to ask myself the same question, but I'm on the way to an improved version of me."

"You two seem happy, no?"

"We're working out the knots. I felt bad about taking her away from her family but her mother and uncle agreed she needed to leave Florida as soon as possible. Her uncle is the man with the cigar business I told you about when I was here for Mama's wedding. These are his cigars we're enjoying, by the way."

"She has no father?"

"No. Killed by the authorities during the civil war there. She joined the rebels when she was fifteen."

"Not many men can claim to have a swash-buckling revolutionary soldier as a wife."

"Who's from a family of thieves and forgers."

This time Drew didn't cough but his eyes went as wide as plates, so Noah explained that part of the story as well.

"Does Mama know about this?" Drew asked when he was done with the telling.

"No, and I'd prefer you keep it between us." And he knew Drew would. Being only a few years apart, Noah had always been closer to him than to his nine-years-older half-brother, Logan.

"I'm not trying to be offensive but do I need to hide my Billie's jewelry?"

Noah cut him a look.

"You just said the woman's a thief, Noah."

"No hiding of jewelry is necessary. I promise."

"Okay. I'll take you at your word."

Silence reigned as they both mined their thoughts. Finally, Drew asked, "Do you love her?"

Noah thought that over for a few long moments before admitting, "I'm not sure but it's probably the closest I'll ever get. I have fun with her, Drew."

Drew smiled, "Then I will love her for you."

Their eyes met and Drew said, "Welcome home, Noah."

Noah nodded and they savored the remnants of Miguel Ventura's cigars in a shared brotherly silence.

"Did you enjoy yourself at dinner?" Noah asked Pilar. They were in the sitting room relaxing together on the settee before bed.

"I did. Your family is very nice. I especially enjoyed Billie and Mariah."

"They're two very special ladies, my brothers are lucky to have them."

"Should I be worried about the party your mother wants to throw for us?"

"No. More than likely it'll be a huge affair but as Logan pointed out, it'll be fun. And as Mariah said, you'll get to shop for gowns and anything else you need or may desire."

"I need a bit of everything. Nightgowns, under-things, ladylike shoes, as you called them."

"Get what you need. Personally, I prefer you without clothes but that might be frowned upon outside these doors."

"Crazy American." She quieted for a moment

and her voice took on a serious tone. "How soon can my mother and sister come for a visit?"

"We can send them a telegram tomorrow if you like."

"Truly?"

"If that makes you happy. Truly."

She threw her arms around his neck. "That makes me happy. Thank you, Noah."

He eased her onto his lap. "You wouldn't happen to have a reward for your very generous husband, would you?"

"How about generosity being its own reward?"

"How about I tie you down the way you did me and pleasure you until you beg me to make you come?"

"Now that sounds interesting."

He threw back his head and laughed. "And you call me shameless."

They both went quiet as they assessed each other. She reached up and gently touched his scarred cheek. "How did you get this?"

"The night I was shanghaied. It was the captain's way of teaching me obedience. He said I was too pretty anyway."

"It was done with a knife?"

"Yes."

She leaned up and pressed soft lips against its length. "Each time we make love I will kiss it so that when you look in the mirror you will think of your shameless Cuban wife, and not that *bastardo*."

Noah's heart soared. He pulled her closer and kissed her with such a deep intensity he heard himself moan in the silence. She was his balm, his angel, his reason to exist. And true to her vow, she planted kiss after fervent kiss on the visible manifestation of his darkness until the scarred flesh pulsed brightly in tandem with his need. They undressed each other slowly, languidly taking the time to pay carnal homage to each unveiled expanse of bared skin. Gloriously nude, they kissed their way into the bedroom and onto the bed. He worshipped his way down the planes of her body, pausing to lick and suckle until she was twisting and open. When he finally entered her, she arched and crooned with uninhibited delight. The first thing he'd wanted to do when he returned home was make love to his wife and he did, again and again, and again, until the energy to breathe was all they had left. And in the aftermath, she kissed his scar one last time, was eased close, and they gave their sated bodies over to the arms of Morpheus.

The next morning dawn was just pinking the sky when Pilar awakened beside her snoring, sleeping husband. She watched him fondly. She was unable to pinpoint the exact moment he worked his way into her heart but he had, somehow, and she enjoyed having him there, even though the aftermath of the nightmare he'd had the night they first made love continued to cause her worry. She didn't know enough about love to call what she felt for him that, but if wanting to be with someone for the rest of her life was a component, then she was in love. Whether he felt the same way didn't really matter. What they had together was more than enough for her to be content.

Slipping quietly from the bed, she eased open the doors on the large wardrobe and took down one of his dressing robes. Soundlessly donning it, she tiptoed from the room. Outside on the verandah the air was chillier than she'd expected but she pulled the heavy black robe closer and curled up in one of the chairs to watch the sunrise. His rooms were on the back of the house and the sight of the mountains against the sky was comforting because they reminded her of home. Yet this was her new home. Were she being greedy, the ranch would be on a wide expanse of water so she could wake up each morning to the sounds and sights of the sea, but the blessings she'd been given were many and she was content with that, too. Now, she had to carve out a new life. Pilar the rebel, soldier, and thief had been left behind, replaced by a woman who resided in a world of wealth and ease. She had much to learn in order to take on the role, but she looked forward to her future and finding her place in it. She wondered if it was too early to approach his mother about the charity work Noah spoke about.

"*Buenos días, querida.*"

She turned to see him dressed in a brown robe, standing in the doorway. "*Buenos días.*"

He walked over and gave her a soft kiss before moving to the railing and looking out at the dawn. "Didn't expect to find you gone when I woke up."

"I wanted to watch the sun come up. I'll leave you a note next time." Had her absence worried him?

He chuckled.

"Do you have plans for the day?" she asked.

"I thought maybe we'd ride into town and send the telegraph to your mother letting her know we arrived safely and to invite her and your sister to visit. Then if you like, we could tour the ranch."

"I'd like that."

"Do you ride?"

"Of course."

"Then after breakfast we'll find you a mount and head for town."

"Does this town have a name?"

"Stewart. It's named after one of the forty-niners who established the first trading post here."

"Forty-niner? Who or what is a forty-niner?"

So while they watched the sunrise, he told her all about California's golden past. They then dressed and headed downstairs to have breakfast with his mother.

• • •

"Where's Max?" Noah asked as he and Pilar took seats at the table.

"Gone to Stewart to help with the construction."

In response to the question on Pilar's face, Alanza explained, "There was a bad fire earlier this summer. Most of the buildings were either burned to the ground or severely damaged. Max is overseeing the new construction."

"How'd the fire get started?"

"It was arson tied to a scheme to abduct Billie and Tonio."

"Drew's wife and son?"

"Yes."

"Oh my goodness."

"Billie engineered her own escape, and Drew found the baby with friends. It ended well, thank heaven, but it all began with the fire."

Bonnie entered with their food. Pilar had been introduced to her last night during dinner and the Irishwoman blessed her with a smile before departing.

"Pilar is not used to an American breakfast, Mama, which is the reason for the skepticism on her face."

She shot him a mock quelling look. "It's not what I'm accustomed to, but I'm getting better with it."

Biting into a strip of bacon, he grinned. "She calls bacon, belt leather pork."

291

"Hush!" she said over a laugh. "Now you're going to get me in trouble. Your mother will think I'm not appreciative."

His mother said, "I do understand, Pilar. We rarely eat the food I grew up on, either, and I do miss it."

"Then may I cook sometimes? I'd like to contribute to the household."

"Certainly."

"Your son frowned on my offer to work in your stables or help clear brush, but he said you do charity work with your church. May I join you sometimes?"

Noah smiled at the surprised look on his mother's face.

She viewed his wife with new interest. "Billie and Mariah have never made such an offer."

"I've cleared brush all my life."

"We have hands for that, but we can certainly discuss you helping in that way."

"Good."

Noah saw that Pilar was pleased and because she was, he was as well.

Chapter 19

At first, Noah had been concerned about Pilar's ability to handle the big dark gray mare she chose to ride on their trip to town, but once they set out and he saw her confident seat and the way she handled the reins, his concerns melted away. "You ride well."

"Moonlight is a good mount. Aren't you girl?" She gave the mare an affectionate pat. "She's faster and stronger than the old plodders I rode back home."

The horses were reined to a walk so he could enjoy her company and she could get a good look at their surroundings along the tree-lined road. "The countryside is much different from Cuba, isn't it?"

"Yes. No bananas or mangoes or coffee bushes. No wild-colored flowers. No sweetness in the air. Everything here seems to be either green or brown."

"We have flowers here."

"Where?" She made a point of standing in her stirrups and looking around as she shaded her eyes and peered off into the distance.

He laughed. "Okay, they may not be readily visible, but we do have some."

"California has its own beauty though."

"Are you throwing me a bone?"

"Yes."

They rode on.

"Where'd you learn to speak English?"

"From my father. My pirate grandfather spoke English as well. My sister and I speak mainly Spanish, as does my mother, but my parents encouraged us to learn both."

"Which do you prefer?"

"The Spanish because it's more beautiful and descriptive."

He agreed, but English was the language of business, so he rarely spoke Spanish away from home.

"If we have children I would like for them to speak both," she noted.

"I'd prefer that as well, and my mother will insist upon it. She speaks only Spanish to Tonio and Little Maria." Noah thought back on their passionate night and wondered if the intensity had created a child. If so, he'd be pleased.

When they reached town, the air was alive with the sounds of hammering. Planks of wood and bricks sat in piles up and down the main street while an army of men worked on the roofs and built walls.

"This is the construction your mother mentioned?" she asked as they dismounted in front of the telegraph office.

"Yes. Looks like they've made quite a bit of headway."

They went inside and a man with gray hair looked up. "Morning, Noah. Didn't know you were home. How are you?"

"Doing just fine, Will. Want you to meet my wife, Pilar. Pilar, this ornery old cuss is Will Sally, a longtime family friend."

"Well, aren't you a pretty little thing. Welcome to Stewart."

"Thank you. Pleased to meet you."

"Same here."

"We'd like to send a telegraph message to her family in Florida."

"Sure. Just write out what you want it to say."

Noah took one of the pieces of paper set out for that purpose and wrote down what he wanted and showed it to Pilar. She approved the wording so he handed it to Will.

"Got a letter for you here, too, Noah. Came in a few days ago." The telegraph office also doubled as the valley's post office.

Noah recognized the handwriting on the envelope right off. It was from his friend and business partner, Kingston Howard. He tore it open and the words made him sigh.

"Bad news?" she asked.

"More disappointing than anything else. He wants to dissolve our partnership so he can spend more time with his wife and children."

"I'm sorry."

"He's been talking about stepping away for over a year now. Guess he made his decision."

"Where does that leave you?"

"For the moment, without a partner, but I'll figure it out."

Will asked, "Noah, do you want to wait for the reply from Florida? May take a while."

"No, just send someone out to the ranch, if you would."

"Will do. Nice meeting you, Mrs. Yates."

"Same here, Mr. Sally."

Noah planned to wire Pilar's family the money for their train tickets, too, so they moved on to the bank. As they crossed the unpaved street, he nodded at familiar faces and stopped to introduce Pilar to some of the people he knew well. Having spent the past ten years mostly at sea, he wasn't as familiar with everyone as maybe Drew and Logan were. To many of the newcomers in the valley, he was known simply as the Yates brother with the scarred face.

Drew, the bank owner, was in the lobby when they entered. "Morning. I expected you two to be still sleeping off all that traveling. Are you just showing my lovely sister-in-law around or are you here on business?"

"Both." When Noah explained what he needed, Drew had one of the two clerks handle the matter.

"I'm looking forward to meeting your family, Pilar," he said genuinely.

"I can't wait to see them."

Noah thanked him. With their goals accomplished, they mounted their horses and rode back to the ranch.

Upon their return, both noticed the large number of carriages and buggies parked near the house. "What's going on?" Pilar asked.

"I have no idea."

As they turned their mounts over to the hands, they paused to watch a large group of women dragging sawhorses out to the field behind the house. Billie and Mariah were among them. When Billie saw Noah and Pilar, she walked over, and Noah asked, "What is all this, Billie?"

"My ladies' gun club. We're meeting here today. Pilar, you're welcome to join us."

"I've never heard of such a thing," Pilar said eyeing the women as they continued to set up.

"We can teach you how to shoot."

"I'm already familiar with firearms but I'd enjoy participating."

Noah had never heard of such a thing either. "You two go shoot. I'm going inside where I'll be safe."

Both women rolled their eyes.

Inside, Noah found his mother in her study and asked, "Are you in here for your safety?"

She laughed. "The first time they met here a few weeks back, someone's bad aim brought down one of the cows. Logan was furious. We've since learned to move the livestock a safe distance away. The hands give the area a wide berth, too." She eyed him silently. "Do you have time to sit and talk to your mother for a bit?"

"I do." And he took a seat in one of the big leather chairs and glanced around. "I've quite a few memories of this room."

"Good or bad?"

"A bit of both. Drew and I spent many a day standing here squirming while you yelled at us for yet another outrageous stunt."

"Like the time you painted yourselves with whitewash and snuck into Aunt Rosita's room in the middle of the night and pretended to be ghosts? You scared her to death. She never came to visit us ever again."

"And you took great joy in scrubbing us with turpentine until we were raw. To this day the smell of it makes my stomach churn." He paused a moment and thought back. "Then there was the time we brought the cows in the house to see if they could climb the stairs."

She chuckled. "It's a wonder I let you two live to be adults. I was convinced you were going to put me in my grave."

"And there were a few times we thought you were going to put us in a grave."

"It's good to have you home again, Noah. Any idea how long it will be this time?"

He shrugged his shoulders. "I'm not certain. I

got this today." He passed her the letter from Kingston and sat silently while she read it.

"Are you going to carry on alone?" she asked and handed it back.

"Again, I'm not certain. I've already been thinking about making some changes. I have a wife now, too. She and I both love the sea, but living aboard ship for the rest of our lives isn't very practical, especially once there are children to raise."

"I like Pilar."

He went quiet as her gamine face shimmered across his mind. "She's given me back the parts of myself I seem to have lost."

"Then my prayers are answered. I miss who you used to be, if I can say that."

He inclined his head. "Understood. I doubt I'll ever be him again, but there are pieces of him inside, and all of me loves you still. Very much."

"I remember when you were born and how tiny and perfect you were. It had been raining for days and we worried whether the midwife would be able to get here, but she made it. I had no name for you though. Your father, Abraham, said, we might as well name you Noah since it appeared we'd be needing an ark if the rain didn't stop."

"It saddens me that I don't remember anything about him."

She nodded. "You all favor him in your own way."

"That's good to hear." He wondered if Drew or Logan shared his lack of memory about the man who helped give them life.

They talked a bit longer about the message he'd sent to Pilar's parents and how well she rode, which of course Alanza was pleased to hear, and about Alanza's plan to take her daughters-in-law on a shopping trip in a few days.

"We'll stay overnight and be back the next day."

"I appreciate you doing this for Pilar. Just let me know how much she'll need."

"I will. I hope you won't mind me spending some of my own money on her as well."

"It wouldn't matter if I did, would it?"

She shook her head.

In turn he dropped his, amused as always by her queenly force-of-nature ways. He might have changed, but his mother had not.

And on that, he rose from his chair. "I'll let you get back to whatever you were doing."

"I enjoyed our visit."

"As did I. It's good to be home."

"Would be nice if you dropped your anchor for a while."

He gave her a crisp salute. "Aye, aye, Captain."

"Out!" She laughed, pointing.

He walked over, placed a kiss on her upturned cheek, and exited.

Up in his room, he walked out to the verandah to see how the gun ladies were progressing. The air was filled with the crack of bullets firing and he wondered if he was in any danger. He spotted Pilar among the dozen or so in attendance. She was behind a raised rifle and appeared to be aiming at two tin cans sitting atop a sawhorse a few feet away. She squeezed the trigger. Her shoulder jerked with the rifle's kick but her bullet didn't hit either can. Billie said something to her and Pilar sighted again. She fired again and again, hit nothing. Chuckling, he went back inside.

"Don't be so tough on yourself, Pilar," Billie said to her. "You'll be fine. You're used to pistols. Remingtons are different."

"I couldn't hit the can though, Billie." She couldn't believe how inept she was.

"At least you're familiar with firearms. When we started out earlier this summer, some of the women were afraid of the gun, the bullets, and the sound of the gun going off."

"And I," Amanda Foster said interrupting, "used to close my eyes every time I took a shot. Accidently shooting one of Logan's cows cured me quick, however."

Pilar asked around a surprised laugh, "You shot a cow?"

She nodded.

Billie grinned. "Logan was so angry. He made all the ladies go home and didn't speak to me for days."

Amanda patted Pilar on the back. "You'll be fine, Pilar. And again, welcome to the valley."

"Thank you."

Pilar jumped in to help with the cleanup and putting the sawhorses back in the barn. Once that was accomplished, she thanked her sister-in-law for her patience and went inside to find Noah.

She got lost on her way to his wing and found herself in a suite of rooms where all the furniture was covered with white dust sheets. Standing there in the hush, she wondered who the rooms belonged to, but since there were no answers, she closed the door behind her as she exited and started out again. Upon hearing faint notes from a piano she followed the melodic sound as if it were a trail of bread crumbs, and when she pushed the door open, there he sat, head lowered, fingers moving over the keys. Whatever he was playing had an airy lightness to it that made her think of a clear, blue-sky day. His skill was well apparent. She remained standing by the door so as not to interrupt, but he glanced up and the smile he sent her way caused her own to curve her lips.

He stopped. "How'd the shooting go?"

"I was awful. Had no idea shooting a good rifle would be difficult. I used to hunt with an old musket but—"

"You hunt?"

"Everyone who lives in the countryside hunts, Noah. If you don't, you don't eat."

"Yet something else your mother-in-law will love about you."

"She hunts?"

"Quite a bit."

Pilar walked to the piano. "What were you playing?"

"A Beethoven sonata."

"I made a wrong turn and somehow ended up in a suite of rooms where all the furniture was covered, then I heard the music and it led me here."

"You were probably in Drew's wing. He and Billie and the baby lived there until recently."

"I didn't mean to interrupt."

"Nothing to apologize for. I was just about done anyway. Would you like some lunch?"

"I would." After the ride into town and the time spent with the gun club, breakfast seemed like years ago.

"Then let's go down and see what we can beg from Bonnie."

Bonnie packed them a picnic lunch and they drove a wagon out to the river that bordered the property. As he set the brake, he said, "It's not the ocean, but it is water."

"And it's peaceful, too," she replied taking in the wide-open land.

"There are some seats down at the edge. We can eat there."

"Lead the way."

Once they were settled they ate in a companionable silence.

"These seats are very convenient."

"Max built them for my mother after my father died so she could come down here and grieve in peace. Everyone takes advantage of them now."

She peered down the bank. "Whose home is that?"

"Drew and Billie's. He'd wanted to build on that spot since we were adolescents. Max designed it and the men of the valley helped with the construction."

"Do Logan and Mariah live near the water, too?"

"No, they're closer to the main house."

"Where do you want to live?"

"Not sure. Didn't think about it much until you came along," he said, showing a smile. "Had planned to spend the rest of my life aboard a ship."

"Not very practical if we have children."

"No." Noah wondered what their children might look like. Would they have their mother's proud chin and expressive dark eyes? Would they be tall and robust like him and play the piano? The only thing certain was that they wouldn't bear his scar and that was a good thing. "Do you mind waiting until I sort out what I'm going to do—now that Kingston is stepping away from our partnership—to decide where we want to live?"

"Not at all."

"My brothers and I each own a parcel of the ranch. Mine is west of here, so if we do decide we want to be here with family, we have a spot."

"Can we go see it?"

"Sure."

They gathered up the leavings of their meal and drove west, where the terrain was more wooded and rugged. The river was wider and the current ran stronger as well. There were huge boulders mid-stream and the mountains on the far bank stood like sentinels against the cloudy sky. Noah had always enjoyed the wild, untamed feel of his portion of the ranch and if he did decide to build a home there he'd have no complaints.

"I like this," she said to him while balancing herself to walk out onto a rocky shelf above the fast moving water. "Reminds me a bit of home. I wouldn't mind living out here."

"Good. It's close to the main house but far enough away to give us all the privacy we need."

"And since I have such a shameless husband, privacy will be needed."

He placed his hands on her waist and swung her down to where he stood and looked down into the face that was altering his take on life. "I'm not the only shameless one."

"And aren't you glad?"

Laughing, he eased her in against him and savored the feel of her arms as they tightened around him. "Have I kissed you today?"

She leaned back and cracked, "If you have to ask, you have some rectifying to do."

"Give me your sassy mouth, woman."

As always, kissing her filled his soul with light, warmth, and joy. He drew back and asked, "How's that?"

She shrugged. "I've had better."

He swatted her behind and pulled her in again, this time kissing her so deeply and thoroughly she softened against him and a quiet purr of pleasure slipped from her lips. "Better?"

"Very much," she whispered.

Suddenly the wind picked up and with it came fat, cold drops of rain.

"Where'd this come from?" she screeched as it began pouring.

Laughing, they ran for the wagon. He pulled a tarp out of the bed, threw it over their heads, and headed the horses towards home.

That evening after dinner they were playing checkers in the sitting room when a knock sounded on the door. Pilar got up to answer but not before giving her pieces a quick look to verify their locations because she'd recently discovered that her husband liked to cheat. "Keep your hands off my men, Noah Yates."

He dramatically placed his hand over his heart. "You wound me, fair maiden."

"Yes I will, if you touch anything."

When she opened the door, there stood Max.

"Message from the telegraph office. It's addressed to you, Pilar."

"Thank you."

"You're welcome."

After closing the door, she excitedly tore open the envelope and read:

Happy.

Leaving soon as possible.

Love,

Doneta

"It's from my sister! They're coming!"

"That's good news."

"Yes, it is. I can't wait to see them. It feels like years since I saw them last."

She looked down at the board, saw his alterations, and looked up into his eyes. "You're truly rotten, do you know that?"

"Me?"

"Be glad I don't have my rapier."

"We definitely have to get you one. That fire in your eyes makes me want to bring out my own sword, if you get my meaning."

Heat scalded her cheeks. "I don't make love to cheaters."

"Really?" he asked in a silken voice that hardened her nipples and increased her pulse. "I'll bet I can make you willingly lie on this table and do all manner of shameless things with me before the clock on the wall strikes the time."

She gave the clock a quick glance. Five minutes.

"And I say you can't." She knew she was destined to lose and in truth looked forward to it, but this was a dance, a game—their own seductive version of *Destreza* and she hoped they'd play it together for the rest of their lives.

He made a great show of slowly removing the checkerboard from the table. His gaze was searing as he went about the task and her anticipation made it difficult to maintain her regal pose.

"I think I want you partially nude," he voiced and she swayed in her chair. "You can start by removing your blouse."

Like a puppet on a string her fingers slowly worked the buttons free. Seconds later, she set it aside.

"Now the corset, but don't remove it. I love the way it frames your beautiful breasts when it's open . . ."

Pilar complied, making sure she did it slowly so she could savor the blaze in his gaze. Seducing him while he seduced her filled her with a decadent sense of power. Holding his eyes, she ran her hand lazily over her bared breasts. He smiled.

"Stand please. Drawers next. You have about two minutes before the clock strikes." She stood and even though he hadn't asked, she lifted her skirt so he could watch her unveil herself and tossed the garment aside.

He soundlessly patted the tabletop. She let her skirt drop and eased herself up onto the edge of the large wooden dining table. He kissed her and the passion possessing them both flared and bloomed. He filled his hands with her breasts, then bent to greet them until she purred and the drumbeat between her thighs quickened.

"Lie back."

She did and he embarked upon a meandering journey that paid smoldering tribute to all she had to offer. Her skirt was skimmed up to her waist and his touches widened her thighs in beguiling invitation. He dropped his head and the lick he placed there sat her straight up with shock. A smile curved his lips and he gave her a brazen wink. The clock chimed. His finger found her, again bringing with it such dazzling delight, she laid down again and let herself be enjoyed until she was arching and twisting and gasping. When the orgasm tore her apart, she screamed so loudly, her hand flew to her mouth to keep from being heard back in Cuba and rode the wave of her completion until she finally washed up on the shore, spent. And as she lay there, shuddering, open, and satisfied, he entered her boldly. Groaning with the glory of his hard pulsing conquering, she greedily took him in and began to move in tandem with his rhythm. It was a memorable evening and she was certain she'd never see their dining table the same way again.

Later that night, while Pilar slept, a sated Noah sat in the sitting room. He picked up the message from her sister and read it. It would be good to see them. He was certain her mother worried how her daughter was faring and he wanted her to see with her own eyes that he and Pilar were making a good go of their life together. There were still issues and questions to be mulled over, like how he would restructure his life now that King wanted out, where he and Pilar might live, and finding something to keep Pilar busy so she could contribute without taking on the ranch with a machete. He smiled. What a woman.

Chapter 20

The following morning, Pilar wanted to take Mariah up on the invitation she'd extended last evening at dinner to visit her dress shop. Noah's plan for the day was to ride into town with Max and Logan and lend a hand with the ongoing construction.

As they got dressed, he noticed her smiling to herself.

"Why the smile?"

"Just thinking about last night. With all this lovemaking there's a good chance we've made a child."

His eyes shone with pleasure. "Would you prefer a girl or a boy?"

"Having seen the havoc Tonio causes in just the short time we've been here—definitely a girl."

He laughed.

"What about you?" she asked. "Do you have a preference?"

"Yes, a boy. It's what most men want, I think. Either way you'll make a wonderful mother."

"I'm glad you think so. I'm not so certain."

"You'll do fine."

She hugged him tightly, then raised herself on her toes and placed a soft kiss on his scarred cheek. "Thank you for your confidence. I'll see you when you return from town."

"It will probably be late in the day."

"As long as you come home to me, I won't care."

He drew her into his body and held her as tightly as she'd held him. "Thank you for marrying me."

And as always, she quipped, "I didn't have a choice."

He gave her a swat on the behind. Laughing, she left the room.

Alanza was seated on the patio having coffee when Pilar stepped outdoors.

"Are you off to Mariah's?" she asked in Spanish.

Pilar smiled at this very special woman and responded in her native tongue. "Yes. She said to follow the trail out front, correct?"

"Yes."

"Is it okay if I ride over? It's been so long since I've ridden on a regular basis, I'm enjoying being on horseback."

"Of course. Feel free to ride anytime, anywhere—except back to Florida of course."

Pilar inclined her head. "I'm afraid it's too late to get rid of me, now."

"Then you're enjoying being here?"

"I am. More than I ever believed I would. Your family has been very kind."

"We take our family ties very seriously, and thank you for what you've done for Noah. He hasn't been the same since being shanghaied but he seems more relaxed now, and I attribute that to you."

"I'm not sure that's the reason but I enjoy being with him and hope he feels the same way."

"He does. I've seen the way he watches you. Having him back is more precious than anything I can ever possess. You'll stay in my heart forever."

Pilar found the words very moving. "Thank you."

"Now go before I begin to cry, but don't forget, we'll be leaving for the train early tomorrow for our shopping excursion."

She'd announced the outing last night at dinner and although Pilar was a bit apprehensive about having to pick out clothes and such, she was looking forward to getting to know the three women better. "I will be up and ready. Oh, before I go: I received a telegram last night from my sister. She and my mother will be here soon."

"How exciting, then we'll wait and have the party for you and Noah when they arrive. Would that be okay?"

"That would be wonderful. Thank you."

"You're welcome. I'll see you later on."

She inclined her head and struck out for the stables.

When she arrived at Mariah's house, she was surprised at its size. Unlike Alanza's big sprawling home, this one was smaller and cozier and the bright flowers blooming on both sides of the porch framed it beautifully.

Mariah opened the door to her knock. "Morning. Come on in."

The interior was as lovely as the exterior. It was well furnished but not extravagant.

"My shop's in the back."

Her second surprise was to see Billie there. Pilar had enjoyed her company immensely at the gun club meeting. "Morning, Billie. I wasn't expecting to see you here, too."

"I didn't want to hear all your secrets second-hand. You're our new sister and 'Riah and I want to know *everything,* especially how you and Noah met. He seems so mysterious."

Mariah laughed. "Can I at least take her measurements before we subject her to the 'Inquisition'?"

"Of course. I'll go out and make sure the prisoners haven't escaped."

Pilar's confusion must have shown because Billie explained, "Our babies. They're playing in the pen we call the Baby Jail."

Pilar laughed.

"And with a third prisoner coming in the spring we may have to add a wing."

"You're carrying?"

"Yes and praying every night and day for a girl this time."

Pilar thought back on the conversation she and

Noah shared earlier. Would she be next in line to bring a new Yates baby into the world? Setting that aside, she glanced around Mariah's small shop and was amazed at all the fabric and notions stored and displayed so neatly. A few dress forms held gowns in progress. "I must say I admire you being able to do all this. I can replace a button and do a few stitches but not much more."

"I grew up working in my mother's dress shop in Philadelphia."

"That must've been fun."

"No. My mother's a witch. I couldn't wait to come to California."

"Do you have family here?"

She shook her head. "Alanza ran an advertisement in the Philadelphia newspaper for a housekeeper for Logan and I got the job and wound up being his wife."

"How long have you been married?"

"Just two years."

"And Billie and Drew?"

Billie stepped back in on the heels of the question and provided the answer. "Drew and I have been married since May."

Pilar was confused.

"I know," Billie replied. "He and I knew each other in the past, which is why our son is older than our marriage. And before you hear it from someone outside the family, I was Drew's whore in those days."

Pilar began coughing, which put quiet smiles on the faces of her sisters-in-law.

"Let's get you measured while Billie tells you the whole sordid tale."

So Pilar listened while Billie talked and Mariah had her turn this way and that, and wrote down numbers. Pilar had no idea what she was being measured for but assumed she would be told the purpose at some point. Billie's story of the abduction of her and Tonio was as heartbreaking as it was frightening.

"But DuChance fell into the bay and drowned," she said, winding down the tale. "Drew found our son and we all came back to the ranch."

Pilar was pleased that the ordeal had ended happily.

"So, Pilar, now your turn. We know you were the pirate that took his boat, but why?"

"Needed it to pick up some guns."

Twin mouths dropped.

Pilar chuckled. "Let me start at the beginning." So she told them about her ties to the rebels and her need of a ship and then about Noah's abduction.

Mariah said, "He was very upset about it when he came for Alanza's wedding but he said nothing about being abducted."

"Manly pride, probably," Billie cracked.

Pilar then told them about Noah showing up at her uncle's birthday party, the sword fight, and his demanding her hand.

"You fought him with a sword?" Mariah gasped.

"And here I thought my marriage was a story for the ages," Billie said in a wondrous tone. "Mine is a child's bedtime story in comparison."

She then told them about the visit from Calvo. "So I had no choice but to ask him to marry me and now, we're here."

"Smart woman," Mariah said. "He probably fell in love with you the moment he set eyes on you that night though."

This was the second time Noah being in love with her had been mentioned that day. "Not sure he loves me, but we're getting along rather well." She thought about last night on the table and couldn't hide her smile.

As if possessing the abilities of a mind reader, Billie quipped, "Our husbands are known for their manly talents."

"Billie!" Mariah gasped around a laugh.

"What?" Billie countered. "Are you saying Logan doesn't make you scream?"

Mariah's fair skin showed her blush to the roots of her hair.

Pilar raised a hand. "No bedroom complaints here."

Laughter greeted that confession and Billie announced, "Pilar, you are now an official member of the Yates Sisters-in-Law Society. Glad to have you aboard."

"Thank you."

● ● ●

In town, Noah was working on the new roof that would top off the new general store when Will Sally appeared below and called up, "Message just came in for you, Noah."

While the rest of the crew continued to work, he came down the ladder and took the message from Will's outstretched hand. "Thanks."

"You betcha."

It was from Lavinia Douglas. His lips tightened.

Will be in Stewart tomorrow.
Father wants to talk to you.
Business proposition.

He wondered what the business proposition entailed. Walter Douglas was one of the most well respected shipyard owners in San Francisco. Whenever the *Alanza* had been in need of repairs, Noah had taken her to Walt. With no way to answer his questions, he pocketed the message and climbed back to the roof.

After leaving Mariah and Billie, Pilar mounted her horse and decided to tour the ranch. She saw the orchards and the grapes, the fields where vegetables were grown, and the small army of workers tending them. She marveled again at how large the Yates enterprise was and the bustling air of the place. It was so different from where she'd grown up. There'd be no foraging for food here or nights sleeping on an empty stomach, which is why she was so set on finding a way to contribute. It would be her way of saying thank you.

Heading back to the house, she came upon some corrals holding horses. She knew from talks with Noah that Logan often rounded up wild horses and brought them back to the ranch to sell. One of her uncles had been an excellent horseman and spent his life breaking them in for the wealthy to ride. She and her cousins often helped and it was a task Pilar particularly enjoyed, but the method being used by these ranch hands made her stop her mount and watch. Apparently preparing the horse for the saddle involved nothing more than a rider mounting and letting him be thrown until the horse tired and gave in, or at least that's how it appeared. Granted, she hadn't seen the earlier process, but she found the practice quite strange. Standing outside of the corral were a group of men egging the rider on and howling gleefully each time the rider sailed off the back of the bucking horse. She watched for a moment more and dismounted.

The animal was a beautiful cinnamon-gold stallion and from the way he was charging around and bellowing, he was not pleased. She walked to the fence and stood next to a man watching the show inside the enclosure.

"Hi there, little lady. Are you Noah's wife? Name's Eli Braden."

"I am. Name's Pilar. A pleasure meeting you."

The rider was tossed again, to the sound of

much laughter and razzing. He dusted himself and scrambled out of the way of the rearing and bellowing stallion.

"What's going on here?"

"Breaking a horse. Been at it a couple days. Doesn't want to take a rider or the saddle."

"I wouldn't want a stranger on my back either after living my entire life free."

He paused and raised an eyebrow.

"It's not my place to tell you your business but an animal as beautiful as that deserves better than to have his spirit broken just so he can be ridden."

"Are you speaking from experience?"

"Yes."

Once again the rider tried to get into the saddle and the stallion did his best to flatten the man against the rails of the fence in an effort to keep that from happening.

"We've been doing this for years, Mrs. Yates."

"Understood, but there are other ways. May I go into the ring?"

"No."

She watched the horse tear around the enclosure at full speed as if seeking the exit. Upon not finding one, it reared angrily and the rider ran to the fence to keep from being a victim of its hooves. "Why not?" She felt sorry for the animal.

"Because if you get hurt, Logan will kill me, and whatever is left, your husband will kill."

"Don't be ridiculous. Does the horse have a name?"

"No. Only been here less than a week."

Pilar debated what to do. The stallion continued to storm around the pen. "I will take full responsibility if anything happens."

"Doesn't matter. Logan will still feed me to a buzz saw."

She sighed. "Have you ever struck or hurt a woman, Mr. Braden?"

"Of course not."

"Good." She climbed the fence and dropped down into the pen.

"Hey!"

The men went silent as the dead. The rider stared at her in confusion. Pilar asked him, "What's your name, sir?" The horse reared and bellowed again.

"Uh, Danny, ma'am," he said keeping one eye on her and the other on the horse.

"Danny, I'm Pilar. Nice to meet you."

He swallowed. "Same here."

"Would you do me a favor and remove the horse's saddle please?"

His eyes shot to Eli.

The horse, breathing heavily, reared and screamed his anger.

"I don't think he's going to let me do that, ma'am."

"Okay. Leave me alone with him then."

His alarm mirrored the others. "I don't think that's wise."

"It's okay. Bring me a bucket of water please. He's probably thirsty."

He looked to Eli, who leaned against the fence and asked, "Mrs. Yates, please come back out here before you get hurt. If something happens, I'll never forgive myself."

"I've done this many times, and please call me Pilar." She made deliberate eye contact with the stallion for the first time. It stared back angrily.

"Please, Pilar."

"A bucket, Mr. Braden. I promise you, I won't be hurt. I know what I'm doing."

As if sensing her determination, he sighed and surrendered. "Okay. Danny, get the water, and Pilar, when your husband and his brothers kill me, have them send the pieces to my lady Naomi in town."

The water was delivered and handed over. Pilar carried the heavy container to the center of the pen and set it down. She sat in the dirt beside it. "Mr. Braden, I need you and the men to move away from the fence and to stay very quiet."

They reluctantly withdrew and once they did, they watched and waited.

When Noah and his brothers returned from town one of the stable hands told them what was going on over at the horse rings and they hurried over. He expected to find her on the ground broken like a rag doll, but instead found her simply sitting in the dirt and talking to the stallion in soft Spanish as it stood watching her warily from the corner of the pen.

Noah asked Eli, "Why's she sitting down? Was she thrown?"

Logan asked Eli, "What the hell is going on?!"

"Keep your voices down. She wants everybody to be quiet."

Noah scanned for any injuries. "Is she hurt?" he asked urgently.

"No. She hasn't tried to ride him. She's just been sitting talking real quiet. Been in there about thirty minutes now. Told me the way we were trying to break the stallion was the wrong way."

Logan gritted out, "Noah, go get your wife."

Noah ignored him for the moment to ask Eli, "Why'd you let her in there?"

"Had no choice. She climbed the fence over my objections. What is it with your wives? They don't listen very well."

Drew cracked, "Aren't you the one marrying Naomi Pearl in less than two weeks?"

"Touché," Eli replied.

Noah was still concerned about her safety. The huge stallion could charge and kill her if he decided to, but she seemed to be perfectly calm.

"Noah," Logan warned. "If she gets hurt, Lanza will feed us to the bears."

"She seems fine, Logan, besides, she might take

a machete to us if we make her come out. How about we just wait and see what happens."

Logan threw up his hands.

Drew asked, "Does she really know what she's doing?"

Noah shrugged. "I've no idea." This was an aspect of his wife he knew nothing about—probably one of many.

Eli said in a loud whisper, "Keep your voices down."

So they quieted.

Logan quietly fumed.

In the pen, Pilar, speaking Spanish, was telling the horse a fairy tale about a poor little country girl who married a prince. She knew the horse had no idea what she was saying, but it was the sound of her voice that she wanted him to become familiar with and when his ears went up a few minutes ago, he apparently was. She also wanted to remove the saddle. It was far too soon in the process for the men to have put the weight of it across his back, but she doubted Titan, as she'd name him, would let her get close enough to do so. For now it would have to remain. "I know you're thirsty," she cooed softly. "Crazy Americans have bruised your pride by capturing you and putting you in this pen." She slowly moved her hand back and forth through the water letting the horse hear the sound. "I'd be angry, too. Come and drink. I won't hurt you or even touch you this time. I promise."

Every now and then the horse would rear and race around the enclosure as if wanting her to know who was really in charge. Pilar kept a keen eye on him but she didn't move.

An hour after taking her seat, half the ranch had drifted over to watch the goings on, including Alanza, Billie, Mariah, and the children.

Finally the horse began a slow approach and then stopped about three feet away. He reared and called a challenge. Pilar eyed him. He eyed her. She continued to speak softly. "I'm not going to move, my bronze titan, so come and drink and we can get to know each other."

And to the amazement of everyone outside the pen, the horse slowly closed the space, dropped his large head and drank. A few cheers went up, but were sharply silenced by those nearby and Pilar was grateful. She'd come too far to have the stallion spooked by loud noise now. He drank almost greedily.

"You've had a pretty rough day, haven't you?" she said sympathetically.

Once the horse drank his fill, he retreated to the far side of the pen.

She didn't mind. She'd accomplished her goal for the day. Rising slowly to her feet, she walked over to the fence, climbed to the upper rung, and simply sat where the silent watching stallion could see her.

Out in the crowd, Noah was grinning from ear to

ear. He now understood her request to work with the animals but he'd dismissed her out of hand. She'd certainly showed him.

Drew asked Logan quietly, "What's she doing now?"

"How the hell do I know, but I think she just got hired, especially if he'll let her ride him."

Smiling at the pride in Logan's voice, Noah turned from his brothers and turned his attention back to watching his incredible wife.

She sat there for another thirty minutes, then climbed down.

As she approached him, Noah asked her, "Can we talk now?"

Amusement sparkled in her eyes. "Yes."

"That was pretty incredible."

"Save the applause for when he actually allows me on his back. And Logan, let him be. No one is to try and ride him. I'd like to come back later and take the saddle off and the bit out of his mouth. It's probably hurting him."

"Okay," he said, eyeing her like he wasn't sure who she might be. "Anything else, boss?"

"No. I think that's it for now. Oh, and I've named him Titan in honor of Cuba's 'Bronze Titan' General Antonio Maceo. I hope that's okay?"

Logan grinned. "It is."

"I know that my way of doing this will probably take longer than what you and your men are used to, but that's a very special animal. Who will his owner be?"

"You. He's the most bullheaded stallion I've ever had. If you can ride him. He's yours."

Her eyes widened with surprise and she glanced back at Titan. "Truly?"

"My wedding gift. So, work your magic, little sister. I just want to watch and learn."

She threw her arms around his waist. "Thank you!"

"You're welcome."

Later, after dinner, night was falling when she and Noah went back out to the corral. Titan was still wearing his saddle. According to Logan in order to get it on him initially, they'd had to hobble his legs, and it had taken every hand he had to accomplish the task. Pilar didn't want the stallion to suffer through that again, but it might be necessary in order to remove it.

Watching the horse race around, she marveled at his beauty. She called to him. His ears perked up and he charged in her direction but didn't stop, and ran right by her. She laughed.

"You're not going back in there, are you?" Noah asked in a concerned tone.

"No, but I wish I wasn't going to San Francisco in the morning, so that I could when I get up."

"You'd rather play with a horse than shop? No woman alive has ever said that."

"Hush," she replied watching Titan rear. "He's

showing off. He knows how handsome he is."

"I think I'm getting jealous."

"And you have good reason. I can't believe Logan offered him to me."

"My brother has a generous soul beneath all that crustiness. He just doesn't like to show it."

She shivered as the night air rolled in. "It's getting chilly. Time to go." She gave her stallion one last look. "Good night, Titan."

He reared. She shook her head at the display and she and Noah walked back to the house.

Chapter 21

As the Yates women left the train in San Francisco, Pilar couldn't contain her excitement. A few days ago, when she and Noah had come through the city, she had no desire to see the sights, all she wanted was to reach the ranch and never see another train, but now, she was embarking on a grand adventure led by Queen Alanza, and the only thing that would've made the day better was having her sister Doneta by her side. Doneta was on her way, however, so Pilar put her longing away and enjoyed her present company. Their first stop was a beautiful hotel. She was certain when they entered the grand lobby that segregation would get them thrown out on their rears but either the place didn't support the demeaning practice or the clerk behind the counter was too afraid of the imperious Alanza to enforce it. Whatever the reason, they were ushered into a luxurious suite of rooms that opened up to each other allowing them each a bed of their own. The window looked out on the bustling city streets below.

Because Billie and Alanza knew San Francisco well, Mariah and Pilar let them lead. They visited shops that sold gossamer-thin night wear, seductive corsets, and silken hose. Pilar had no idea what she was doing, so Billie and Mariah jumped in and picked out garments for her that were in some cases scandalous—like a little black corset with emerald buttons—and beautiful, like an indigo silk kimono. They chose bedroom attire that would for sure make Noah's eyes pop from his face and roll around on the floor, and Pilar couldn't wait for him to see her wearing it and then slowly strip it away. There were shoes to try on and purchase, hats to laugh over, and other items to add to their haul. They made sure Pilar purchased day gowns and shirtwaists and skirts. Because she had no coats, Alanza gifted her with two. By the time it came to consider trudging back to the hotel under the mountainous weight of their purchases, Pilar was stunned by all the money they'd spent but giddy with the joy of the hunt. Who knew shopping could be so exhilarating. On the way back, Alanza insisted on stopping at her favorite chocolatier, an establishment known as Ghirardelli's, and the ladies bought a bevy of the sweets. As they left the store, Pilar saw a shop that had something displayed in its window that immediately caught her eye. "I have to go in here."

The others followed. The interior was an eclectic mix of goods ranging from toys to writing implements and paints and brushes to music boxes and beautifully ornate fans. She selected some oil paints for her husband as a thank-you to him, and while Mariah and Billie conversed over the toys, Pilar asked the gentleman behind the counter, "How much is that rapier in the window?"

He looked her up and down and sneered. "Probably more than you can afford."

Pilar stilled. "Excuse me?"

"And even if you could afford it, I wouldn't sell it to a woman."

She closed her eyes to keep her temper in check. "Are you the owner?"

"I'm his eldest nephew."

By then Alanza had stepped to her side. "What's the problem, Pilar?"

"I would like to purchase the rapier displayed in the window but this one says I can't afford it and even if I could he wouldn't sell it to me because I'm a woman."

"What does a woman know about swords?" he tossed out.

"If I geld you with it beforehand may I purchase it?"

He laughed. "Of course, but as I am classically trained and you know nothing about such things, why don't you just pay for what you have in your hand and leave the store?"

Pilar, muttering murderously in Spanish strode over to the window, grabbed the rapier and stalked back.

The clerk's eyes went round.

"Choose your weapon!" she snapped.

His laugh was thinner. "Surely you don't expect me to—"

"You just insulted my skill, my gender, and my purse and you expect me to simply titter and go away? Get a sword, and if your classically trained arse has to go home to retrieve one, I will wait."

The other customers in the store began gathering and whispering.

An older gentleman came out of the back. Seeing the steel in Pilar's gaze and her equally steely hold on the rapier in her hand, his shocked eyes flew to his red-faced nephew, back to Pilar and then to the silent but coldly furious Alanza, standing at her side. He cleared his throat. "What's going on here?"

From behind Pilar, Billie said, "Aldo. How are you?"

His eyes widened. "Billie?"

"Yes. How've you been?"

He coughed and sputtered, "Uhm, fine. Been fine."

"Your nephew has insulted my sister-in-law. Told her she can't afford the sword she's holding and that even if she could he won't sell it to her because of her sex. She's challenged him to a sword fight. You might want to have the other customers leave. I hear she's very good with that thing, and you don't want them to see all the blood that's going to flow when she teaches him some manners."

His eyes popped. He turned and glared at the nephew before smacking him smartly across his forehead. "We are here to sell merchandise! Go in the back!"

The nephew fled. Aldo adjusted his vest and visibly drew in a breath. He smiled. "My apologies, ma'am. My nephew is an idiot. Of course you may purchase the rapier."

"Thank you."

So the purchase was made. Aldo even threw in the jewel-encrusted leather scabbard for free as a token of goodwill. Pilar was pleased.

Once outside, Alanza turned to Billie. "I'm almost afraid to ask, but how do you know him?"

"When I first started working at the Black Pearl, he was one of my best customers."

They laughed and walked the short distance to their hotel.

That night, as Pilar lay in bed, she thought back on the wonderful day. She'd actually learned to shop for herself, with help of course, but when the time came for purchases in the future she wouldn't feel so lost at sea. She wondered how Noah was doing and if he missed her. The same held true for her beautiful stallion. She couldn't wait to get home and see them both.

That morning, Noah awakened in bed alone. He'd become so accustomed to Pilar's warmth beside him he'd slept fitfully without her and decided she could never spend the night away from him ever again. He could fully imagine her reaction was he insane enough to actually make such a demand, but he did miss her. Luckily for him, she and the rest of the family's ladies would be home later in the day. It was his hope that she'd had a good time and made purchases that she found pleasing. It was also his hope that the gift he had for her upon her return would please her as well. While traveling the world, he'd seen many beautiful things, but one of the most beautiful was a ruby necklace shown to him in India. He'd purchased it on the spot with the intentions of presenting it to his mother because he knew he'd never have a woman in his life worthy of it, but for some reason he never did. It was as if a part of him knew it wasn't meant for her even though the stones spoke to her fiery personality, so he'd locked it away along with a small treasure trove of other fine pieces in the family safe. He planned to retrieve it and ask his mother to present it to Pilar as a gift from her. Granted, him presenting it to Pilar personally would undoubtedly put a feather in his cap but he didn't want her to think he was attempting to buy her affections, nor did he want her to turn it down because she deemed it too expensive. He remembered the shock on her face when he paid for the room in St. Louis.

In the meantime he looked forward to the visit by Walter Douglas and Lavinia. He was interested in hearing what the man had to say, especially now that his own enterprise was presently at loose ends. With the *Alanza* at the bottom of the sea, he was still in the market for a ship to replace her, so he planned to talk to Walt about having a new one built or choosing one from any that might be available for sale in his shipyard.

After getting dressed, he headed downstairs for breakfast. He entered the dining room to find Max and his brothers already at the table and the babies close by in their high chairs. Little Maria was eating and having a toddler conversation with Logan while Tonio was happily decimating orange slices in his chubby little hands. Pulp clung to his face and there was juice all over his clothes. Drew sounded a tad frustrated as he told his son, "Antonio, either eat the oranges or I'm going to take them away."

Tonio continued to mangle the fruit. Drew confiscated the slices that were still "alive" and Tonio cried in protest. Drew used a napkin to rid the tear-filled face of the orange pulp. Retaking his seat he groused, "I can't wait until Billie returns."

"You should have had a nice, quiet little girl." Logan offered.

Drew said wryly over his coffee cup. "I'll remind you of those words when she gets older and the boys start coming around."

"That's what shotguns are for," Logan pointed out and popped half of a biscuit in his mouth.

Noah helped himself to the mountain of scrambled eggs in a bowl in the center of the table, and added bacon and Bonnie's excellent biscuits to his plate.

Max said, "I hear Pilar's folks are on the way."

He nodded and began eating. "She's been missing them terribly. It'll be nice to have her mother and sister here for however long they plan to stay." He then told them about the business meeting with Walt and Lavinia Douglas.

"Any idea what he wants?" Max asked.

"No."

"Weren't you keeping time with her once upon a time?" Drew asked.

"Once upon a time."

"Does she know you're married?" Logan asked.

He nodded. "She was at the train station when Pilar and I arrived. When I made the introductions she made some thinly veiled snide comments."

Max stated, "Hope she minds her manners while she's here. Your mother's liable to take a bullwhip to her otherwise."

Noah agreed and hoped Lavinia would be on her best behavior—for her own sake.

After breakfast, Logan and Drew took their children and the Baby Jail over to Lupe Guiterrez's, one of the ranch's employees to spend the day; then, accompanied by Max, they rode into town.

While Noah waited for his guests to arrive, he went up to his room and sat down at the piano. A musical composition had been running through his head for the past few days and he wanted to begin working on it. He already knew what it would be called: *Pilar's Sonata.* Taking out some paper, he penned in a few opening measures and began to play. He wanted the piece to be the musical embodiment of their relationship: the mystery of their initial encounter, his quest to find her again, and the danger and excitement of the sword fight—a movement he planned to title "La Verdadera Destreza." It would be followed by another representing the passion they found in each other, but for the moment, he'd concentrate on the sonata's beginning.

Two hours later, Bonnie interrupted him to let him know his guests were waiting in the parlor. He thanked her but was keenly disappointed about being pulled away from the piano. The notes had flowed well and he'd made quite a bit of progress. Rather than be rude and make them wait, he tucked the sheets away and left the room.

As he entered the parlor Noah was taken aback by how thin and gaunt the formerly robust Walter appeared.

"Pretty shocking, aren't I?" Walt cracked thinly.

"I have to agree, yes."

Lavinia looked sad.

"Docs say I have six months tops, so you and I need to talk."

Lavinia interrupted him. "Is there a boardinghouse where we can stay? I didn't see anything in town when we got off the train. We'll be heading back tomorrow."

"You're more than welcome to be our guests here. We've plenty of room."

"I'd like that," Walt said with a smile. "Haven't seen that beautiful mother of yours in a dog's age."

"She and my wife and sisters-in-law are in San Francisco but are due back later today."

"Vini said your wife's a foreigner?"

Noah could fully imagine how Lavinia must've described Pilar. "She's Cuban, Walt. How about I have Bonnie bring some refreshments out to the patio and we can sit and talk there."

They agreed and once they were settled, Walt said, "Beautiful place you have here."

"Thank you. It's all my mother's doing."

"I've yet to meet your mother," Lavinia pointed out. "You never brought me here to meet her."

"I'll amend that when she returns."

"Vini's been spitting nails all week about your new wife. Told her years ago you weren't going to marry her. A man's not going to buy the cow when he can get the milk for free." He laughed at that, which brought on a fit of coughing. He pulled out a handkerchief and dragged it across his lips.

Lavinia's eyes burned fiercely.

Hoping to derail the embarrassing trajectory of the conversation, Noah asked, "So, Walt. What did you wish to discuss?"

"Want to sell you my shipyard if you'll have it."

That surprised him. "Why me?"

"Because you know ships and the sea, and you'll do right by what I've built. She wants me to leave it to her but she's a woman. No man's going to want to do business with her, which means my yard will be broke and shuttered within a year."

"I've worked in that shipyard since I was nine years old," Lavinia protested in defense of herself. "I know the business like the back of my hand. I've kept the ledgers, approved drawings, planed wood."

"Doesn't matter, Vini. You're not getting it. And neither is that foreigner you found. Man doesn't know a sail from a porthole."

"He'll let me run things though."

"I don't care. Don't like the looks of him."

She sat back against her chair and blew out a disgusted breath.

Noah wondered who the man was. Noah would be the first to agree that Lavinia's smarts and confidence made her more than capable of owning and running the shipyard, but unfortunately her father was correct. The times being what they were, closed-minded men would only see her gender. His mother had faced similar barriers while building the ranch, but as word spread about the quality and virility of the prize bulls she'd leveraged her last dollars to invest in, cattlemen eagerly brought their cows to Rancho Destino to be bred and didn't care that the bulls were owned by a woman. Shipyards were a different matter. There were many quality establishments up and down the coast. If buyers or captains chose not to patronize Walt's yard because of Lavinia's hand on the tiller, they could take their business elsewhere and be assured of the same level of service.

For the next hour Noah and Walt talked about the shipyard's workers, pending orders, and other aspects of the business, but as the afternoon waned, it was plain that Walt was tiring.

"How about I show you up to your room so you can rest?" Noah asked.

He sighed. "Hate that this sickness makes people coddle me like a child, but I'll take the offer. We can finish this later. Just need to know whether you're interested or not though."

"I am. I'll want to see your ledgers to make a final decision but I'm pretty confident we can work out a deal that benefits us both."

"Good." He struggled to his feet. Lavinia reached out to help, but he angrily pulled away and set his cane. "Quit your fussing."

Her lips tightened.

Noah watched silently.

"Thanks for hearing me out," Walt said to him. "Had circumstances been different, would've been proud to have you as a son-in-law."

Noah offered no response and escorted them inside.

Bonnie prepared adjoining rooms for them in his mother's wing. Once Lavinia got her father settled, she rejoined Noah on the patio and sat down heavily.

"He's blessed to have you," Noah said.

"Someone needs to tell him that."

"None of us knows how we'll respond when death stares us in the face." For a moment memories of the island flitted across his mind. He forced them away.

She picked up her glass of lemonade. "True, I just wish he'd see clear to leave me the business."

"It's the times."

"To hell with the times. I've given that shipyard my life's blood and it isn't fair. Nor is it fair that you've replaced me with an ill-dressed—"

"Don't say it. I never broached marriage with you and we both know it, so for you to malign my wife in my own home is tasteless and uncalled for."

Her chin rose. "My apology."

And then, as he struggled to control his temper he heard the sweetest sound he had all day: "We're back, Noah!"

Pilar's smile as she strode towards him was all he needed to forget about Lavinia. "You look stunning," he said. She was dressed in a fashionable well-cut ladies' suit the color of dark sapphires and there was a saucy little hat of the same hue on her head.

Only then did she notice he had company and from the way her eyes cooled, she wasn't pleased. To head her off at the pass, he said, "Pilar, you remember Lavinia Douglas?"

"Of course. How could I forget?" she replied with a false smile.

"She and her father are here about a business matter. He's upstairs resting. They'll be our guests until tomorrow."

"Welcome to our home. I hope you and your father will enjoy your visit."

"Thank you," Lavinia responded tersely.

"Noah, you'll not believe what I found. Wait here. I'll be right back."

Whatever Lavinia was thinking she was wise enough to keep it to herself.

Pilar returned carrying something wrapped in brown paper. Due to the odd size it was impossible to guess what it might be. She set it on the table and her eyes shone excitedly as she tore the paper away. When the scabbard appeared, he laughed. "Oh my."

"It's so beautiful, and just the right weight." She unsheathed the rapier, took a few swipes at the air, and her grin matched his.

Lavinia sneered. "Why on earth would you waste Noah's good money on that?"

The point of the rapier was suddenly an eyelash away from the hollow of her throat and she froze, her eyes wide.

"Just in case I have to defend my family," Pilar replied meaningfully. Drawing the blade down, she turned to Noah. "I'll let you finish your business."

She and the rapier made their exit. Noah wanted to cheer at the way she'd put Lavinia in her place.

When Pilar stalked into the house, Alanza took one look at her face and asked, "Whatever is the matter?"

"Nothing. Noah has company and she wanted to know why I'd waste his good money on this?" She raised the rapier. "So, I answered her."

"She isn't bleeding all over my beautiful patio, is she?"

"No ma'am."

"Good. Bonnie told me Walt Douglas and his daughter Lavinia are here. I met him years ago. I've not had the pleasure of meeting her, although I know Noah kept company with her off and on over the years."

Pilar found that news pleasing. If Noah had never brought her to the ranch to meet his mother, he couldn't've been that serious about her. Pilar told her about meeting Lavinia at the train station.

"Was she unpleasant to you?"

"Yes and she made a few snide comments about how badly dressed I was."

"Well, truthfully, you were, but it was very rude of her to mention it aloud."

Pilar chuckled. Walking over she gave Alanza a

kiss on the cheek. "Thank you for the shopping trip. I had fun."

"You're welcome."

"Now, to change out of these clothes and go say hello to my horse."

"Have fun."

Pilar was standing by the fence watching Titan race around and the sight of him warmed her heart. She noted the saddle was gone and was pleased by that as well. Calling his name made his ears perk and he stopped running to watch her just as Logan and Eli rode up.

"Figured you'd be here," Logan said. "Mariah said you ladies had a good time buying up everything that walked by."

She laughed. "We did indeed. I see the saddle's gone."

Eli said, "We had to hobble his legs though. Pitched a fit."

"Poor baby."

"Some baby," he cracked.

"What did you do with the saddle?"

"In the tack room."

"Can it be placed in the corner of the corral instead, so he'll get accustomed to seeing it?"

"I suppose," Logan replied doubtfully and shared a look with Eli, whose expression mirrored his. "Where'd you learn this?"

"From my uncle." And she told them about his

employment by wealthy Cubans. "Sometimes he would sleep in the pen with the horses he was training. I knew you and Noah wouldn't allow me to do that."

"You're right."

Eli said, "Never ever heard of anybody sleeping with a horse to break him."

"It's not breaking, Mr. Braden. It's training."

"If you say so."

Logan asked, "What's next?"

"A few more days of sitting with him and once he knows I'm not a threat or plan to hurt him, I want to tie two long leads to his halter so that we can walk together and I can begin to voice-train him to stop and go."

Logan studied her. "That works?"

"Yes, it does."

"So what did your uncle do with horses that didn't want to be broken—I'm sorry, trained—no matter how much patience he showed them?"

"Then he would do something he learned from a slave who once had a master in Texas. He'd take the horse out to deep water in the bay, mount it and make it swim and stay there until it got so tired that once it was back on firm ground, Tonio would be able to ride it."

Logan stared.

"A horse can't buck if its feet don't touch the ground. According to the Texan, some of the people who live on the Gulf train horses that way."

Eli looked astounded. "Never heard of anything like that."

"I watched him do it more than once."

Logan shook his head. "I'll have to keep that one in mind. Well, we'll leave you to your horse. Eli and I have chores to finish before dinner so I'll see you then."

Eli added, "My Naomi's anxious to meet you. She and Mariah and Billie are good friends."

"I look forward to meeting her, too."

They turned their mounts and with a touch to their hats, rode away.

Chapter 22

The Douglases joined the family for dinner and as always it was a happy affair. The women told stories of their adventure—especially Pilar's confrontation with the clerk over the purchase of her rapier, and the men talked about Tonio putting Drew through his paces. From where Pilar sat next to her husband, Walter Douglas seemed to be enjoying himself, though he looked very frail. He smiled kindly when the two of them were introduced, but his daughter Lavinia alternated between shooting daggers Pilar's way and watching with what appeared to be envy as Pilar and Noah interacted and shared whispers.

They were finishing up dessert when Alanza announced, "Before we all go our separate ways for the evening, I'd like to thank Walt and Lavinia for joining us. Please feel free to visit us again."

Walt nodded. Lavinia offered a tight smile.

"And, I have a gift to present to my newest *nuera*."

Pilar gave Noah a quizzical look but he shrugged his shoulders in response.

From the pocket of her skirt, Alanza withdrew a long black velvet box and walked over and placed it on the table in front of Pilar. "Open it please."

While everyone watched eagerly, she undid the lid and gasped at the sight of the beautiful ruby necklace inside. Her hand flew to her mouth and tears sprang to her eyes. She stared up at Alanza, who said softly, *"Bienvenida a la familia."* Welcome to the family. Pilar stood and hugged her through her tears.

Noah appeared moved as well. "Thank you, Mama."

"I gave diamonds to Mariah and emeralds to Billie and now rubies to you for your fiery spirit." She placed a kiss on Pilar's cheek and retired to her seat at the head of the table. At the other end, Max raised his glass to his wife and smiled.

Applause and cheers filled the dining room; even Walt Douglas clapped with enthusiasm. His daughter didn't but Pilar didn't care, she was too busy staring wondrously at the rubies strung like small flecks of fire on the intricately worked gold chain.

As dinner ended, Mariah and Billie each gave her happy hugs and marveled over her rubies. Noah walked over to give his mother a hug and a kiss on the cheek. They spent a few more minutes laughing and conversing until finally Billie and Drew and Mariah and Logan left to pick up their children from Lupe so they could head home. The still awed Pilar picked up her rubies and walked over to Noah sitting at the table with Walt. "I'm going to go up," she informed him.

"I'll join you as soon as Walt and I finish our business."

"That's fine. Nice meeting you, Mr. Douglas."

"Same here."

She gave her husband a quick kiss and walked to the staircase. Looking back she saw Lavinia watching her. Pilar ignored her and climbed the stairs.

Up in the room, the first thing she did was marvel over her gift. Never in her life had anyone given her anything so costly or beautiful. Removing it carefully from the box, she draped it around her neck and after managing to do up the clasp, she studied herself in the bedroom's stand-up mirror. It was exquisite. She had no idea where she'd wear something so elegant but just being able to gaze at it was enough. Only a short time ago, she'd been a poor woman from the country-side whose main mission in life had been her country's future, and although her hopes for it continued to burn bright in her heart, she was now wearing rubies. It was quite a change and she wasn't sure how to reconcile the two or even if she should. On the one hand, she thanked the saints for the incredible family she'd married into but on the other hand, she thought of what the money spent on the necklace could buy back home: food, guns, books for the makeshift schools scattered across the island, medicine. She'd never dishonor Alanza by pawning the gems, but there had to be a way for a woman married to a man as wealthy as Noah to help back home, or better yet, maybe she could convince Logan and Eli to hire her to help with the horses so she could earn her own money and not have to rely solely on Noah's funds. It was something she decided to talk to him about when she got the chance. Until then, she glanced around at the many bags holding all the new clothes and things she'd purchased in San Francisco and smiled.

When Noah entered the sitting room an intoxicating scent floated lightly on the air. He drew it in deep even as he wondered what it was and slowly closed the door behind him. "Pilar?"

"In here," she called back.

He walked into the bedroom and saw a wealth of garments spread out on top of the bed. Skirts, shirtwaists, corsets that made him grin and when he finally turned his eyes to his wife her sensual attire stole his breath. The indigo-colored nightgown was held up by two small frogs, one on each shoulder, then flowed in open panels down to the short-heeled black velvet mules on her feet. His rubies on her necklace glowed like beads of fire around her throat.

"Do you like?" she asked and twirled. The gown lifted and split, showcasing the gleaming sides of her hips, thighs, and legs, and he was instantly as hard as a beam.

He cleared his throat. "Very much."

"How about this?" She picked up a black French corset with tiny emerald-colored buttons and held it against herself. Imagining himself freeing the buttons hardened him further. "Planning on spending the rest of your life in the bedroom, are you?"

She laughed and set the corset down. "I purchased something for you."

"Better than the corset?"

"Maybe, maybe not. You can decide." She handed him a large box. He recognized the name emblazoned on the front and what he felt for her in his heart multiplied a hundredfold. Opening it showed neatly nestled pots of oil paints and water colors. There were pencils and pieces of colored chalks and charcoal, and three brushes with heads of varying sizes.

"I hope this makes up for my selling your painting to the man on the dock—at least a bit."

That in the excitement of shopping with his mother, she'd taken the time to bring him back something so personal . . . "It wasn't necessary, but thank you, Pilar."

"You're welcome. Have you finished your business with Mr. Douglas?"

"For the moment. If all goes well, I'll be buying his shipyard."

"Oh my."

"Mama will probably want to take her bullwhip to me because it means we'll be moving to San Francisco. Would you mind?"

"No, of course not. A woman follows her husband, especially to a place that's on the water. Throw in the fact that I really enjoyed being in the city and I'll be ready to go whenever you give the word."

"How about we try and find a home on the water or have one built?"

"That would be wonderful."

"If you don't mind, I'm going to take the train back to San Francisco with them tomorrow and look over the books. I want to get this done as soon as I can. Walt's not sure he'll see the new year so . . ."

"I understand. I think I can spare you for a few days so you can secure our future."

Taking in her beauty and savoring her spirit, Noah had no doubts he loved her—fully, totally, and forever. He had no way of knowing if his feelings were reciprocated but it didn't matter. She was willing to be with him in spite of his imperfections and the brokenness that still lingered inside and he loved her for that as well.

"Now," she said, "I truly missed your kisses while I was away. Would you care to offer me a few to welcome me home? Then you can decide if this gown meets with your approval. Your hard-earned money purchased it, after all," she quipped, making reference to Lavinia's words of earlier.

His glowing eyes roamed over her in the way his

hands longed to. "We should probably move the things off the bed first."

"Agreed."

So under the soft light of a turned-down lamp, Pilar received a bevy of passionate and humid kisses to welcome her home, and Noah found that he approved of the gown so much, he'd be handing over his hard-earned money so she could purchase more—as soon as possible.

The following morning Noah and the Douglases made their departure. Walt slept most of the way to San Francisco and Noah noted that he seemed to have withered further overnight.

"Thank you for letting Father and me stay with your family last night."

"You're welcome."

"I wish someone would gift me with rubies that way."

"My mother's very generous."

"So I saw. That necklace would have looked lovely on me, don't you think?"

Noah didn't reply to that but instead said, "Tell me about the other buyer your father mentioned."

"He's from Brazil, and although he doesn't own a shipyard, he's incredibly wealthy. He's moving to California and is looking for businesses to buy and invest in."

"But Walt turned him down."

"Yes. Which I find very shortsighted, considering

Martinez is prepared to pay a sizeable sum. I'm willing to throw in with anyone who'll allow me to be at the helm."

Noah couldn't fault her for that.

"Would you allow me to be?"

He thought that over. "You're more than capable, Lavinia, and I'd've been open to discussing your continued ties had you been more gracious with my wife. Pilar's very important to me. I'll not have her subjected to your snide and belittling comments."

She didn't like that. "Then for old time's sake, will you at least meet Mr. Martinez?"

"Is this the man you're championing?"

"Yes."

"Why? Your father's already made me the offer."

"I've told him about you and he'd like to meet you to talk about possibly being an investor."

Noah saw nothing wrong with that. "That'd be fine but I'm heading home tomorrow."

"Then I'll send a note around to see if he's available for dinner this evening."

Noah nodded. If Martinez wanted to invest, Noah would be a fool to not at least listen.

Walt awakened when it came time to leave the train. "I'm going to let Vini show you around, Noah. Too tired for anything else today."

"I understand."

"When are you going back to the ranch?"

"I was hoping to sometime tomorrow."

"Okay. Look at the books tonight and come see me in the morning. I'll have my lawyer meet us with whatever papers we need to sign to close our deal."

"Agreed, and thank you again for your faith in me."

"You're welcome."

A driver was waiting for them at the station and once they reached the Douglas home, Walt was met by the nurse hired for his care and was slowly ushered into his bedroom.

"Is there anything I can get you before we leave?" Lavinia asked. "Something to eat or drink, perhaps?"

"No, thank you. Let's just get on our way, if you don't mind."

"Just give me a moment to send one of the servants around with a note to Mr. Martinez."

Once that was done, they climbed back into the coach.

The ride through the city and down to the docks showed how San Francisco was growing. New buildings were cropping up everywhere and the traffic was thick. The city being one of the largest and busiest seaports in the nation, they passed all manner of waterside operations on the way to the shipyard: from ramshackle saloons and gambling dens, to docks both large and small that accommodated everything from whale-oil production to those tied to horses and hay. The sights and smells made him long to be on the water. He'd asked Drew to draw up the papers to dissolve his company and to send Kingston his share of the profits, but he wondered how feasible it might be to resurrect the import-export business as an offshoot of the shipyard. In theory, such a merger sounded feasible but in practice he wasn't sure. He'd have to investigate it further once he'd owned the shipyard for a while.

The Douglas shipyard was nestled along a stretch of similar-sized establishments, and its wharf and docks were busy with activity as wooden hulls and masts were moved around on pulleys and small cranes and sent to the various stations to be turned into seaworthy vessels. The air was loud with sounds of hammers, machinery, and the voices of men. Some of the workers stopped to watch his approach and he inclined his head in greeting. The gesture was returned, albeit warily. He wondered if they were aware that the business was up for sale. Lavinia offered no such greeting, however. He asked himself if her aloofness was rooted in her gender and she didn't want to encourage familiarity, or did she look upon the men whose labor provided the money for her fancy hats and suits as simply workers and therefore beneath her acknowledgment? Knowing Lavinia he figured it was a bit of both. The office was set back from the wharf in a large warehouse.

The men inside were building, too, but these hulls were larger and sleeker. "Cutters?" he asked.

"Yes. It's a commission from the Coast Guard, our first. If they approve the final product and we get it done on time, I'm hoping they'll let us build more—well, you, since you'll be the new owner."

He found that news encouraging. Having a government contract would go a long way in adding not only stability but profits as well.

For the rest of the afternoon, he viewed the files that held pending orders, met some of the supervisory workers, and walked around both inside and outside to see what he could see. By the time the yard closed down for the day, he was a little tired and a lot hungry, but he was pleased with the operation.

"Are you ready for dinner?" Lavinia asked.

"Yes, but do you want to go back to your house and check on your father first?"

"No. The nurse is there. I'm sure she has everything in hand. Do you have a room for the night?"

"Not yet, but I have the names of a few hotels. I'll seek them out after we're done with dinner."

"You're welcome to stay with Father and me. We have the room."

"No, thank you."

"Are you afraid I'll slip in and ravish you in the middle of the night? I know you claim to be happily married, but I wouldn't mind playing the role of mistress, Noah."

He sighed impatiently. "I don't need a mistress, Lavinia."

"If you change your mind, let me know."

"Let's go meet your man." Would she never stop? How she could even think he'd want to share himself after meeting his beautiful wife was beyond him. He hoped this would be the end of the matter once and for all, because her constantly throwing herself at him was tiresome.

The restaurant was not a place where he'd eaten before but it was well appointed and clean.

"Ah, he's already here."

Noah looked in the direction she indicated and swore his eyes were deceiving him. His surprise must have shown.

"What's wrong?"

"That's Martinez?"

"Yes. Have you met him before?"

"Oh yes, but not as Martinez. I know him as Victorio Gordonez."

As they approached the table, Gordonez smiled at him through the white powder on his face. "Ah, Mr. Yates, we meet again."

"Gordonez. I hear you're calling yourself Martinez now."

"I'm known by many names. Please, have a seat. I hoped you enjoyed touring the shipyard with the lovely Senorita Douglas."

"I did."

Lavinia seemed taken aback, but no more than

Noah. Knowing Walt Douglas, he'd taken one look at the man and turned down the offer flat. Noah didn't blame him.

"And did you ever find little Banderas?" he asked.

"I did," but offered nothing else. He was fairly certain Lavinia had already told him about his unsuitable Cuban wife so unless Gordonez inquired further, Noah had no intentions of discussing Pilar.

As they reviewed the menu, Noah asked, "Why in the world are you looking to buy a shipyard here?"

"I have various interests all over the region, so why not? San Francisco is a thriving city. A shipyard would be a sound investment and having my own ships would facilitate the movement of some of the goods I deal in."

"I see."

The waiter appeared to take their order and afterwards departed.

"So," Gordonez asked, "how much gold would it take for you to back away from her father's offer?"

"Pile it as high as the Great Pyramid in Giza and that still wouldn't be enough."

"Suppose I dangle your wife's location under the nose of the Cuban authorities? I hear she's wanted for questioning."

Noah raised his wineglass. "Then I will kill you."

Gordonez stiffened. Lavinia gasped.

Noah added coolly, "It's been over ten years since I took a man's life, but endanger Pilar and I will happily send you to hell. Do not doubt me."

"Such passion."

"Such truth."

"Then we are at an impasse."

"Yes, we are."

Gordonez raised his glass. "To your health, Mr. Yates."

It was yet another threat, but he chose to ignore it. Instead, he stood and tossed some bills on the table. "My portion of the meal. If you'll excuse me, I'm no longer hungry."

Without a backwards glance, he walked out of the restaurant.

In his room at a small hotel later that evening, a weary Noah closed the ledgers he'd been evaluating and swiped his hands down his tired eyes. The Douglas accounts met with his approval but he was still thinking over the surprising confrontation with Gordonez. How did Lavinia meet him? was his first question, and was she aware of his sordid history? After witnessing what she had at dinner would she be so blinded by her quest to take possession of her father's business that she'd ignore it out of hand and continue to champion the Cuban? Noah had no answers and truthfully, they didn't matter. The only thing that did was the certainty of Gordonez's death should anything happen to Pilar.

The next morning Lavinia met his knock at the door of the Douglas home.

"Good morning, Noah. Interesting dinner last evening."

"You'd do well to distance yourself from your new companion, Lavinia. He's more than he seems."

"Father's waiting for you in his study."

"Thank you." He didn't plan to argue with her over the matter. If she wanted to dance with a viper, so be it.

His meeting with Walter and his lawyer went well. The papers were signed and dated and as soon as they were filed with the proper entities, Noah would become the owner. Contrary to what Lavinia believed Noah would be forking over a significant sum as his part of the deal, but it was money well spent. He'd now be able to provide a future for his wife and family. "Thank you again, Walt."

"Thank you again, Noah. I can now go to my grave in peace."

Noah was saddened by the thought of his imminent passage. He was a tough but fair man and the world would be a poorer place without him in it. He shook hands with the lawyer and they spent a few more moments talking business as the man showed him out. Noah didn't see Lavinia.

Chapter 23

The day Noah left for San Francisco, Pilar spent the morning with Titan. The stallion still remained wary of her presence but he protested less. He even deigned to eat from the feedbag of oats while she held it, but when she reached out to touch him he raced away. It was disappointing in some ways but she felt encouraged, too. They were making progress.

She was sitting on the patio having lunch with Alanza when Drew appeared. "Afternoon, ladies."

He was greeted in return.

"Pilar. I want you to close your eyes."

"Why?"

He shook his head. "I have a surprise."

"What is it?"

He looked up to the sky as if seeking strength from the heavens. "Why are Yates women so hardheaded? Can you do what I ask please?"

Alanza interjected. "Go ahead, Pilar. He'll just whine until he gets his way."

He shot his mother a look of amused censure.

"Okay, Drew," Pilar said, "but if it's something that scares me, I will get you."

"I'm terrified, little sister."

She closed her eyes and waited.

"Now, you may open them."

And on the patio stood her mother and sister. She jumped up with a scream and for the next few minutes there was much hugging, rapidly spoken Spanish, and tears of joy.

"Oh, it so wonderful to have you here," Pilar proclaimed enjoying the feel of being embraced by her mother. "I've missed you and Doneta so."

"We've missed you, too," her mother whispered back. "So much."

She and Doneta shared a hug and tears.

The elated Pilar finally remembered her manners. "Mama, this is Noah's mother, Alanza Rudd. Alanza, my mother, Desa Banderas, and my sister, Doneta."

"Welcome to Rancho Destino. We're honored to have you here. Your daughter has given me much joy."

"Thank you. We're honored to be here. She's been behaving herself?"

Drew tossed in, "Of course not."

"May I punch him, Alanza?" Pilar asked laughing.

"Not now, let's get your family settled in first."

But Pilar had a question for him, "How did you find them? Where did you find them?" She noted her mother's and sister's reserved manner upon meeting Alanza but told herself it was to be expected. They had no way of knowing how Pilar was being treated by Noah and his family. Later, once she was alone with them she'd reveal the truth because she dearly wanted them all to get along.

In response to her question, Drew explained: "The depot manager sent a messenger to the bank to alert me to tell Noah of their arrival. Since he's away, I drove to the depot to pick them up and— *voila*—we're here."

Pilar gave him a kiss on the cheek. "I take back wanting to punch you. Thank you."

"You're welcome. Senora Banderas and Doneta, welcome to California. It's been a pleasure meeting you both. I'll see you tonight at dinner."

He bowed and departed.

Alanza said, "Mrs. Banderas, give us a short while to ready your rooms. In the meantime, Pilar, why don't you take them up to your wing so they can relax and the three of you can talk. I'll send Bonnie up with refreshments."

Pilar found that agreeable.

Winding their way through the hallways to her and Noah's suite, her mother said, "This house is very grand, Pilar."

"Yes it is. His family has lived here for many years. They're old Spanish but not stuffy or formal at all."

She opened the door and gestured them inside, and both women stared around in awe. Doneta asked, "These are your rooms?"

Pilar nodded. "When his mother became wealthy enough to afford it, she added this wing so that

Noah and his two brothers could have their own space away from the main house. Noah said they made too much noise and monopolized the lone bathing room."

Doneta went to the verandah doors, while Desa continued to stare around. Her gaze rested on the piano. "Who plays?" she asked curiously, "or is it simply for show?"

"Noah does, and extremely well. He also paints and composes music."

"Really?"

She chuckled in response to her mother's unmasked surprise. "Here, sit. Or do you wish to sit out on the verandah? You can see the mountains from there."

Doneta made the decision by opening the doors, so they followed her lead.

"This is lovely," she said, standing at the railing and looking out. "And his family owns all this?"

Pilar nodded. "There's cattle and chickens and orchards and grapevines. Noah's father died when he was very young and Alanza built all this practically with her own hands. She's an amazingly wonderful woman, Mama. Reminds me of you in many ways. She's been incredibly kind to me."

"And Noah?" her mother asked pointedly.

Pilar thought about the wonderful man she'd married and her heart soared.

Doneta laughed. "Look at her smile, Mama. Pilar, are you in love?"

Pilar beamed.

Doneta cried, "You are, aren't you! I am so jealous."

They all laughed.

"We get along far better than I ever dreamed we would. He's been incredibly kind, too."

Doneta held out her hand. "Pay up, Mama."

Pilar eyed the exchange curiously.

Doneta explained, "I told Mama the night you left that he was in love with you and that she wouldn't have to worry about how he'd treat you."

Desa chuckled and fished around in her handbag for her coin purse. Extracting one, she placed it on her daughter's open palm. "You know extorting your mother is a sin."

Doneta turned to Pilar. "Where is he?"

"In San Francisco on business. I'm expecting him later today, unless something's detained him."

"Drew is very handsome. I know you said both his brothers are married. Does he have any unmarried cousins?"

Pilar laughed. She was so happy to be with them again, especially her sister. "I haven't been here long enough to meet any cousins yet, but I will keep an eye out for you."

Bonnie arrived a short time later bearing a tray with tea and sandwiches. As they ate, they caught Pilar up on things in Florida.

"Our cousins have *novios*!" Doneta informed her excitedly. "A set of twins who are only a few years older. Tio Miguel and Tia Simona are ecstatic."

Pilar was pleased to hear that. She hoped they'd be as happy as she and Noah.

The talk moved to the house Desa had been considering buying when Pilar left Florida. "We moved in last week. It has three acres of land and the house is in need of some repairs but Miguel will take care of that and promises everything will be ready by the time we return."

"How long are you planning to stay?"

"Our tickets give us two weeks. Would that be an imposition?"

"Of course not. In fact, I hope you will decide to stay longer. I love it here and I know you will, too." Pilar couldn't stop grinning. She couldn't believe they were truly there.

Alanza came in a short while later to let them know their rooms were ready. "I'll see you at dinner," she said.

They were given the wing that Billie and Drew once called home and the visitors again marveled at the suite's size and scope.

Doneta took a seat on the settee and declared, "That's it. I'm not going back to Florida, Mama. I'm finding a husband and living right here for the rest of my days. This is exquisite," she added, looking around the well-appointed space.

Pilar and Desa chuckled.

"Good afternoon, ladies."

"Noah!" Pilar shrieked. She ran to him and he caught her up and they held on to each other as if they'd been apart for a lifetime.

"How are you?"

"Wonderful, now that you're here. Mama and Doneta are here, too."

"So I see. Welcome to California. I hope you plan to stay with us for some time. How was your trip?"

As Pilar settled in beside her husband, she doubted there was another woman in the world happier than she.

Eventually the talk came to an end, and Pilar and Noah stood to leave so Desa and Doneta could rest up for dinner. Pilar shared a parting hug with her mother and again whispered, "I'm so glad to be with you again."

"I feel the same way."

She shared a hug with Doneta as well. Wiping at her happy tears, Pilar and Noah departed.

In their room, they shared a welcome home kiss. "I missed you," he said holding her tightly against his heart.

"I missed you as well."

When they finally parted, they walked out to the verandah and took seats. "How was the trip?" she asked and then listened as he told the story. "So you now own a shipyard."

"I do and sometime soon you and I need to go to San Francisco and begin the search for that house we talked about. I'm letting you tell Mama we're moving."

"Coward."

"Definitely."

"This is all very exciting."

"Yes it is. There was a fly in the ointment though."

"Meaning?"

He told her about Gordonez.

She stared. "He was in San Francisco?"

"Yes and he wants to buy Walt's shipyard. Lavinia wanted him to be the owner."

"Is she out of her mind to be on the same side of a snake like him?"

"My sentiments exactly. He asked if I'd back out of the deal. When I told him no, he threatened to reveal your location to the Spanish authorities."

Her heart stopped. "Would he really do that?"

"I promised to kill him if he did."

The cold truth in his eyes raised the hair on the back of her neck. She realized he was not kidding. She also realized there was a man beneath the surface of Noah Yates that she didn't know and that gave her pause. Was he the man who had the nightmares? She sensed that questions about that would open a Pandora's box, so she let it be. "Let's hope it doesn't come to that."

They talked about his trip for a short while longer and then he asked, "How's your horse?"

Her worries about Gordonez negatively impacting

her life momentarily faded and she smiled. "He's coming along rather well. I want to take him with us when we move."

"That means we'll need a place with some acreage."

"Will we be able to find something that has water, too?"

"I don't know but we'll certainly try our best."

That filled her heart. "You are so kind to me, Noah Yates."

"I don't ever want you to regret marrying me, Pilar. I want us to be happy."

"As do I."

His arm across her shoulders drew her closer, and as she rested her head against his chest, she wondered if this was how it felt to be in love.

That evening at dinner, Pilar introduced her family to her in-laws and the babies, and Alanza declared, "Next weekend will be the party to celebrate Noah and Pilar's marriage, and to let our neighbors and friends meet Desa and Doneta. All in favor say aye!"

The answering ayes could be heard in Denver.

Rancho Destino spent the next week gearing up for the party. A small army of hired workers retrieved tables and chairs from the warehouses, along with linens, china, and tableware. Food orders were placed with local providers like Eli's Naomi, now happily working out of her brand-new restaurant, while fresh fruit was gathered and stored for the gallons of sangria that would be consumed. Alanza and Pilar, accompanied by Desa and Doneta, drove all over the valley to find the peppers, yams, and other vegetables needed for the Cuban dishes Pilar planned to prepare as her contribution to the festivities. And Pilar finally learned why Mariah had taken her measurements during that initial visit to her shop. It was for a gown.

Mariah presented it to her one evening at dinner and the deep red gown was so beautiful, Pilar cried.

"I wanted it to match your rubies. You are planning to wear them, correct?"

"I will now. Thank you, Mariah."

Mariah kissed her cheek. "You're welcome."

Later as she and her mother and sister viewed the gown her mother asked, "What was that about rubies?"

Pilar explained.

Doneta stared shocked. "You have rubies?"

She nodded. "You'll see them at the party. They're in the safe now."

Desa said, "I'm getting jealous of your mother-in-law. There's no way I can compete with that."

Pilar gave her a hug, "There's no way my love for her will ever surpass my love for you, so please don't be. She's my mother-in-law and I adore her, but you're my mother. Okay?"

Desa nodded and smiled.

The party was yet another grand Alanza affair. There were no juggler or dancing bears but the people of the valley turned out in droves to meet and greet the newest Yates wife and her family. Only a few of Alanza's many relatives were able to attend due to the short notice but those who did come were as pleased to meet her as she was to meet them and they were ecstatic that she had Spanish roots and spoke the language. Wearing her beautiful gown and the rubies around her neck, she felt like a queen. And her king, decked out like a Spanish grandee in his well-cut black suit and snow-white ruffled shirt, was so handsome and elegant he looked good enough to eat.

As they moved through the crowd mingling and garnering hugs and well wishes, he said to her, "I can't wait to get you alone tonight. The only thing you'll be wearing are those rubies."

Her senses flared. "You look so handsome I was hoping to maybe sneak off and make you do all manner of scandalous things."

"You're a woman after my heart, but my mother would kill us both."

"As would mine."

"So hold on to that thought."

"You do the same."

She and Noah received hugs and congratulatory kisses on the cheeks from his brothers and their wives. They were all beautifully attired as well.

Drew raised his glass of sangria. "A toast to all

the women who weep this day because the last Yates brother has married."

The brothers raised their glasses. Their wives rolled their eyes.

A short time later the musicians arrived and music filled the air. She smiled at the sight of her sister doing a *rumba* with one of Alanza's young male cousins. He was among the small battalion of unmarried men competing for her attention. Doneta looked to be having fun and Pilar was pleased. Her mother looked happy as well. She was seated with Alanza, Max, and some of the aunts, drinking sangria, eating, and chattering away in Spanish.

Noah left her for a moment to speak with the postmaster, Will Sally, about a package that had arrived for him and she continued to thread her way through the gathering.

Naomi stopped her. "Pilar, what are these? They're delicious. You have to show me how to make them."

"Certainly. They're called *chatinas*. They're fried green plantains."

"I could eat these for the rest of my life."

Eli had introduced the two women to each other a few days ago and Pilar genuinely liked her. "May I make some for your wedding dinner?"

"Would you?"

"I'd be honored."

They spent a moment discussing the wedding

that was only a few short weeks away and Naomi went off in search of more *chatinas* and her *novio* Eli.

Noah made his way back to her side.

"What did Will say about the package?"

"It arrived yesterday. He would've brought it with him but he was so anxious to get here, he rode off and left it. I'll go pick it up Monday morning. I'm hoping it's the paperwork from Walt's lawyer."

"Have you told your mother we're moving yet?"

"No. If I had I'd be dead and you'd be making love to a ghost tonight."

She laughed.

"Would you care to dance, *mi pequeño pirata*?"

The endearment made her heart soar. "I'd love to."

Later, as dusk fell, the party began winding down. The musicians packed up their instruments and the hired help started to clear the tables. Surplus food was given to all who wanted to take some home—there wasn't much left, and Noah and Pilar said good-bye to each and every guest and thanked them for attending. Alanza's relatives would be staying overnight but would be heading for home at first light.

A happy Doneta gave her and Noah hugs. "I had a wonderful time."

Noah said to her, "I hope you told your army of suitors that we're sleeping in the morning and that anybody arriving before dawn will be shot."

She hit him playfully on the arm. "I doubt there'll be any demand at all."

Pilar said, "You might be surprised. I saw a few of them talking to Mama."

Her sleepy eyes widened. "Really?"

"Yes."

"Now I'll be unable to sleep, wondering who it might have been."

Pilar chuckled. "Go on to bed. Sweet dreams."

" 'Night." And she headed inside.

Noah draped an arm around her waist. "Are you ready to go in?"

It was a beautiful night. "Just let me stand here for a minute." She looked around at the torch-lit grounds and thought back on the glorious time she had and knew she'd remember this day for the rest of her life. "Your mother really knows how to throw a party."

"I wanted dancing bears," he groused.

She laughed and they went inside.

Upstairs in their room, just as promised, he slowly removed her gown and left her dressed in only the ruby necklace. The love they made was so hot and scandalous the party wasn't the only thing Pilar would remember for the rest of her life.

Chapter 24

Pilar and Noah rose at dawn, along with Alanza to see the relatives off. After their departure, all three want back to bed. When they all gathered later for breakfast they learned that one of the relatives had stayed behind. His name was Cristopher Vallejo, the only son of one of Alanza's cousins. He wanted to spend some time with Doneta and had apparently received Desa's permission at the party. When he joined them at breakfast he only had eyes for Doneta and Pilar could tell that Doneta was quietly ecstatic about his presence. Pilar didn't know anything about him, but apparently Noah and his brothers knew him quite well.

As they began eating, Logan started things off: "So, Christopher, you'll be with us for a few days."

"Yes."

Noah asked, "How old are you now?"

"Twenty-four."

Pilar caught Doneta's smile.

Drew added, "You do realize that before you formally court Doneta we'll have to approve."

Pilar hid her smile at Doneta's surprise.

Noah said, "We are her brothers-in-law and because her father is deceased, we stand in the gap with her mother."

Desa beamed.

Christopher didn't and neither did Doneta.

Noah forked up some eggs. "Just wanted you to be clear on how this will work."

"Thank you," Christopher said.

Doneta shot Pilar a look of misery. Pilar shrugged in reply.

So, for the rest of the day, wherever Doneta and her potential beau went, Noah or one of his brothers followed. When they went riding, Logan did, too. When they had lunch on the patio, Drew joined them. When they went walking, Noah trailed them like a six-foot-plus duenna.

As the women of the family relaxed together in the parlor, Desa remarked, "I had no idea they would be so protective."

Alanza replied, "Christopher is a fine young man but he has a reputation as somewhat of a heartbreaker. The boys are just reminding him to treat Doneta with respect."

Mariah cracked, "And Logan is practicing for when Maria comes of age."

Billie shook her head. "All I have to say is Drew has a lot of damn nerve."

The room erupted with laughter.

That evening, after dinner, Pilar went up to spend some time with Doneta and their mother in their suite.

Doneta complained, "Can you please do something about Noah and his brothers? With them around I'll never get married."

Pilar took a seat. "Weren't you the one who said you didn't want Noah to be any girl's brother-in-law but yours?"

"I was obviously delusional."

Desa said, "You're a member of their family now, 'Neta, and they're taking their job seriously. I'm very pleased."

"I'm not."

"How long will Christopher be staying?"

"The way the day went, I'll be surprised if he doesn't sneak away as soon as it gets dark."

"If he does, then he isn't the one," Desa pointed out.

Doneta fell into a chair. "I suppose."

"He is quite handsome," Pilar added.

Doneta smiled. "He is indeed."

That night as Pilar lay in bed cuddled next to Noah he asked, "How mad is Doneta?"

"Pretty mad."

"We aren't going to let her be courted by just anyone; she's family now."

"Mama explained that to her. She thinks Christopher is going to sneak away under the cover of darkness."

Noah chuckled. "If he does then he isn't as serious about her as he claims to be."

"I agree."

"I'm serious about you."

Pilar turned to him. "Actions speak louder than words, *Americano*."

"Come here," he growled playfully.

For the next hour, he treated her to more action than words and she decided he was very serious indeed.

Monday morning, the family resumed their normal routine. With the construction in town all but completed, Max went to the sawmill to pick up some lumber for a new home he'd been asked to build. Logan rode off to meet Eli to mend fences. Billie wasn't feeling well so Drew stayed home to help with Antonio while she rested. Doneta and Christopher sat in the parlor under the watchful eyes of Alanza and Desa. Pilar headed out to spend the day with Titan and Noah set off for town alone to retrieve his package from Walt.

On the ride to town he thought about how perfect his life seemed. He had a wife he adored, a new business enterprise, and a family filled with love and laughter. He was also pleased that Christopher hadn't snuck off and hoped that his cousin would be all that Doneta wanted him to be.

Suddenly, he heard the crack of gunfire and pain erupted in his back. A second bullet rocked him, lower this time and he lost his grip on the reins and fell to the ground in agony. Clawing for the gun in his holster all the while trying to locate the shooter and manage the increasing pain, he managed to draw, only to have a another bullet explode in his arm and send the weapon flying. Lying there in the road, growing woozy from pain and all the blood he knew he was losing, he sucked in air and fought to get to his feet. Wobbling, he felt himself tottering on the edge of blacking out. Determined not to succumb, he willed his legs to move. He was no more than a mile from home. If he could just focus he might make it back. He took one step but the second one was his undoing and he fell face-first on the road. As he slid into the blackness, the last thing he saw was a man wearing a black hood standing over him.

Pilar was with Titan when Alanza ran up. "Noah's horse came back without him. There's blood all over his saddle. I've sent hands after Logan and Drew, but I'm going to look for him, now. I already spoke with your mother and sister."

Her heart stopped. "I'm coming, too."

"We'll take the wagon, let's go!"

They ran to the stable. A hand had the horses hitched and the wagon ready to go, so Alanza slapped down the reins and they were off.

The wagon wasn't moving fast enough for Pilar, but rather than be upset about that, she prayed and kept her eyes peeled so they didn't roar past him if he was lying in the vegetation lining the road.

When they found him, he was so motionless Pilar just knew he was dead. She jumped down while an equally distraught Alanza did the same and they ran to his side.

"Noah!" Pilar called. He didn't move. "Noah!"

She glanced in horror at the blood pooled on the back of his denim shirt. "Oh my God. How many times was he shot?"

"Noah!" Alanza cried. The bloodstain was spreading. He groaned faintly, but the sound put tears of joy in their eyes.

Drew came thundering up and dismounted in a flash. "What happened!"

"He's been shot," Pilar said.

A grim Alanza told Drew, "Help us get him in the wagon and then ride for Dr. Lloyd. Have her meet us at the house."

Between the three of them they managed to get him to his feet. His head hung forward and he was like dead weight. Pilar said encouragingly, "*Querido*, move your legs. Help us please. Just to the wagon."

His eyes fluttered open. "Pilar?" he questioned in a ragged voice. She bit her lip, determined not to cry. His glassy eyes found Alanza. "Hurt so bad, Mama," he whispered.

"I know, but you must walk, son," she urged. "We have to get you home."

Where he found the will, Pilar didn't know, but he somehow managed to propel himself forward a tiny step at a time. He was breathing so harshly by the time they reached the wagon, she wasn't sure he had the strength to climb in. He did, with aid from Drew, but not without crying out. A tear slid down her cheek and she dashed it away.

"We'll find out who did this, believe that," Drew pledged angrily. He'd found Noah's gun, and after passing it to Pilar, he ran to his mount and rode like hell up the road towards town.

"We have to slow this bleeding," the worried Pilar said to Alanza. Seeing nothing in the bed that could be used, Pilar stripped off her shirt waist, tore it in half, and stuffed the pieces against the wounds before easing him back down. "Okay, Alanza, go!"

With her unconscious husband's head cradled in her lap, Pilar held on while a tight-lipped Alanza turned the wagon around and drove for home.

Dr. Renee Lloyd, who'd trained back east in Pennsylvania and had recently moved to the area, was blunt about his chances for survival. "He's lost a significant amount of blood," she told the assembled family. "I removed three bullets and cleaned and stitched the wounds. All we can do now is wait. Those of you who have God's ear should start your prayers."

Alanza offered her a room so she could stay with them and she accepted.

Logan and Eli, who'd set out to see if they could track down the person responsible, returned that afternoon with a man in the bed of the wagon.

"We found nothing but a Spanish man. Said he was thrown by his horse. I think his leg's broken."

"Spanish?" Pilar asked.

Dr. Lloyd asked Alanza, "Would you mind if he was brought into the house?"

"No."

Eli and Logan had the hobbling man held up between them as they helped him inside. As soon as Pilar saw his face, she picked up Noah's gun she'd laid on a table, and before anyone realized what she was about, she stuck the gun hard beneath the man's chin. "So, we meet again."

Everyone stilled and stared.

She told the wide-eyed man in a cold and deadly voice, "If you even blink I will blow your head off. Put him in a chair, Logan."

"Pilar, I—"

"Do it, Logan! Now!" She drew the gun back but she watched the man with hate-filled eyes.

As he was helped to a chair, the room went quiet as a tomb and he viewed Pilar warily. "I don't know who you think I am—"

"Oh I know who you are." And to prove it, she said to him in her crone's voice, "Who's your master?"

It took him a moment to remember meeting her on the docks that morning so many months ago, but when he did, he began shaking.

"You remember now. I was in disguise the day we met, but you weren't. And now, I'm going to ask you once. Did Gordonez send you to kill Noah Yates?"

She heard gasps behind her but ignored them.

"And don't lie to me. Noah is my husband and this is his mother's house. The men you see are his brothers."

"I—don't know what you're talking about."

She shot him in his broken leg. His scream filled the house.

Ignoring his sobs of pain and terror, she promised, "The next one will be between your legs. Did Gordonez send you to kill my husband?"

He looked around and pleaded, "Someone help me!"

No one moved.

Pilar pointed the gun at his thighs and he froze, took in her deadly purpose and spat out through his tears, "Yes, you bitch, he did! He and the Douglas woman! Don't shoot me again, please!"

Eli said, "I'll go for the sheriff."

Pilar put the gun on the table and left the room to go sit with her husband.

The next few days were a living nightmare for Pilar and his family. Because of Noah's perilous condition, the doctor didn't want him carried all the way upstairs, so he was put in a spare bedroom on the first floor. Pilar asked to have a cot added so she wouldn't have to sleep away from him and one was brought in. Family members took turns sitting vigil with her, including her mother and Doneta. She apologized for not being able to make the rest of their visit the merry time they'd all envisioned, but they understood and vowed to stay with her until the crisis passed. Alanza spent most of the time sitting by his bed, too, leaving only to go to her chapel to light candles and pray.

Logan sat with her for a while during the third day. Because she hadn't left Noah's side, she had no idea what happened after Gordonez's man confessed, so she asked him to tell her.

"Doc Lloyd removed the bullet and set his leg. The sheriff arrived a bit after that and took him away. I checked with him yesterday. Lavinia has been arrested for attempted murder and the U.S. Marshals grabbed Gordonez just as he was boarding a ship to leave the country. He's been charged as well."

"May they all rot."

"You stood up for Noah in a way that scared the hell out of everybody in the room, Pilar. Thank you for your fearlessness." He kissed her cheek.

"You're welcome."

As three days turned into four, Reverend Paul Dennis from the local church stopped by to offer prayers of comfort, as did Tom and Amanda Foster, and longtime family friends Lucy Redwood and her daughter Green Feather, who'd be leaving in a few days for her second year at Hampton in Virginia. Even Felicity Deeb and her husband Jim came over—although most believed it was just Felicity's attempt to get back into Alanza's good graces after not being invited to the wedding or Noah and Pilar's party due to her rudeness to Billie when they were initially introduced last year. Naomi Pearl arrived to sit, too, and to assist Bonnie with the food. Pilar and the family were grateful for the shows of support.

Noah made it through the first four nights, but Pilar worried. When he wasn't lying as still as a corpse, he was moaning, crying out, and thrashing around. During one of the violent episodes, Drew, in an effort to keep him calm, took a fist in the jaw.

"I think he's having one of his nightmares," she said as Drew tenderly worked his jaw to make certain it hadn't been broken.

"What nightmares?"

"I don't know what they are about, but he wakes up shaking." And angry, she reminded herself.

Drew eyed his now calm but still fretfully sleeping brother. "Has he told you he was shanghaied?"

She nodded. "But only that it happened. He hasn't offered any details."

"I wonder if the nightmares have anything to do with that time. Something terrible must have happened, because he was so different when he finally returned to us."

Pilar couldn't say.

"Let me get some ice for my jaw. I'll owe him one for this when he's up and around again."

"I refuse to believe he won't recover."

"He will. Noah's too ornery to die."

She smiled for what seemed the first time since finding him facedown in the road.

"You love him, don't you?" Drew asked her quietly.

She didn't hesitate. "I do with my every breath."

"He loves you, too. It'll take more than a couple of bullets to keep a Yates man from his wife." Drew gave her a kiss on the cheek. "Hang on. And by the way, if anything like this ever happens to me, I want you standing right next to my Billie."

"I promise."

"Good." And he left her sitting by Noah's bedside.

Drew's prediction was right. On the morning of the fifth day, Noah opened his eyes. Pilar wanted to shout with joy but held it in so as not to scare him into a relapse. "Good morning."

"Where am I?" he asked groggily.

"In a bedroom downstairs. You were shot by one of Gordonez's men." She placed her hand on his forehead. It was still feverish but not as skillet hot as it had been.

"I remember you and Mama, but not much else." Then as if his mind finally allowed the memory to form, he went still. "I remember the pain in my back. I was shot, wasn't I?" He looked to her as if seeking verification.

"Yes. One high, the other lower, and one in your arm."

"Where's the man now?"

"In jail, along with Gordonez and Miss Lavinia Douglas. She was in on the plot as well."

"Good, then I won't have to hunt them down. Poor Walt must be devastated by her complicity."

Pilar was sure he was, but she was happy. The family prayers had been answered. Noah would live.

Chapter 25

Noah's recovery was slow, so slow that by the end of the first week, he was growling like a tiger at anyone close enough to be a target—except his mother, his wife, and Dr. Lloyd, none of whom paid any attention to his demanding to get out of bed, ride his horse, or take the train to San Francisco to begin running his business.

His brothers, on the other hand, tried reasoning with him in an effort to make him understand why he was restricted to bed rest.

"Look," Drew said to him that morning. "Your bad mood isn't going to help you leave the bed any earlier, so you may as well play along with Pilar and the doctor. I took care of the package you were after the day you were shot. Inside were your copies of the paperwork from Walt's lawyer. He wired me two days ago to say your foremen are running the shipyard in your absence and doing just fine without you."

Noah bored him with a hostile glare. If he had to stay in bed one more day he was going to go mad.

Logan added. "And were you a better patient we might throw our weight behind you to try and get you a reprieve from the wardens but you aren't ready. No sense in letting you up just so all those stitches can break free and you wind up flat on your arse for another two weeks. Stop being such a baby."

"Get the hell out."

"Gladly!" Drew and Logan said in unison.

Alone, Noah blew out a breath. No, he wasn't being the best patient, but were they in his shoes, or bed, they'd be no better. He was being forced to use a bedpan, for heaven's sake. Where was the dignity in that? So, because he knew he was right and they were wrong, he sat up. His back protested but he paid it no mind. Breathing through gritted teeth and ignoring the sweat suddenly drenching him, he swung his legs to the edge of the bed and sat for a moment to try and catch his breath. Fueled by stubbornness and sheer will, he haltingly stood on legs that had not been consulted beforehand and they promptly gave way.

Pilar entered the room carrying a tray and found him lying on the floor. Rather than be concerned she set the tray down. "How's the ceiling look from there, *querido*?"

He growled.

"No cracks or signs of water damage?"

She walked over and stooped down beside him. "You're an idiot, do you know that? And if I didn't love you with all my heart, I would let you lie there for oh, three or four hours just to teach you a lesson."

His startled eyes met hers. "You love me?"

"Of course, why else do you think I haven't

gone back to Florida? You've been rude, short tempered, and impossible to be around."

He smiled. "I love you, too."

She leaned over and kissed him. "Good. Now, I'll go and get your brothers so they can help you back to bed. Their ridicule alone should make you never attempt to do this again until Dr. Lloyd says you are ready. Are we agreed?"

"Agreed."

And because he kept his pledge, one week later he was able to leave the bed. He couldn't do much more than walk to the water closet, which pleased him immensely, and out to the room's verandah to take his meals and bask in the sunshine and fresh air, but each day he got stronger.

Another week of resting allowed him to attend Naomi and Eli's wedding. He still tired easily so they left the reception early. As they got ready for bed, he said to her. "I'm ready to make love to my wife."

Pilar, wearing one of the nightgowns he enjoyed removing, sidled close. "Are you sure you're up to it? Think how embarrassing it would be if I had to go get your brothers to put you back in the bed, with us being nude and all."

That earned her a swift but playful swat. "A wife is supposed to revere her husband not poke fun at him."

"Then you can poke me as punishment," she took him by the hand. "Come on."

He was very much up to it, and when they were done, she drifted off to sleep in his arms and with a smile on her face.

As October arrived, the time came for Pilar's mother and sister to return to Florida. They'd extended their stay to help Pilar and Noah through the crisis.

"I will miss you, very much," Pilar said through her tears as she hugged her mother at the train station. She'd become so accustomed to having them in the house when she awakened each morning, it was going to be a difficult adjustment knowing they were no longer there and thousands of miles away again.

"I'll miss you, terribly, too, Pilar, but we'll return, and Noah has promised me you will come and visit us."

She turned to him with surprised eyes. It was the first she'd heard of this.

He explained, "Since your uncle and I remain business partners, I'd like to go down and look over the operation once I get caught up at the shipyard, and since Drew and Logan have invested, too, maybe the entire family will want to go, and we can chip in for a private car so we don't have to ride with the pigs."

Pilar thought that a grand idea. That he'd not said anything to her beforehand didn't upset her. She was glad he'd made the pledge.

Her next hug was for Doneta. Her she'd miss the most. Billie and Mariah were wonderful sisters-in-law and she loved them dearly but her love for Doneta held a special place in her heart. "Going to miss you, too."

"I'll stay longer next time and maybe we can find me a husband like Noah," Doneta said, hugging her tightly. Christopher hadn't worked out. At some point during the aftermath of the shooting, he'd gone home, but Pilar had no idea when and Doneta hadn't wanted to talk about it.

Pilar kissed her cheek. "You have a deal."

The train chugged into view, spitting smoke and brimstone from its stack. Pilar was glad to see her mother throw her arms wide for a hug from Noah and he stepped forward without hesitation. "Take care of my daughter," she said.

"Always. Travel safe."

He and Doneta shared a hug as well.

The conductor announced it was time to board. With her tears running freely now, Pilar watched them disappear inside. Soon she saw both faces in a window and then their waves. The whistle blew shrilly and the train began to move. As it chugged away, Noah slipped an arm around her waist as if he knew she needed his solace. "I will miss them so much."

He kissed her forehead. "We'll see them soon. I promise."

Pilar was a bit melancholy for the rest of the day and that evening, as she stood outside watching the moon come up, she hugged herself in response to the chill. "How much colder is it going to get?" she asked Noah as he stepped out to join her and fit himself against her and circle his arm around her waist. "Just a bit."

She twisted around to look into his face. "Is that the truth?"

"No."

She playfully jabbed him with an elbow.

"But as I promised, I'll keep you warm. In fact, how about I take you inside and warm you up right now. Give you something else to think about besides missing your mother and sister."

"You'd do that for me?" she asked, turning fully this time to face him.

"For you, I'd be willing to make any sacrifice."

"I'd like a nice soak in a warm tub. Do you think you can sacrifice enough to join me?"

He made a point of thinking it over. "Yes, I believe I can do that."

She eased herself closer and purred, "Thank you. And for being such a wonderful husband you get to choose what you want me to wear after we're done in the tub and remove it when you're ready."

"Have I told you I love you today?"

"Not sure but you can tell me while we're getting warm."

• • •

In the weeks that followed, Noah threw himself into his job as the new owner of the Douglas Shipyard and looking for a house. Noah planned to keep Walt's name on the sign out front in honor of his passing away right after the attempt on Noah's life. He was certain Lavinia's involvement stole the last few precious moments her father thought he had left, but his death spared him having to witness his daughter's trial. The man she and Gordonez sent to kill him was given immunity from prosecution in exchange for his testimony and was promptly deported back to Cuba. On the last day of the trial, Pilar and Noah sat in the courtroom as Lavinia and Gordonez were sentenced to life in prison.

"They got what they deserved," Pilar remarked as they sat in the buggy he'd rented for their stay. They planned to return to the ranch the next day. "And in a way my father received justice today, too. My mother will be pleased."

"I'm sure she will."

"We've all waited a long time to see Gordonez being taken down, too bad you almost lost your life."

"But I've recovered and that's a blessing. And speaking of blessings I have a surprise for you."

"What is it?"

He chuckled. "Why do you always ask that?"

"Because I always want to know."

He leaned over and placed a quick kiss on her forehead before returning his attention to the thick afternoon traffic. "I think I may have found you and that horse of yours a perfect house."

"Really?"

"Do you want to see it?"

"Now?"

"Yes, my love. Now."

"I do!"

And it was perfect. It was outside of the city but there was plenty of room for Titan and the edge of the property fronted the waters of the Bay. "I love this, Noah."

"It's a former horse farm."

"I can already see Titan running through the fields." The property had been cleared but tall trees ran across the back acreage.

He drove them through the wooden fence and up the lane to the house. "It's big," Pilar said noting the windows on the first and second floor. Of course, it wasn't as large as Alanza's but how many homes were?

"It needs a new roof and some other work," he added. "But that's why we have Max."

She grinned. "Can we go inside?"

"Not yet. I wanted you to see it and get your approval before I make my bid to the bank."

"You have my approval and my love, Titan's love, too." Her stallion was trained well enough now to ride and she couldn't wait to mount up and explore their new home when the time came.

"So, do you think you'd like raising a family here?"

"I would. Thank you for finding this place, Noah."

"For you, the world. How about some dinner before we go back to the hotel?"

"That's a great idea."

They had a wonderful dinner to cap off a wonderful day. As they left the restaurant, Pilar hooked her arm in his. "You know," she began to say, but her words faded when she realized he'd stopped and was staring ahead. His scarred jaw throbbed and his eyes blazed. She saw an old man approaching. By his rough attire and cane, it was apparent that he'd seen better days. When he came abreast, he stopped and smiled smugly.

"Well, if it ain't the pretty Mr. Yates. How are you, boy?"

"Why do you care, Simmons?"

His cackling laugh brought on a coughing spell and he spit the phlegm onto Noah's boots. "Still mad, are ya? Don't know why. If it weren't for me and that island you'd still be a mincing little fop sucking on your mama's teat. I made ya a man!"

Pilar felt Noah stiffen and she urged softly, "Come on, Noah, let's go."

The man turned rheumy eyes her way. "Aren't you a pretty little thing. He bugger you the way I heard the boys used to bugger him?"

Noah's fist erupted in the old man's face and it

knocked him down. Grabbing him by the lapels Noah dragged him up and rained down blow after blow.

"Noah!" Pilar screamed. "Stop!" She pulled at him. "Stop it! Noah! You'll kill him!" He paused and turned but he was not the man she loved. The seething eyes holding hers were feral, maddened, frightening. Then they cleared and he dropped the man to the pavement. He stared down emotionlessly as the old man lay moaning, with blood streaming from his mouth and nose.

"He needs a doctor," Pilar said urgently.

"Yes he does." He dragged him to the nearest doorway and tossed him inside. "This man need a doctor!" That done, he turned to her. "How's that?" And he started up the street again as if he didn't care whether she followed or not.

He didn't speak to her for the rest of the evening and she was awakened much later by his shouts and cries as he wrestled within the throes of a nightmare. It was the most awful night of Pilar's marriage.

Or so she thought.

He had very little to say on the train ride back to the ranch. When they returned home, Drew was the only one in the house and in response to his normal questions about the trip, Noah was aloof. Then as if he'd wanted nothing else to do with them, he left the parlor without saying a word. Pilar dropped into a chair.

A visibly stunned Drew asked, "What happened?" She related the details of the fight.

"What did the old man do to deserve such a beating? Who was he?"

"I don't know." Drew was her favorite brother-in-law and she knew how close he and Noah were, so she told him first about the phlegm on the boots and then what the man said.

Drew's eyes widened. "*Dios!*" He whispered, "No wonder he came back from the island the way he did. My poor brother. I think I'm going to be sick." He ran his hands over his hair. "Oh God! Oh God! I need to talk to him."

"No!" She sensed Noah wouldn't approve of her sharing what she'd heard, but Drew was already running inside.

Noah was in his room seated out on the balcony when he heard the knock. He ignored it. More knocking followed, stronger this time. He ignored it.

Then came the muffled sound of Drew yelling, "Noah, open this damn door or I swear I'll break it down."

He doubted Drew was strong enough but thought Logan might be able to if they were out there together, so he stood and went to the door, undid the lock, and opened it. "What?"

"Pilar told me what happened."

"What do you want?"

"Have you been this surly with her?"

Noah did not want to have this conversation. All he wanted was to be left alone. He backed away from the door and Drew followed him inside.

Drew asked, "Well, have you?"

"That's none of your concern."

"Then the answer's yes. You plan on treating Mama the same way?"

"Dammit, Drew, what do you want?"

"To help if I can."

"You can't. Did Pilar tell you what Simmons said, too?"

Drew nodded.

Noah wanted to break something.

"Let me try. You're my brother. I love you."

"Are you after the full story? Is that why you came up here?" he yelled. "They raped me for three consecutive nights. I convinced a guard to trade me a machete for the gold St. Christopher medal around my neck and when they came for me that fourth night, I sliced up the ringleader so fiercely his arms were hanging from his shoulders by a thread. He bled to death at my feet and I was glad. His friends who'd watched and laughed those first three nights scattered like sheep." He met his brother's horrified gaze. "Now you know."

"Noah, I'm so sorry," Drew whispered.

"So am I." And he turned and walked back out to the verandah. The parts of him that loved his brother knew he'd been ugly and harsh, but the part of him being ruled by horror and pain didn't care.

Alanza came home a few hours later. Pilar was seated out on the patio with Drew.

She took one look at their faces. "What's wrong?"

"Noah's nightmares have turned him mad," Pilar said.

"Nightmares? What nightmares?"

Pilar couldn't bear seeing any more heartache, so she got to her feet. "Drew will tell you. I'm going to ride Titan and clear my head." She knew she was taking the coward's way out, but at that moment, she was tired of being strong. Every fiber of her being wanted to help her husband but she didn't know how.

When Pilar returned she knew Drew had told his mother the story because Alanza's eyes were red and puffy. With her blessing, Pilar holed up in the suite her sister and mother had vacated and spent the rest of the day there. By evening, her spirit somewhat restored, she went to her own rooms to see if Noah wished to talk. He was in the sitting room and said accusingly in a flat, cold voice, "How dare you tell my brother something so private."

She closed her eyes as her heart broke again, but she didn't apologize. "Your brother loves you, so do I."

She steeled herself for an argument, but instead he said, "I'm going for a ride. No need for you to wait up."

Hours later, she was awakened by the sound of the piano. Slipping from the bed, she eased open the door to listen. It sounded like a storm on the sea, much like the painting that once hung in his quarters on the *Alanza*, complete with the musical equivalent of rumbling thunder and flashes of lightning, and a darkness that was at once angry yet beautiful. She didn't know if the composition was his own or created by someone else. Still wanting to help but not knowing how, she went back to the bed and sat and listened to him play for hours. When she finally fell asleep he was still playing.

The following morning, he walked into the bedroom at dawn and announced that he'd be going back to San Francisco.

Pilar was certain that he hadn't slept. "Will you be back this weekend?" In the past he'd always come home Friday evenings.

"I don't know."

She sat, silent while he packed. More than a few times she saw him look her way and there was a bleakness and an anguish in his eyes that seemed to rise from his soul. He was in hell and because he was, she was, too.

He finished packing, gave her a final glance and walked out of the bedroom. He didn't say good-bye.

Chapter 26

Noah rented a room in San Francisco and hoped to keep his demons at bay by working, but it didn't help. For the next two weeks, the nightmares haunted him every night, as did the hurt he saw reflected in Pilar's eye when he left her, and he knew something had to be done. She deserved so much better than to be married to someone who slipped into madness because of his dreams.

One evening after the men had gone home for the day, he stood on the silent dock and looked out at the bay. There was a storm coming. The waves were rising with caps of white and the wind was blowing hard enough to catch the edges of his coat. The conditions mirrored how he felt inside— angry, raw, so raw he'd nearly beaten an old man to death and done maybe irrevocable harm to his relationship with his family and more important, his wife and his marriage. The pain in Pilar's eyes was his fault and his alone, but how could he fix that when he couldn't fix himself? For a long time her love and the life they were building had been his salvation. There'd been no nightmares, they'd been happy, playful—perfect. And then, Simmons appeared and his sneering words brought back the terror, the horror, and yes, the shame, and all he wanted to do was make it stop even if it meant taking the man's life. He sighed and ran his hands down his face. Ten years had come and gone and the happenings on that island still held him in thrall like a slave in chains, and no matter what he did he could not break free. If he went back and confronted his ghosts would that help him begin to heal? He knew he'd never be able to banish the memories of what happened there entirely but if he could make peace enough with it and with himself, could he get on with his life? He didn't have an answer but it was all he could think to do. To not do anything was to live with the reality of having broken Pilar's heart and that was more than he could bear.

So he took the train home the following morning. When he arrived she was sitting with his mother in her study.

His mother said, "Noah."

"Mama."

She didn't say welcome home, or ask how long he'd be staying but he supposed he'd stopped earning such a loving response. She, too, was owed a respite from the hurt he'd seen in her eyes.

He turned his attention to Pilar. "May I speak with you?"

Alanza rose from her chair. "I'll let you have some privacy."

She exited and closed the door softly.

"So, what do you wish to speak with me about?"

He'd been away for two weeks without a word

to her and her bluntness was expected. "I'm going back to the island where the nightmares began. The old man I beat so badly was the captain who shanghaied me."

"And the one who gave you the scar?"

"Yes. I'm hoping if I return I can rid myself of all this darkness and hurt."

"When will you leave?"

"As soon as I can."

She didn't respond at first and he wished he knew what she was thinking. Finally, she said, "Then go—with my blessings, so you can come back to me and to our child."

He froze.

She offered a bittersweet smile. "Yes. Dr. Lloyd said the baby will be born late spring."

His knees went weak. "How long have you known?"

"A few weeks. I wanted to tell you, but . . ." She shrugged as if no other words were needed.

He understood fully and was at once embarrassed and contrite that he'd treated her so badly she didn't think he cared enough to want to know.

"May I ask a large favor?"

"What is it?"

"Can I hold you? Please?"

Tears filled her eyes. She studied him for a long moment but slowly stood. He closed the distance between them and as he eased her in against his heart and tightened his arms, the strong swell of emotion made him ache. "I'm so sorry for hurting you, Pilar. I do love you. I may not have acted like it these past few weeks, but I do. Fiercely."

"I love you, too," she whispered. "But I can't live this way, Noah. I won't live this way."

"I don't blame you for wanting to leave me, but please, don't."

She leaned back. "Then go and do what you need to. The baby and I will be here when you return." After placing a soft kiss against his scar, she was gone.

His mother came back in and he said to her, "Mama, I want to apologize for all the hurt and chaos."

"From what Drew told me, you earned the right to them both, but you've treated Pilar abominably."

"I know. I'll make it up to her. I promise." He then revealed his plan.

"It can't hurt. Do you have a boat?"

"I've leased one and have a crew."

"Then go and come back to us as whole as you can. Make peace with your brother first though."

"Yes, ma'am."

"And your mother needs to hug you before you go."

He walked into her outstretched arms and thanked God for her love. "You will watch over Pilar?"

"No, Noah, I'm putting her and my newest

grandchild out of my house just as soon as you leave. What a ridiculous question, and besides, Pilar can take care of herself. Ask that man who shot you. If she hadn't intervened Gordonez and Lavinia might be still plotting ways to kill you."

He had no idea what she was referencing. "What are you talking about?"

"Pilar never told you?"

"No."

So she told him the story of what transpired while he had one foot in death's door, and when she finished, he stared in amazement.

"We all assumed she told you."

"My God. No."

"You're married to a very special woman, Noah Yates, and the fact that you're willing to travel all that way and walk in the shoes of your past shows you may have figured that out. Now, go and talk to Andrew."

"I love you, Mama."

"I love you, too, my youngest."

"Is Drew at home or in town?"

"Home. Billie and Mariah are up in Seattle to deliver a dress to one of Mariah's clients. Little Maria went with them but Tonio the Terror was left behind with his father."

Riding to Drew's, Noah hoped to get another look at Pilar before he departed in earnest but when he looked up at their verandah, he didn't see her.

Drew answered the door. The look on his face showed his displeasure, so to keep from having the door slammed in his face, Noah said, "I came over to apologize."

"That's a good start. Come on in."

The house was in shambles. There were toys and dirty little boy's clothing and shoes strewn about along with glasses and saucers and napkins and so many other items that Noah had to stop looking at it all. Then Tonio appeared—butt naked. Noah glanced at his brother.

"He will not keep his clothes on. Short of dressing him and tying him to a chair—Lord, how does Billie do this? How did Mama do this—there were three of us!"

"In truth there were only two. Logan was forty years old at birth."

Tonio ran to Noah screaming, "Unca Wo-wa."

It was toddler speak for "Uncle Noah." Noah picked him up. "How are you, Tonio?"

"Fine."

"Are you being good for your papa?"

He shook his head. "No."

Holding on to his laugh, Noah put him back on his feet and the boy ran off and disappeared.

Noah said, "Mama also had a bullwhip."

"Maybe I'll have somebody give me one for my next birthday—better yet, a wig because by then I'll be bald from tearing my hair out."

"How long has Billie been gone?"

"Two days. Due back tomorrow and if she comes home and finds the house this way, I'll be sleeping in the barn."

Noah hoped that when Pilar had their baby he'd be better at child maintenance than Drew was, but he probably wouldn't be.

"So you were apologizing. Come in the kitchen. He's yet to destroy the chairs in there."

In the kitchen Noah was stopped short by the big red circles drawn on one of the cream-colored walls.

Drew gestured him to a chair and said by way of explanation, "Billie's lip paint. He did that about ten minutes after she left. Writing my obituary now because I have no idea how to remove it."

Noah dearly hoped he was better. "As I said, I owe you an apology. You were just trying to help."

"I was. I'm sorry that happened to you, Noah. It's enough to give anyone nightmares."

Noah then shared his plan about returning to the island.

"I'll go with you if you think that would make it easier," Drew responded.

Noah shook his head. "Thank you for the offer but I need to do this alone."

"You've talked to Pilar?"

"I have. I feel so bad about the way I've treated her. She told me we have a baby on the way, but you probably already know that."

"I do. The whole family knows."

Noah looked away. "I love her with every beat of my heart."

"I know you do, so go back and face whatever you find."

"I will. I feel like a fly caught in a piece of amber."

"You'll be in our prayers."

They shared a strong hug. Noah said, "You'll say good-bye to Logan for me and tell him what I'm planning?"

"I will. He wants his brother back, too."

"He just wants me around so he can whip me at arm wrestling."

"There is that."

Their smiles met. "I love you, baby brother," Drew said with true affection.

"Love you, too, Drew. I'll look for a wig for you. Oh, I need you to do something for me."

He explained what he wanted and Drew nodded and smiled. "I will take care of everything."

"Thank you," Noah said gratefully.

At that moment the house was rocked by a loud crash.

Drew shouted, "Antonio! Travel safe, Noah." Drew rushed off.

Noah let himself out.

A few days after Noah's departure, Pilar sat on the verandah and thought about her future. She didn't want to live apart from Noah, but if he returned still broken and angry, she would have to. Raising a child in a house filled with so much sorrow was unthinkable. Not having him in her life was unthinkable, too, because she loved her husband. It was her hope that he'd return as healed and as well as possible because the alternative would further break her heart.

Chapter 27

Noah's crew set the anchor and he rowed to the island alone. He thought back to his first sighting of the place all those many years ago and how scared he'd been about what he'd find there, especially when he and Kingston were met by the armed soldiers. Now, as he rowed closer, he saw no evidence of the dock he and the other prisoners had worked so tirelessly on. In fact, as he waded in and pushed the dinghy onto the beach he saw no evidence of human life at all. The silence echoed eerily. Armed with a machete and a pistol, he walked inland. By his estimation it would take him about an hour to reach the prison.

The open expanses of felled trees were now filled with waist-high brush, and for a short period of time, he lost his way. Using the machete to hack his way through the thick vegetation, he finally reached his goal. He stopped and stared. The gates that the guards once locked the men behind at night were still there but the rest was rubble. Piles of tumbledown stones were everywhere. He wondered if the place had been felled by an earthquake. He made his way around the pillars holding the gates and into what was left of the interior. Looking around he tried to get his bearings to gauge where he and King were once housed and when he did he moved in that direction, careful not to turn his ankle or trip on the varying sizes and shapes of the piles of stones. Along the way the memories returned and for the first time he didn't fight them; he let them all rush back, and as they did he heard the ghostly voices, the screams, saw the rats and the fires. And although he didn't want to, he let himself relive those first three nights with the hope that by facing it, the horror would somehow lose its power over him. So he sat, let his mind go back and as it did, he began to weep for the man-child he'd once been and his brutal initiation into a terrible world he never knew existed. He sat for a long time, remembering how he'd prayed to be found, only to give up when he decided God wasn't listening. But something moved him now to pray for all the men who'd lost their lives to the senseless violence of the place; for Pilar and his family, who continued to love him in spite of his moments of madness. He prayed for his father and Walt Douglas and all the other men who'd touched his life and had moved on. Lastly, he prayed for himself and recited a string of prayers he'd learned at church and from his mother that he didn't realize he remembered. Prayers of forgiveness, contrition, and thanks. Prayers for strength, healing, and grace. And when they finally came to an end, a profound sense of peace washed over him and he exhaled a shaky breath. He had no idea if God had answered, but he felt as if his soul was no longer in hell.

He wiped his eyes and stood. Glancing around, he froze at the sight of the tiger standing no more than ten feet away. By its size, he knew it was a big male. He thought about the pistol in his pack and whether he could get to it quickly enough should the cat decide to attack. It didn't. Instead it stood there and eyed Noah for a second or two longer, then turned and slowly went on its way. When it disappeared, Noah left the ruins and did the same.

Six months pregnant but still feeling good, Pilar stood on a cinder block to give Titan his daily currying. A few days ago, Dr. Lloyd had forbidden her to ride anymore until after the baby arrived and the ban weighed on her sorely. The willful parts of herself wanted to eschew the advice and take one last glorious ride but should something happen to the baby she knew she'd never forgive herself. Titan now depended on Alanza to get his exercise as she was the only other person he'd allow on his back. Logan said the horse was spoiled. She and Alanza explained Titan simply had discriminating taste. Logan didn't buy it.

Pilar hadn't heard anything from Noah. She tried not to be anxious because it wasn't good for her or the baby, but she missed him terribly and prayed every night that he'd return to her safely and soon.

She was convinced that once he did return, the issues they had could be worked out, and just like in the love novels Doneta had taken to sending her while he was away, she and Noah would live happily ever after.

Pilar looked up to see Alanza walking in her direction. She was carrying her youngest grandchild, Billie and Drew's son Logan Abraham. He'd been nicknamed Abe to differentiate him from his proud-as-punch uncle.

"I have a surprise for you, Pilar."

Pilar rolled her eyes. "What is it with you Yateses and surprises? I suppose I should close my eyes?"

"Please, and turn your back."

Pilar blew out a breath and complied.

A few seconds later she heard a familiar male voice say, *"Buenos días, mi pequeño pirata."*

Tears were already in her eyes when she turned and he took her in his arms. So happy to see him, she wept copiously, to the point of embarrassment, but they were tears of joy. His eyes were wet as well. "You're home," she said looking up into his handsome scarred face. Alanza had magically disappeared.

"I am and with no plans to ever leave you again."

"Good. I missed you terribly."

"I missed you, too. How's our baby?"

"Doing well, according to Dr. Lloyd, and as you can see, I am no longer *pequeño.*"

He moved a caressing hand over her round stomach, then eased her against him again. "But you're still beautiful."

"Bless you."

He leaned back and asked, "So do you want the baby born here at Destino or in our house on the Bay?"

She stared with wide eyes. "You bought the house?"

"I did. Drew took care of the details in my absence and Max handled all the repairs. It's ready whenever we are."

"Oh my goodness." Pilar quickly did the logistics in her head. "How about we move in but come back here for my appointments to see Dr. Lloyd and for the birth?"

"Agreed."

"So your mother knows we're moving?"

"Yes. Drew had Max break the news to her. He figured she wouldn't kill her own husband."

Pilar felt all her worries drop away and her world tilt back into its proper place. "Just hold me, so I know you aren't a mirage."

"No mirage, *querida*."

"Are you better?" she asked seriously.

He nodded. "Yes."

"You owe me so many kisses, *Americano*."

She heard the rumble of his chuckle in her ear against his chest.

"Then how about we go in, go up to our room

419

and I begin my penance? After that we can talk about my trip."

"Agreed, they can only be kisses though."

"Understood, but I'm sure I can come up with some scandalous ways to comply within those boundaries."

"I can't wait."

"And afterwards, I'll play for you the beginning of the concerto I composed for you."

"For me?"

"Yes. For you and only for you."

As they headed to the house, Titan reared and bellowed.

Noah yelled back, "Sorry horse, I'm home and she's mine. You'll have to get your own woman."

A laughing Pilar punched him in the arm and basked in the knowledge that he was indeed home and that he was her love and she was his.

Epilogue

In Pilar's eighth month, she and Noah were stunned to learn from Dr. Lloyd that she wasn't carrying one baby, but two! The twins were born in early June, six minutes apart. First came Desa Alanza, followed by Javier Maxwell. The attending grandmothers cried. The boy was named to honor Pilar's father and to honor Max for the bang-up job he'd done on their house. To everyone's surprise Max cried as well.

Later, after the rigors of birth, Pilar looked down with love-filled eyes at the healthy twin babies in her arms, then up at their proud father. "Do they make rapiers for babies?"

He threw back his head and laughed loud and long. "I hope not." Once he gained control of himself again, he said, "Thank you for our beautiful children."

"You're welcome."

"Do you want me to take them and put them in the bassinets so you can sleep?"

She yawned, "Yes, please. And when you're done, tell Max to get started on a new Baby Jail. I think we may need it."

He kissed her gently, took each baby in turn and once they were sleeping as soundly as their mama, the very grateful Noah thanked God for his blessings and tiptoed out.

Author's Note

Getting to know the Yates family has been a pleasure, and I hope you enjoyed this final book in the series. The research tied to Pilar was very eye-opening. I had no idea of the role played by General Maceo, the Mambis, or the Afro-Cubans in the country's history. The freedom Pilar and the rebels worked so diligently to obtain finally came to fruition in 1898, but it was a bittersweet victory. The Cuban people were not allowed to participate in the negotiated settlement hammered out between the United States and Spain.

Here are some of the resources I used to bring *Destiny's Captive* to life:

Carr, Chomsky, Smorkaloff eds. *The Cuba Reader*. Duke University Press. Durham and London. 2003.

Staten, Clifford L. *The History of Cuba*. Palgrave Macmillan. New York, NY. 2003.

Gates, Henry Louis, Jr. *Black in Latin America*. Amazon Digital Services. 2003.

In closing, I wish to thank my readers for their continued prayers, love, and support. It means the world to me.

See you next time,

B

Center Point Large Print
600 Brooks Road / PO Box 1
Thorndike, ME 04986-0001 USA

(207) 568-3717

US & Canada:
1 800 929-9108
www.centerpointlargeprint.com